WHAT HE WANTED

Meg swallowed. "I begin to conclude that tonight you do not want sympathy."

"No," he replied.

What he wanted fairly glowed in his eyes, despite, or maybe heightened by, their being shadowed by the bruise and the curtain. Meg did not, however, think of backing away. She resented him for putting her continually to the test and had no inclination to perform such an undignified maneuver again.

"You set your payment yourself, sir, last night," she said, tossing her head. "You cannot collect it until you have earned it. Otherwise you are a thief."

"Did not the performance just now convince you that there is more than one way to skin a cat?"

"You did say you sympathized with the clown."

"There is nothing funny about the way I feel about you."

Meg shivered from wanting his hands caressing her. "There is nothing funny about the way I feel about you, either, my lord. That is because we have an arrangement, you and I."

BOOK YOUR PLACE ON OUR WEBSITE AND MAKE THE READING CONNECTION!

We've created a customized website just for our very special readers, where you can get the inside scoop on everything that's going on with Zebra, Pinnacle and Kensington books.

When you come online, you'll have the exciting opportunity to:

- View covers of upcoming books

- Read sample chapters

- Learn about our future publishing schedule (listed by publication month *and author*)

- Find out when your favorite authors will be visiting a city near you

- Search for and order backlist books from our online catalog

- Check out author bios and background information

- Send e-mail to your favorite authors

- Meet the Kensington staff online

- Join us in weekly chats with authors, readers and other guests

- Get writing guidelines

- AND MUCH MORE!

**Visit our website at
http://www.kensingtonbooks.com**

In Pursuit of a Proper Husband

Glenda Garland

ZEBRA BOOKS
Kensington Publishing Corp.
www.kensingtonbooks.com

ZEBRA BOOKS are published by

Kensington Publishing Corp.
850 Third Avenue
New York, NY 10022

All Kensington titles, imprints, and distributed lines are available at special quantity discounts for bulk purchases for sales
promotion, premiums, fund-raising, educational, or institu-
tional use.

Special book excerpts or customized printings can also be
created to fit specific needs. For details, write or phone the
office of the Kensington Special Sales Manager: Attn. Special Sales Department, Kensington Publishing Corp., 850
Third Avenue, New York, NY 10022. Phone: 1-800-221-
2647.

Zebra and the Z logo Reg. U.S. Pat. & TM Off.

ISBN 0-8217-7819-6

First Printing: July 2005
10 9 8 7 6 5 4 3 2 1

Printed in the United States of America

For Cheryl,
because I would be poorer today
if Mom and Dad hadn't fined me
so many nickels over you.

Acknowledgments

I want to thank the members of the Beau Monde who always provide invaluable assistance. Without you guys, I would never make it out of the library. Jennifer Ashley deserves much credit for reading drafts. I would also like to thank my editor, Kate Duffy, for working so hard to keep Regencies alive.

Chapter One

"You have taken your sweet time getting back," said Lizzie Grantham to her aunt by marriage. "I do not understand your long walks."

"Am I back?" replied Meg Grantham, rifling through the post that rested upon a salver on a table in the trim little foyer of her brother-in-law Sir George's manor house. Sir George's manservant had taken her admonishments to heart and removed the tarnish from the salver. But this detail provided gratification rather than satisfaction.

Meg was finding herself less satisfied by the day, as thoughts of what could be possible cast their frustrating lure. She knew she could do more with her life in England than her slow takeover of Sir George's household. Her circumstances, however, had fenced her in. At least until Lizzie married. Then there might be more possibilities.

But in the meantime, she walked and could not explain so that anyone in the household understood, although she had tried at first. Sir George, his wife Tessa, and their daughter Lizzie were good people. They had saved her from loneliness by insisting she come live with them after her husband, Sir

George's younger brother, had been killed in the Peninsula. Their imaginations, however, did not run in the same roads as Meg's did.

She had tried to describe how, upon first coming home from the war, she had needed the mindlessness of a daily route, putting one foot surely before the other, or how the progress of ice-slicked bud to flower to leaf delighted her, or how the smell of wind and rain made her feel alive, or, more recently, how sometimes she needed to explore, taking the measure of the varying ground of a new hill or meadow or forest.

They had looked at her with confusion or polite skepticism.

"Do you claim you are not back?" Lizzie asked. "You do delight in teasing me, Aunt."

Meg tried not to sigh. At seventeen, Lizzie considered calling someone aunt who was seven years her senior something of an absurdity and, by consequence, an imposition. Worse, she knew that little escaped her aunt's eyes.

"Have you never continued a thought despite being in a new place?" Meg asked Lizzie. "That is what I meant."

"Oh, well, when I think about my music," Lizzie said, "but you don't think about music, so what would you be thinking about?"

Meg shook her head, and said gently, "This and that."

Lizzie relaxed a little, although Meg could not determine whether empathy played any part in it. "Wherever you are," Lizzie said, "you must think about being here now, for Mama and Papa are entertaining a gentleman in the drawing room who has come calling for you."

"His name? Regiment?"

"He was not wearing a uniform," Lizzie said, and her voice took on a wistful note. "But he did appear handsome and excessive fine from the window. I peeked in."

"You did not give yourself away by—"

"No, I did not trip, or fall against the door," Lizzie said, annoyed. "I wish you would stop worrying so. I have not broken anything in days."

Thank God for that, Meg thought. "Do you know the gentleman's name?"

"Yes, and do stop looking at me like that. His name is Dodd. You have never mentioned—"

"Dodd?" Meg asked, alarmed. "Did you say Dodd?"

"Yes," Lizzie said. "What does that mean?"

Meg took off her bonnet and laid it on the bench next to the table that held the salver. She straightened the skirt of her dark blue walking dress.

He could be here for any number of innocent reasons.

He could be someone else. Meg hoped he was someone else.

"You cannot intend to go in there as you are," Lizzie said. "Your petticoats are an inch thick in mud."

"Precisely," Meg replied.

"Precisely?" Lizzie asked and followed in Meg's wake.

The withdrawing room faced north, so that it was never the wrong time of the day to greet visitors.

Meg opened the heavy door and said into the dim room overfilled with blue jacquard-woven settees, "Sir George, there you are. Do you know your prize bull became positively enraged this afternoon when I passed him? He charged the fence, and such a noise it made. Is he going to be moved to the upper pasture soon?"

"You are unharmed, sister?" Sir George asked, standing.

Another gentleman also stood, and Meg decided she could now take notice of him. "I am quite all right, thank you. So sorry, I did not realize you had company. Tessa, my apologies," she said to Sir George's wife, who fluttered her hands and lashes. "I was so concerned about the wretched creature that I have burst in on you in my dirt. Please excuse me."

Meg had learned the first of what she needed to know. The gentleman was not some elderly relative of the Dodd she knew about. The best she could hope for was that he was a close cousin of the man her dear friend Anne had described in her letters.

> *I could not love a man who did not tower over me, Meg, so he has fulfilled this expectation. Broad shoulders, fine frame, the darkest hair one wants to sink one's fingers into like the ocean at twilight. And did I mention, the most delicious hazel eyes? This one, my dearest, could match you for intelligence. I want him, and I shall have him. So never worry. Here is a reason beyond friendship why I would never betray you.*

The delicious hazel eyes drank in every detail of her as she drank in every detail of him. An impeccably tailored blue coat and tan trousers, a simply tied but perfect cravat, and one gold watch fob proclaimed a simple, elegant taste. Dark sideburns highlighted the refined but forceful lines of his face. He had a dimple in his right cheek that likely embarrassed him, for he smiled only from the other side. Too bad, too, for on a woman that mouth would be described as kissable.

Meg and Anne had spent many an agreeable assembly arguing over what made a man handsome. This Mr. Dodd would have appealed instantly to Anne. Meg, however, decided that the cool, ironic gleam in his eyes bespoke an arrogance she would do best to avoid. She had never got on with men who thought they owned the world and all its appurtenances.

Never got on. That was an understatement.

At least this specimen of an arrogant aristocrat did not seem inclined to possess what he saw: a woman of four and twenty, taller than Anne by some three inches, too thin for English taste, with eyes that let the weather decide their color, her blondish hair partially blown from its confining pins, and her dress unfashionable and muddy.

"No, no, sister," Sir George said, "do not go yet. This gentleman has come to call upon you."

"Indeed?"

The gentleman bowed. "Yes, Mrs. Grantham." He had a deep, resonant voice that reminded Meg of Spanish pomegranates. To her surprise and unease she almost licked her lips.

"We have not met, sir," she said. "Such a mystery."

"His name is Dodd," Sir George said, "and he has come on a commission from Viscount Reversby."

Maybe he *was* a cousin. Could anyone be so arrogant as to pretend to be on a commission from oneself? Yes, Meg thought, for she had seen worse manifestations of arrogance. She said, "How very kind. I am all astonishment, though, as to why Lord Reversby would send you, sir."

"There is no mystery, ma'am. He sent me to give you this." With long, well-molded hands, he took a packet from his pocket and gave it to her. As he did, his hand touched hers, and a sharp but indefinable feeling made Meg draw her breath in sharply. He likewise appeared startled.

"I, I cannot think of what Lord Reversby would want to give me," Meg said.

"Open it, Aunt, do," said Lizzie and promptly bumped into Meg's elbow. Meg grimaced, and Lizzie tightened her mouth.

"This is my daughter, Miss Grantham, sir," said Sir George.

"Your servant, Miss Grantham," said the gentleman.

"A pleasure, sir," replied Lizzie. "Open it."

"Make a proper curtsy," Meg told Lizzie. "You must get into the habit of it."

"Are you going up to London for the Season?" the gentleman asked.

"Yes," Lizzie said, curtsying without falling on her face. "But I am hopeful that by the time we reach there, my aunt will stop acting like a sergeant drilling troops."

"Lizzie!" Sir George said, while Tessa fluttered her hands.

"I have known many a young woman," the gentleman said, "who would be thankful to know that their manners will flow smoothly when they are faced with one of the Patronesses."

Lizzie sighed, and Meg knew what she was thinking.

Why should she expend courtesy on a man who ran errands for other men? Lizzie could not know this man was likely Viscount Reversby himself.

"Thank you, sir, for that reassurance," Lizzie said begrudgingly. "Now open the package, Aunt."

Meg turned the package over, broke the wax seal that held the heavy paper closed. Inside, surrounded by cotton batting, lay an achingly familiar garnet broach in the shape of a Maltese cross. Arrogant or not, Mr. Dodd or Lord Reversby, he had given Meg something precious.

She looked up at the gentleman to thank him from the bottom of her heart, and understood from the tick in his cheek—the same one that held the dimple—that this visit was not about generosity. It was a test.

"A simple jewel," Lizzie said. "Look, Mama, garnets."

"This belonged to Anne. Lady Reversby, I mean."

Tessa and Sir George crowded up to take a look. "Very pretty," Tessa said. "You grew up together, is that not right, sister?"

"Yes," Meg said. "After my parents died, I was all alone in the world until I came to live with my Neville cousins. Anne and I were only six months apart."

"When did she die?"

"In '12, when I was yet in Spain. Sir, please thank Lord Reversby for me, but this cross belonged to Lady Reversby's mother. It should, properly, go to her brother, Mr. Neville."

"It was, apparently, Lady Reversby's dearest wish that this cross come to you, Mrs. Grantham. Lord Reversby regrets only that it has taken so long to bring it to you."

"We have another mystery, then, sir, for I have been living here in western Leicestershire the better part of a year, with my late husband's family." She smiled in Sir George and Tessa's direction.

"That is why he is particularly annoyed."

"That is why he sent you, sir?"

"Precisely, ma'am," he said.

Lizzie snorted and fell back inelegantly onto a settee, kicking a small table and making it jump. "Well, Aunt, finally I may say I have met someone else who says 'precisely.'"

The gentleman raised his brows, but did not comment upon Lizzie. "I hope you will keep the cross, ma'am."

"I feel now I may accept it with gratitude and thanks." Meg closed her hand around the brooch. Its clasp bit comfortingly into her palm, its garnets pebbly beneath her fingers. "I no longer had anything of Lady Reversby's." Would the gentleman reveal himself now?

"I am sorry for that," the gentleman said. "Her loss was a loss to us all."

"Yes," Meg replied, studying him. No irony lurked in his hazel eyes now. If he was Reversby, he had loved his wife as much as Anne had represented in her letters.

But Meg now recalled a reserve that had entered her friend's letters when mentioning her husband. Meg could not remember how long the honeymoon had lasted, but Anne had hinted at something awry in the garden. Had his arrogance dimmed Anne's appreciation of his good looks?

"Do you stay to dinner with us, Mr. Dodd?" Tessa asked. "You would be most welcome."

"Yes, indeed," Sir George said.

Meg expected him to beg off, but he said, "Thank you so much for your kind offer. I should be most pleased."

With more than a little disquiet, Meg excused herself to change into more suitable clothing. She chose a muslin patterned with small, dark purple flowers, pinned the garnet cross on its lace fichu, and asked Hemmie to repair her hair. Then she dismissed the maid and took Anne's letters from her secretary.

The outermost two had lost most of their words to the rushing waters of the Tagus during one of their many crossings. A soldier in the regiment had rescued the packet for her. Meg found the one she wanted. Touching the letter, as she reread the passage that had so often puzzled her, made her feel closer to her friend.

This letter was among the last she had received, shortly before Anne's death.

> *I adore Reversby, never doubt that. But lately I have felt as if I were skating on a lake, with decided boundaries and no thin ice. He would have me be all too safe. How I wish I could be with you, living all that excitement.*

Meg shook her head, as she had every time upon reading it. She had written Anne that there was little of excitement following the drum, mostly death and survival. Anne had not believed her, claimed Meg uttered platitudes to calm her. And in the cold, bloody time between the storming of Ciudad Rodrigo and Badajoz, Meg had not the patience to disabuse her.

Why was he here, with his delicious but piercing eyes, garnet cross, and false name? What test had he wanted her to pass? What ordeal did he yet expect to put her through?

Why did his voice remind her of pomegranates, her most treasured fruit? They were a lot of work, but their sweetness could quench the bitterest thirst.

Meg replaced the letters, and not a moment too soon, for Lizzie burst into her room.

"You must do something!" she said, all tragedy.

"About what? Do calm yourself and tell me."

"My pianoforte! Papa has word from your beau Mr. Black—"

"Mr. Black is not my beau."

"Whatever. You sent him to oversee its removal to London. You promised that it would come with us to London. How can I hope to impress gentlemen callers when I have no pianoforte?"

Meg had sent Mr. Black to hand-carry the instrument if necessary, but not because she felt that Lizzie would fail to secure someone's hand because of its lack. Meg had sent Mr. Black after the pianoforte so he would not come after Meg. "What has happened?"

"He says that it has met with some sort of accident being loaded onto the barge at the Oxford Canal, and awaits instructions." Lizzie's voice rose to a screech.

"Has your father given him instructions?"

"Papa wants to speak to you about it, for he does not understand from Mr. Black's letter just what the problem is."

Meg wished she knew who was responsible for

breeding such hesitation into the Grantham brothers. "There is nothing we can do today."

"Why ever not?"

"There is the matter of our gentleman caller. Where is he, by the by?"

"Papa let him into the garden."

Let him? Like a dog? "Alone?" Meg asked.

"Certainly. Papa was not going to discuss my pianoforte before him," Lizzie said indignantly.

Meg pressed her fingertips over her eyebrows.

"Do not say, 'God give me strength,' like you usually do. *You* left him alone to change. After you started talking to him looking like you did."

Meg took a deep breath. "And you should go change, too."

"Do you ever admit you might be wrong?" Lizzie said with patently false sweetness.

"No," Meg replied in a like tone.

Lizzie scowled and retreated. Meg went downstairs to the little garden that flanked the north drawing room. There she found the gentleman gazing across the rosebushes, perennials, and stone portico to the larch that dominated the stand of trees across the lawn. A mist was coming in, forming in whorls around its upper branches.

"It is one of my favorites, too," she said by way of greeting.

"It does have character. An imposing one, though."

"Is there not some ancient expression about like recognizes like?" she asked.

"*Similis agnoscit similim,* perhaps?"

"Perhaps. Everything sounds better in Latin."

"Yes, but do we know each other well enough to

hazard guesses upon each other's characters?" he asked in that plush voice of his.

"I believe I passed your test earlier, sir."

He raised a brow. "You do not seem ruffled by the notion."

"That is because I could be ruffled about a more important matter entirely."

"Oh? Miss Grantham's itinerant pianoforte?"

"No, but I am sorry my husband's family has abandoned you over the subject."

"I shall survive."

"They would not have, did they know you are Reversby."

He smiled slightly, which made him appear winning, and thus more handsome. "It is refreshing to be treated like a lackey. Quite braces the constitution."

Inwardly Meg winced. But she said, "You do not deny it, then? That you are Reversby?"

"I am surprised you have kept the secret this long."

"I still will. Sir. It would be an abuse of hospitality, do you not think?"

"And if I meet you in London?" The irony curled into roguishness.

"You and your cousin Mr. Dodd share an uncanny resemblance."

"You are able to go to great lengths to keep a secret," Reversby said.

Roguish and winning he might appear, but now Meg knew how he wanted this conversation to tend. Fear stirred within her, gripped her about her throat. She tossed her head to make the feeling go away. "You seem quite focused on the secret itself, sir, when I would prefer to focus on the harm it would do to innocent bystanders."

"Is that, in your mind, the only justifiable reason to keep one?"

"The only moral one," Meg replied.

He considered her, and Meg was aware of his will as she suspected few ever were. "So for you the white lie, or the lie of omission?"

Meg wanted to have him ask her directly, to stop the shilly-shallying. "Tell me you have never employed such a tactic, and then you may use that tone with me. You came here to ask me something, so ask it."

He turned away to regard the larch tree and the broad swath of greens. When he turned back, he said, "It is quite amazing to me that you and my wife were such good friends. She would never have addressed me in so blunt a fashion."

"Anne had other skills," Meg said.

A sad smile tugged at his mouth, and Meg wondered what memory he relived. "I found some of your correspondence to her. You make reference to a secret you carried for her."

Meg nodded. What she had feared had come to pass. Her respectability, and thus her life, hung in the balance. *Curse it, Anne, you should have burned those letters.*

Meg should have burned hers, too, and had not.

"I want to know what that secret is," he said.

"I cannot tell you," she said.

"Cannot, or will not?" he asked, his hands clasped behind his back so that his shoulders appeared larger, broader.

"I am very sorry."

"No, you are patently not sorry, Mrs. Grantham. I did not know what to expect when I came down here. Certainly not this."

"Is that why you tested me?"

"Yes."

"Did I pass?" Meg asked.

"Yes. I could tell you loved my wife."

"I did, sir, which is why I do not betray her secrets."

"The only person left in her family is her brother, and I cannot think of what might serve to embarrass him."

Meg had to give him that. Reversby knew his man. Xavier Neville had not a bone in his body capable of being embarrassed.

"So I must conclude I am the one who would be embarrassed," he said.

"May I suggest, sir, that you be careful about what you conclude about something unknown?"

"It appears I have made the wrong conclusion about you," he said. At Meg's uplifted brows he continued, "I thought you would care enough for her to put her husband at ease."

Meg put her head up as straight as she had almost seven years ago in faraway Portugal, when Colonel Seward, another man with the same easy arrogance, had confronted her. "I owe you no obligation, sir. You have no power over me." *Thank God, this time it is true.*

"You are quite correct. I don't."

"Besides, I hardly consider your seeking after secrets as complimentary to my friend, your wife."

"That is a blow, isn't it? If I told you I still needed to know, for private reasons, and would not repeat what you told me to another living soul, would you tell me?"

He was trying to be winning again, and all Meg's hackles rose. He spared her from replying, though, by saying, "No, you are quite correct to refuse me. After all, you only know me through Anne's letters. I tested you. Now you test me. Put me through my paces. Let me prove to you that I could learn what you know and treat it as a gentleman should. Where are you going?"

Meg stopped. "Sorry. I tend to walk when I think."

"Very well. We may walk. You think." They strolled about the house, counterclockwise, toward the front. He kept pace with her very nicely, and Meg experienced one of those tricks of memory where the past and the present blur. For a dizzying moment she was marching along a road in Spain, speaking to a man who wore the uniform of the 43rd Foot, a major she admired and respected.

"Letters," she had said, "do not tell the whole tale. Be cautious, sir."

The memory vanished with startling abruptness.

Reversby held her elbow. "Are you unwell?" he asked.

"No, thank you," Meg said, her confusion at how she felt to be touched by him replacing her confusion over the sudden shift from past to present. The sharp feeling returned, but with it a heady warmth, as though she had stepped into a hot spring.

She started walking again, toward the house's southwestern side, where Sir George had his library. Reversby followed her, curious but forbearing.

"I do not accuse you of ungentlemanlike behavior," she said.

"Perhaps not, but you do not trust me to—"

He broke off as Lizzie's voice sailed through the lace curtains. "But, Papa, Aunt Meg says she will not speak to you about it today."

Meg backed up toward the gravel drive to put distance between them and Lizzie. Meg could no longer bear the notion of Lizzie's pianoforte, not with him here, pressing her. But how to extricate herself? Then the notion presented itself.

"You wish a test, sir?"

"Well, so long as it does not involve wrestling Sir George's surly bull yonder," he said, a wicked smile playing toward his dimpled cheek.

Was he teasing her or relieved that she could not come up with anything challenging? He had underestimated her, then. "I sent a gentleman, an officer in the 15th Dragoons, to oversee the removal of Miss Grantham's pianoforte to London. He has encountered a snag, in Oxford."

"You mean for me to untangle him? That is my test?"

Meg nodded.

"I am glad we could come to an agreement," he said.

"Yes," Meg said and kept her expression bland. She had made no agreement, but better that his mistake left him believing she had. She would not let another man like Seward try to best her, and steal her last remaining shreds of dignity and honor, no matter a pomegranate voice she could drown in.

Chapter Two

"You have taken your sweet time getting back to London," said Noel's best friend, Viscount Fitzhugh, as he was shown into the library of Noel's London house.

"My sweet time? This from the man who wintered in Yorkshire," Noel said, standing. They clasped hands and clapped each other on the shoulders. "You look good, Fitzhugh. How is Lady Fitzhugh? Does she grieve much for Lady Howard?"

"More than she thought," Fitzhugh replied, settling himself in a brown leather chair next to Noel's. "She is following me down presently, after she settles a few matters. Lady Howard left her the house in Yorkshire."

"In truth?"

"It was a big surprise to Esme. But she will be here for most of the Season."

"Continuing your campaign of respectability? The more she is seen with her dashing husband letting her have as much latitude as possible and using it not at all, the better?"

Fitzhugh smiled the smile Noel wished he could have used successfully against a fierce widow, the kind that had little to do with mirth and everything to do with threat. But no matter, he would soon have his way.

"I have endeavored, while you were rusticating," Noel said, "to brush up on my fencing so I might offer you some practice."

"You are too kind."

"My shooting, of course, has never deviated from superb."

"Did I not recall it, you would remind me," Fitzhugh said.

They grinned like the two school friends they had been.

"So, where were you?" Fitzhugh asked.

"Oxford." Noel stood. "I have not offered you refreshment. How rude of me. What would you like?"

"Tea?"

Noel eyed him. "Tea."

"Tea." Fitzhugh relented. "With a little brandy thrown in for good measure."

Noel rang for tea and cold cuts. He realized he had missed dinner while traveling and must adjust to later London suppers.

"So, Oxford."

"The story starts back at Reversby Lodge," Noel said, sitting down and propping his feet upon a hassock. He told Fitzhugh of finding the letters Anne had kept from her friend Meg Grantham, and how Mrs. Grantham had implored Anne to keep their secret.

"I was wild to know what the secret was," Noel said.

Fitzhugh frowned. "I can well understand the desire to know, but unless it is a triviality, is it not something better left alone? Forgive me, Reversby, but she's been gone these two years now."

For the first time in the better part of a decade, Fitzhugh had made him mad.

"Calm down, Noel," Fitzhugh said.

Noel took a breath. "It is no triviality. Mrs. Grantham would admit a peccadillo in a heartbeat."

"She has so little honor?"

"She would consider it not worth her time. She impressed me as a woman who has a firm grip on practicalities. It is something important, Benedict. I hate to think it of Anne, but I can't stop this thought, like something from a bad dream. I am sitting down to cards with some right twiggy bastard, who could no more raise his hand to me than he could hold up his head without the pound of starch on his shirt points helping him. I get itchy just thinking about it. So I'm trying not to scratch while I have him pressed at the last bet. He has not a sou left, but he says in a nasty whinge that he has other coin to offer. He can tell me whether my wife progged so-and-so, and is it worth my while?"

"He sounds like your brother, Malcolm."

"So my imagination is lazy. I still can't rid myself of the image."

"No one would ever say that to you."

Noel snorted in disgust. "Maybe not, but I can see him, and until I know, every man I meet is thinking it. You of all people must understand."

"I do understand," Fitzhugh said, his expression hard. "But it is not an easy thing you are trying to do. Tell me about Mrs. Grantham."

"She is the widow of one Lieutenant John Grantham, recently of the Peninsula, now living with her

late husband's family in western Leicestershire."
Noel thought of her cool appraisal of him, the way
she had commanded attention despite not being
as pretty as Lady Grantham nor her daughter Miss
Lizzie Grantham. The servants deferred to her, and
she could silence Sir George with a look. "She is a
hawk among the pigeons, let me tell you. Well, I do
take that back. The brother- and sister-in-law are pigeons. The daughter is a jay."

Fitzhugh said, "I would have come with you, you
know."

"Which is precisely why I did not ask you."

Fitzhugh folded his arms and raised his brows.

"I did not know what to expect. I had even hoped
I might find out casually."

"How? Say 'Hello, I'm Reversby. What have you
and my wife been keeping secret?'"

"No," Noel said with exaggerated patience. "That
would be silly. No, I tried the old give-my-family-
name trick. Don't smirk. She saw right through
me." Noel wished she had not seen through him
with such fine, speaking gray eyes. He wished she
could have been a homely shrew.

"Serves you right. I'm sorry, Reversby. Must have
been embarrassing."

"The only thing Mrs. Grantham excels at more than
ordering me about her business is keeping secrets.
Don't ask questions yet. I'll get to it. Where was I?"

"Keeping secrets."

"Yes. She kept my identity secret while I stayed
to dinner. And let me tell you, I do not much want
the rest of them claiming an acquaintance. I have
rarely lived through such dull company. The chit
prattled on and on throughout dinner, the mother

fluttered her hands, and the father kept his mouth full. I was not required to make conversation."

"You expect them in London?"

"The chit is coming out."

"How shall you get away with—"

"I am my own first cousin. I shall have to affect a monocle or some other dashed thing."

Fitzhugh rolled his eyes. "Do not lisp, I beg you. I will have to cut you."

"But you could put up with a monocle?"

Fitzhugh looked dubious. "Perhaps we will be very lucky, and they will not travel in the same circles."

"I look for no ray of sunshine, Fitzhugh. At the least I must meet with Mrs. Grantham about the results of the errand she sent me on."

"Oxford."

"Yes, Oxford. She proposed that I show whether I am capable of hearing this secret of hers by performing a small errand for her in Oxford. The jay's pianoforte had become stalled in transit here to London."

"I am quaking. Is the blasted contraption here now?"

"That would be telling," Noel said. "Ah, here is our tea." He thanked his butler for having poured the stuff, and for thinking ahead to the brandy that went with it. Then he and Fitzhugh picked up cold cuts with their fingers as they had done as schoolboys, and he resumed his tale.

"I found out the fellow Mrs. Grantham had sent to entrust the thing's safe delivery to had holed up at the Mitre."

"Holed up? Was he confused?"

"He was very confused, for all he is an officer in His Majesty's 15th Dragoons."

"Why—"

"Did she send him? I have my suspicions about that. He was very keen she think well of him. Very keen."

"Hmmm?" Fitzhugh mumbled. His mouth was full of roast beef.

"I think she wanted to get rid of him."

Fitzhugh raised his brows.

"So there he was in one of their most excellent booths, stuffing himself with shepherd's pie and strawberries and ale. Necessary, too, really, for a ray of sunshine by him would shine right through."

"I am *very keen* to know how you introduced yourself to this paragon of efficiency."

"Mrs. Grantham had thought of that."

"The devil she had. I am beginning to wish I knew Mrs. Grantham."

"Do not work yourself into any sort of anticipation. She cannot hold a candle to your lady."

"Oh," Fitzhugh said.

"Wipe that look off your face. You don't know what you're talking about. I feel no attraction for the lady. Quite the contrary."

Well, there had been that odd, breathless moment when he had touched her hand, and the heady feeling he had experienced when Sir George had said something inane and he had met Mrs. Grantham's gaze to find his amused horror reflected in hers. She had not blushed as he might have expected, were there some attraction for him on her part. Instead she had stiffened, and his sense of affinity had smashed like glass on stone.

"Of course you do not," Fitzhugh said.

Noel decided it was best not to pursue the subject. What did it matter if he could remember every whorl of her braids and the line of her cheeks, lips, and throat? She was far too good at getting her own way, and was the keeper of a secret he had to know. Of course he had studied her.

Would that she had showed any weakness other than a desire to walk and a decided intolerance of fools. Regrettably, he felt very much like a fool with her.

"So I introduced myself, with her letter."

"As Dodd?"

Noel nodded.

"How did the dragoon take the change in command?"

"I did not need to mention my ability with a pistol, if that's what you mean."

Fitzhugh grinned. "What was wrong with the pianoforte?"

"It sang while it was being transported, with 'a ghostly loneliness sufficient to unnerve the local wagoneers.'"

"He said that? What is this clunch's name?"

"Black."

"Nathaniel Black?"

"Possibly. Why?"

"Sommers was one of your challengers, wasn't he?" Noel asked. "Long on talk, short on skill?"

"That's him."

"So Black didn't just tip them more, or replace them, and get on with it?"

"I do believe he had figured out that this favor he

did for Mrs. Grantham would take him far longer than anticipated."

"Ah, the devious law of diminishing returns."

"There was nothing to be done that night, other than to delight in his chagrin, which could not support the better part of a quarter hour. So I perforce went early to bed and had the thing uncrated the next morning, a local artisan on hand to inspect the instrument. I now know more than I need to about the inner workings of a pianoforte, but it was a fairly easy thing to determine that the dampers had come loose and sharp motions had caused the strings to vibrate."

"Amazing," Fitzhugh said.

"Yes, well, I had the instrument recrated and sent along its way down the Oxford Canal. It came into London a mere hour before I arrived. I had it sent on to the house the Granthams have taken. On Sudbury Street."

"And what of Mr. Black?"

"I wished him good-day. To his face."

"And to the devil otherwise."

Noel nodded.

"Much like Mrs. Grantham did, I do suppose."

"Yes, yes, I know. She did a fine job of getting rid of me, too. But it is a temporary situation, I do assure you. Except . . ."

"What?" Fitzhugh asked.

"Nothing." Nothing except that Black had called her Mrs. General Grantham, with much admiration, and her late husband, Noel had also learned, had been a mere lieutenant. Such a sobriquet fit her, all too well. It *was* amazing to think of Mrs.

Grantham and Anne being friends. They were so very different.

Except . . . for all her having sent him on a hideously tedious errand, Mrs. Grantham interested him in a way he had not been interested in any woman but Anne. It was her holding that blasted secret. She presented a challenge, an obstacle he must overcome. Simple as that. Once he knew it, he would have whatever it was to deal with, and that would probably distract him enough that he would cease fussing over Mrs. Grantham.

Thank you, ma'am, and good day. I wish you the best for a happy life.

Or words to that effect.

"So, when do you approach the lady for your pat upon the head?" Fitzhugh asked.

"I wrote a note already."

Fitzhugh took a few long sips of his tea, pulling back the corners of his mouth at the bite of the brandy. Then he said, "You are quite certain you want to know what this secret is?"

"I am prepared to be unhappy, but not unprepared, if that is your point."

"You may depend on us, you know," Fitzhugh said.

Noel nodded. "What are your plans for tonight?"

"I have promised my Aunt Bourre I will attend her niece's ball."

"Miss Tunbridge? Yes, that is right. She did not take last year, did she? And will Miss Bourre attend as well?" Noel asked.

"Yes."

"Relations between you and Miss Bourre remain strained?"

"If I must say that I regret anything about marrying Esme," Fitzhugh said, "it is that I have hurt Dorrie."

"You may regret hurting her, but Miss Bourre could have had you any year these past four. She chose not to. You and Lady Fitzhugh are damnably well suited. That alone could rub someone the wrong way."

Fitzhugh smiled a little, embarrassed. "It is a ticklish situation. With such an advertisement, I do not suppose you would like to come?"

"I should be pleased. My last night in society monocle-free."

Chapter Three

"Our first night in society!" Lizzie said, in a squealing whisper, her hand dug into Meg's arm. "How very grand it all is! Only look at the mirror running down the entire wall."

"You will be very much on display," Meg replied, trying to be steadying, and unimpressed. But it was her first London ball, too. She had attended various country assemblies and private parties, but the scale of London did overwhelm.

Did her deep green silk and lace compare at all favorably to the other ladies' attire?

"Yes, yes," Lizzie said, "I will mind my manners. But tell Mama to put her fan down before she does herself an injury."

There was no time, for they had come up to their hostess, Lady Tunbridge, a reed-thin woman dressed in the most exquisite fashion, who greeted them with every cordiality. When she asked after Tessa's sister, she answered Meg's unspoken question about why they should be invited to this ball and so quickly. They had arrived in London only that noontime.

Arrived to find a pianoforte, uncrated. Lord Reversby had succeeded far too quickly and easily. A frisson passed up Meg's spine and settled between her shoulder blades, although that was likely attributable to the low back of her gown.

She had to tear herself away from her apprehension to greet some others standing next to Lady Tunbridge. First, Mrs. Bourre, Lady Tunbridge's sister, a woman with a sweet face except for the firm lines around her mouth. This lady, Meg thought, would be a worthy ally. If one needed an ally, that is.

Despite being a pretty blonde dressed in the very first stare of fashion, her daughter Miss Bourre seemed ill at ease. She kept putting up her hand as though she would take the arm of the gentleman next to her, and then putting it down.

"Lord Fitzhugh, meet Mrs. Grantham," Mrs. Bourre said.

Meg had heard much of Lord Fitzhugh, mostly through Tessa, of the "thrilling" courtship between Viscount Fitzhugh and the woman who had been the notorious Dowager Countess of Iddesford. She had listened because she knew Reversby called Fitzhugh friend, and because Tessa enjoyed the simple pleasures of gossip. It had seemed churlish to deny her them.

Lord Fitzhugh was a tall man, with light brown hair and warm gray eyes. Not as handsome as Reversby but engaging. Meg did not wonder at Miss Bourre wanting to cling to such a man. Meg did wonder what the new Lady Fitzhugh thought of it, though, and where she was.

Fitzhugh's expression quickened with interest. "Mrs. John Grantham?" he asked.

"Yes," Meg replied, and hoped she hid the curse

forming in her thoughts. Reversby and Fitzhugh had talked.

"I should very much like to dance with you, if I may be permitted?"

"I was not planning to dance tonight, my lord."

"Surely you are not going to deny the gentlemen here that pleasure. The third?"

"Fitzhugh is a wonder on the dance floor," Mrs. Bourre said fondly. "No one ever appears to disadvantage with him."

Maneuvered thus, Meg assented, and their party moved down the stairs and into the ballroom proper.

"He did not ask me to dance," Lizzie said.

"He is married, anyway," Meg replied.

"Do you want me to believe you old married couples stick together?"

Meg winced. She could not help it. But she reminded herself that Lizzie was only being peevish and could not know what a sudden, unexpected thrust her comment was. "I am no old married couple, remember, niece?"

Lizzie took the reprimand with less than good grace. "Lord Fitzhugh is married, but that is just why being seen with him would be a coup. He married Lady Notorious."

"We are not going to continue this conversation," Meg said as quietly as she could for the burgeoning noise. "It makes your expression appear to disadvantage in the mirrors."

Alarmed, Lizzie studied her reflection without trying to look like she was. They went to join Tessa and Sir George near the tables where the punch was laid, and Lizzie spoke long about the fashions of the other women and how grand everything was.

But as the interval passed and the second dance began, this entertainment paled, and Lizzie began acting fretful again. Meg opened her mouth to admonish her and say that since they were not well known yet in London society, it would take some time to have introductions performed, etc.

But Sir George spoke first. "I say, is that not our new acquaintance, Mr. Dodd?"

Tessa and Lizzie began speaking at breath-neck pace about how they must attract his attention so he might begin the process of social introductions.

The sudden fluttering in Meg's throat prevented her from adding her opinion right away. "Is he speaking to Lord Fitzhugh?" She had to ask it twice before Lizzie said yes.

"Then that gentlemen is likely not Mr. Dodd, but Viscount Reversby. He and Lord Fitzhugh are friends, and, as Mr. Dodd mentioned to you, he was not coming to London."

"He looks very like," Tessa said.

"Some first cousins do," Meg said.

"Yes, but—"

"Some punch, Sir George?" Meg asked, to distract them.

It served, although not for Meg. She watched a gentleman join Fitzhugh and Reversby, blond and a few years younger than they, with a mischievous smile. He handed Reversby something. Then the gentlemen disappeared in the crowd while Lizzie and Tessa watched hard for them. All very mysterious.

Meg sipped her punch and tried to control the fluttering in her throat. She had not expected to see him this first night in London. The pianoforte had been enough of a shock to her system. How unfair of him to be here.

The crowd disgorged Fitzhugh and Reversby, the latter wearing a monocle on a ridiculous blue-and-yellow striped ribbon. Meg choked on her punch, and swallowed lest she spray it in Reversby's face. The effort brought tears to her eyes.

"My dear Mrs. Grantham," Fitzhugh said, "are you quite all right?"

She held out the cup, which Reversby took with an ironical glint to his eyes, and fanned herself furiously. Sir George, Tessa, and Lizzie, as well as any number of those nearby, looked at her with varying degrees of curiosity, alarm, and distaste.

This was not the Peninsula, Meg reminded herself. This was not the place where she could have, had she wanted, ordered from several outcomes desirable to her. Here she was where she had started: with no position except what others gave her. She wanted to growl and hit out at the lot of them.

"I am fine," she replied.

"I am happy to hear it," Fitzhugh said. "Would you all please permit me to introduce Viscount Reversby to you? I understand you recently met his cousin, Mr. Dodd."

"That is right," Sir George said, "at our home in Leicestershire. I must thank you, my lord, for your consideration in sending him to us. Most kind. Most kind."

Reversby bowed. "Indeed the pleasure was mine, Sir George," he said in a languid voice.

Meg instantly hated it. *Pomegranates*, she thought. *We must have pomegranates*. And she ruthlessly pushed down the blush that threatened and the feelings that prompted it.

"I had no idea that you and your lovely family would come up to London for the Season," Reversby said. "I was unavailable, and I so wanted to ensure that Mrs. Grantham got the cross."

Sir George made happy noises.

Tessa interrupted his next effusion. "But you and Mr. Dodd look so very much alike."

Reversby squinted around the monocle.

"His mother and aunt were identical twins," Fitzhugh said gravely.

Meg, however, saw the slight rise of his eyebrows as he said it, and the answering lift of Reversby's brows in thanks.

"Indeed," Tessa said, with a happy little frown. It was precisely the sort of circumstantial puzzle she enjoyed, along with hen's teeth and four-leaf clovers.

Her exploring that little fiction with Fitzhugh gave Reversby the opportunity of inviting Meg to dance the fourth. She hesitated before accepting—realizing that it would be as good a time as any to discuss the pianoforte.

Reversby then turned partially away and patted in his pockets. Fitzhugh handed him a handkerchief. Reversby removed his monocle, polished it, and stuck it back on before pasting a smile on his face and inquiring whether Miss Grantham would do him the honor of the third?

Lizzie accepted with what could only be described as a squeal, and Meg looked away from Reversby's ironic gaze. She had, after all, predicted that Lizzie would treat Viscount Reversby very differently than a mere Mr. Dodd. She took no pleasure in being correct, though. Quite the opposite.

Lizzie had been such a different child before they had begun making plans for London. Not pleasant exactly, but interesting. Then the temper had started, the rebellions. Meg hoped for Lizzie's sake that she would settle down once she married. And for Meg's sake, a married Lizzie would be a grateful, needy Lizzie, whose household might need an aunt who could manage its affairs, leaving Lizzie to her music.

Would that Reversby had never found those letters.

With the exception of watching Lizzie step on Reversby's foot during the dance—not badly, not enough to cause general notice, thank God—Meg spent a pleasant time with Lord Fitzhugh. As she was careful what she said to him, he talked more than she suspected he was wont to. By the end, Meg had gathered that he was a Corinthian, knew horses backward and forward, and was madly in love with his wife.

Meg elected to reserve judgment on whether Lady Fitzhugh deserved such a man being so in love with her. Meg had seen many a stupider situation, her own included.

"I will thank you not to use those dreadful tones with which you entertained my family," Meg said when she and Reversby began their own dance.

He raised his brows, but whether in mock offense or just mocking, she could not tell. Either way, he annoyed her.

"My speech bothered you?"

"Between it and the monocle, you would appear the fop."

"Do you not think I can carry it off?"

He danced almost as well as his friend, and with a sort of assurance that hinted he could do other things well. The impression disconcerted her. From Anne's letters, Meg had regarded him as a gentleman who spent his time as he cared to, as having no ambitions other than to live well. It was, she told herself, what made her resent his arrogance. Meg particularly despised selfishness when manifested as lazy pointlessness.

"Not if you intend to keep your friendship with Lord Fitzhugh realistic," she said. "There is nothing of the fop about him."

"You approve of my friend," Reversby said.

"Yes, I do."

"Thought so."

"How can you tell?"

"Your expression . . . softened."

Meg did not like that Reversby saw so much. How much did he know from her letters to Anne? Impossible to ask. "He is a nice man."

"And a fine friend. He arranged for the monocle tonight. We did not think I would need it so soon."

"I thought that the person who got you the monocle was the blond-haired young man with the devious smile."

"Smith-Jenkins?" Reversby asked. "He is pleased to assist Fitzhugh. Would that he could have provided a sturdier shoe as well."

Meg elected to ignore his comment about Lizzie's lack of poise. "You must blame Lady Tunbridge's friendship with my sister-in-law's sister."

"The Kemps are exceptionally loyal. Both Lady Tunbridge and her sister, Mrs. Bourre, were born Kemps."

"Does he really love his wife as much as I think he does?"

"More, likely. Fitzhugh is dreadfully understated."

"Unlike yourself."

"Quite unlike myself. I am much fonder of the grand, sweeping gesture."

"Else why would you come all the way to Leicestershire to find me?"

"No, ma'am, that has nothing to do with grand, sweeping gestures, and everything to do with practicality."

"There is nothing *practical* you can learn from me. Annie is gone, my lord. I grieve for her, but she is gone."

The irony deserted him under her blunt assault. She hated to do it, but he needed to leave her alone. She did not want a man who could be competent and determined near her secret. She did not want to feel the feelings he had stirred within her, feelings she had dwelt on during the time she had spent packing the family and relocating to London.

Pomegranates. Luscious, sweet red juice catching on her lips, dripping from her fingers, and she, sucking it off.

He had been Anne's husband. Monocle or no monocle, Meg had developed an unhealthy lust for Anne's husband. He was Anne's husband, and her potential doom.

"What do you think of Miss Bourre?" he asked after they had passed through another set of figures.

He has not given up, Meg thought. She decided to follow his game of small talk. "She seems an amiable girl."

"Lady Fitzhugh will not come down to London for another week or more."

Meg smiled a question.

"Yes, Mother, the child will explain his cryptic remarks."

Meg flushed. "I do not think I like you, sir. You tease too much. It presupposes a connection we do not have nor will ever have."

"Not what someone called 'General Grantham' is used to, I daresay."

Meg breathed in so sharply her breath sounded like a hiss. "Where—?"

The dancers around them looked startled. Reversby squinted around his monocle with a hatefully sunny smile. "Chocolates," he said to the dancers nearby. "The lady is new to London and wants to know where I buy my chocolates. Not a trivial matter."

"I should say not," the woman said. "You must go to Gunter's, 7 Bedford Square. Everyone who is everyone goes there. The creams and nougats are divine."

"Yes, but Natarain's in Piccadilly has better varieties in caramels and nutmeats," the portly gentleman accompanying her said. "What sort of woman are you?"

Meg blinked.

The portly gentleman flushed. "That came out unpardonably. My apologies."

"On the contrary," Reversby said, as he turned Meg beneath his hand, "it is precisely the question."

He smelled of warm, tangy lemons. "Fruit," Meg said. "I like fruit."

"Cherries dipped in chocolate," the portly gentleman said.

"Raspberry nougat," the woman said on a sigh.

"I think you are a Gunter's sort of woman," Reversby said.

"Definitely," the lady said.

"Thank you," Reversby said.

The couple's effusions of welcome and further advice carried them through the end of the dance.

"You look like you need a draft of cooling air," Reversby said, and, taking Meg firmly by the elbow, began leading her toward the French doors.

"I do not need cooling. How ungallant of you to say so. What I need is letting alone."

"Too late," Reversby said.

"I beg your pardon?"

"Well, for one thing, you have not said thank you. You have avoided the subject the entire dance, and I cannot say I appreciate your ducking it."

No, he had definitely not given up. "I am sorry. Lizzie was overjoyed to see her pianoforte. Thank you," Meg said, tacitly agreeing to have this conversation, as she could not release herself from Reversby's hold without causing a scene.

The balcony outside stretched some fifteen to twenty yards away from the house and ended in a stone balustrade that sloped down to follow steps at each end. A garden lay beneath them shadowed by lantern light. One other couple, a matron and an older gentleman, stood at the far left, talking softly, their bodies inclined eloquently toward each other.

Reversby directed Meg to the far right. He turned so that he could let the monocle drop. "Devilish uncomfortable thing," he muttered. "And do not tell me it is self-inflicted, for I know that."

"If there is any God," she said, likewise muttering.

"What? If there is any God, what?"

"You will suffer the headache from having to wear it."

"Why do you not like me, Mrs. Grantham? You did not appear to resent my presence so heartily in Leicestershire."

"Next you will be reminding me of the many others who appreciate you."

"Well, I'm a likeable fellow. Only look at how I discovered where you should go for chocolates."

"How do you know I eat chocolates?"

"What? I am all amazement. You must be the first woman I know not to eat chocolates."

"Suppose I said I got out of the habit while following the drum." It was a lie, but it would have silenced Sir George.

It affected Reversby not the least. "You may pick up new habits if the mood seizes you."

"You would have me pick up the habit of confiding secrets that don't belong to you."

"No, I would have you pick up the habit of making good on your contracts."

"What are you talking about?"

"Oh, no," he replied, and his hand slid up from her elbow to her shoulder to join his other hand on her other shoulder. "Do not make the mistake so many women have before you."

Meg held her chin up. She would not be forced into unpleasant choices, not ever again. "And what is that mistake?"

"Of thinking that a beautiful face and lovely body will convince every man to forgive a faulty memory."

"Stop that," she said, looking at his hand on her right shoulder. The contact of his glove against her bare shoulder started those thoughts she would as soon never have.

"Or what?" he asked softly, but with an intent note that sent fresh frissons racing between her shoulder blades.

It must stop.

"Or you will never learn what the secret is."

Chapter Four

Noel stepped back as though stung. What had he been thinking—making up to Anne's friend? Surely he did not think her desirable. Surely she did not think him desirable. Surely he had not lost his touch with women to such an extent that he could judge so poorly?

Still, as they had danced, he had glimpsed a passion in her that had little to do with protecting secrets or being the person one would call "General Grantham." Even when he had teased her, she had followed his lead with an enviable poise, putting her own stamp on her moves, bending a wrist in a nice decline, or tipping her head just so to reveal the delectable hollow of collarbone and throat.

Her shoulders had felt perfectly formed under his hands, and now that they were outside, he could catch her faint scent of orange and cloves. Probably from some emolument or soap she used. She was likely not the kind who applied perfume.

Her hair, which he had not thought remarkable, glowed, backlit from the ballroom light. She struck him, suddenly, as a trimmer version of the subjects of so many Renaissance paintings. She possessed all the mystery and allure that came from a knowledge no man could ever hope to grasp but could identify enough to paint.

Hell, blast, and damnation, he thought.

"We have a problem," he said.

"No, my lord. You have a problem."

Her blunt rejoinder angered him. "And I will overcome it that much quicker do you but tell me what you promised you would tell me."

She studied him, gray eyes hooded, full lips drawn in at the corners. "I never promised you anything."

"But you—" Noel broke off, recalled the conversation they had had in Sir George's garden. He had proposed she test him, but she was right. She had made no promises. Stupid, stupid, stupid.

"You see," she said, and it was not a question.

"You are an exceptionally tricky, managing sort of woman."

"Thank you."

"You take that as a compliment."

"Indeed I do, sir. Being an exceptionally tricky, *managing* sort of woman kept me and others alive."

"So now you embrace 'General Grantham,'" he said.

"What else am I to do? Do I not, you will continue throwing it in my face at inconvenient moments. I did not appreciate the name while in the Peninsula. It drew unnecessary attention from the general officers."

"The official ones, you mean."

"Just so, sir," she said, lifting her pointed chin. "Nor will I appreciate the sobriquet when in the presence of my late husband's family, if you please."

"Why?"

"What else did you and Mr. Black speak about?"

"Oh, no. I will not be fobbed off so."

"And I will not answer your question."

Standstill. Unless he could shock her again. "He is in love with you. Black, I mean."

She pursed her lips and folded her arms. It made the bodice of her green dress bow, revealing more of her bosom than she likely would have considered seemly. Noel did not call this fact to her attention. She had an excellent, compelling bosom.

"You did know it," Noel said. "That is why you sent him after the wretched pianoforte." He laughed. "We must make an inscription upon the thing on a pretty gold plaque: 'I am the instrument by which Mrs. Grantham strikes the right chord with her suitors.'"

"Follow my adagio along the canal," she said, her eyes sparkling.

"A standard fifth progression—"

"But no allegros, thank you."

"In a minor key. E for the middle of Meg, perhaps?" he asked.

The sparkle in her eyes died.

A sting of conscience pricked Noel, as though he had bullied her. That, however, was patently fallacious. This ferocious, tricky woman matched him will for will.

"Black told me he was coming to London," Noel said. "Have you another wild-goose chase planned for him?"

"No. One per customer."

"You think he will be dissuaded so easily?"

"He is cautioned."

Noel leaned against the railing. "You are quite

the most amazing woman I have met this last half year."

"And frustrating, too, I fear sure you will say."

"Frustrating, yes, but I still stand by amazing."

"You must not have as wide a circle of acquaintance as I was led to believe," she said.

"I begin to think I have not been in the right places."

"What—oh, by all that's unholy," she muttered. "Do reattach your first cousin."

Charmed by her phrasing, Noel did not comprehend what she meant.

"Stop looking vacuously at me, my lord. Put your monocle back in. Now. And do not look over your shoulder first."

"There they are," Miss Grantham said with an overzealous wave. "Yoo-hoo, Aunt Grantham."

She and Smith-Jenkins, followed closely by Fitzhugh and Miss Bourre, stepped onto the balcony. Smith-Jenkins looked as though someone had clubbed him. Miss Grantham had had that effect on Noel, too. Then Noel realized he might wear such an expression now from talking to Mrs. Grantham.

"Triple hell," Noel said, under his breath but no less violently for all that.

"Does not begin describe it," Mrs. Grantham said in a murmur. Despite the monocle, he did not miss the sparkle returning to her eyes. Noel began to fear those sparkles. But she had not chided him for his profanity. Interesting.

"Do you see, I told you they would be out here," Miss Grantham said.

"And here we are," Noel replied, playing at First Cousin.

Smith-Jenkins emerged from his stupor. "I say, Reversby—"

Miss Bourre elbowed him. When he turned, affronted, she shook her head slightly at him and winked.

Fitzhugh, however, stood as impassive as a burial urn. Smith-Jenkins had once found Fitzhugh and the former Dowager Countess of Iddesford kissing in a garden. The resulting scandal had been most impressive.

"Never you fear, now, sir," Noel said to Smith-Jenkins, "entirely appropriate, eh? Not in any dark corner."

"Are you, Lord Reversby," Mrs. Grantham said sweetly, "known for being a rake?"

That was coming it a little too brown. Pomposity would answer. "You are a widow, ma'am, so rules may be more relaxed for you, even in London."

"Thank you very much, my lord. I would not want to appear," Mrs. Grantham said, and paused for emphasis, "untutored."

Noel almost lost his monocle, and cast about for something fabulous to say.

Mrs. Grantham appeared to be holding her breath, except that her mouth also looked rigid and she was shaking. The wretched woman was trying hard not to laugh.

"Reversby is no more a rake than any other unmarried gentleman in London," Fitzhugh said.

"No one has introduced me to this gallant gentleman, who has been so concerned with propriety," Mrs. Grantham said, stepping forward and smiling at Smith-Jenkins, who puffed himself up under the approbation.

Miss Bourre and Miss Grantham frowned. Fitzhugh raised his brows, but a tip of his head signaled Noel that he should be the one to do it. "Mrs. Grantham, allow me to present Mr. Smith-Jenkins. Smith-Jenkins, Mrs. Grantham."

They made polite noises to each other, Smith-Jenkins still a little bewildered but willing to be dazzled by Mrs. Grantham's sudden smile. She had a lovely smile, when she chose to employ it with no ulterior motive. Almost Noel could see her as the girl she had been before she had gone off to war.

That train of thought disconcerted Noel. Why had he had it? What did it mean?

Smith-Jenkins was trying to secure a dance.

"You may not have the seventh, sir," Noel found himself saying, "for she has quite promised it to me."

Mrs. Grantham gave him a hundred-paces stare, then she smiled at Smith-Jenkins and accepted for the eighth. "That way, I cannot be tempted outside for a breath of air."

Smith-Jenkins, thought Noel, rot his lack of discernment, could not determine that she was joking. She was joking, right?

"I should say," Smith-Jenkins said, glancing at Miss Bourre.

"Then I am free the eighth, Fitzhugh," Miss Bourre said.

"Very good, Dorrie," Fitzhugh replied, his expression indicating that he would be taking Smith-Jenkins aside sometime later that evening. Noel did not envy him the experience.

Mrs. Grantham studied them all, and Noel was

blessed if the wretched woman had not also picked up on some tension.

Of mutual accord, they headed back into the ballroom, where the rhythm of a lively country dance could be felt in one's bones. Certainly the perfume assaulted one's marrow. "We must return you to your mother," Mrs. Grantham said to Miss Grantham, who promptly pouted.

Brat, Noel thought.

"We last saw Lady Grantham by the far wall," Miss Bourre said, "third mirror up."

"Would you be so kind," Mrs. Grantham asked her, "to show us? I feel quite lost in your aunt's beautiful ballroom."

Patently untrue, wretched woman, but Miss Bourre had no option but to acquiesce. The three ladies curtsied, although Miss Grantham did so only after Mrs. Grantham tapped her on the arm with her fan.

"Smith-Jenkins," Fitzhugh said, "do me a kindness and get Miss Bourre a glass of punch on her way back. She looks a trifle heated, and it would never do for me to tell her so."

"Right away, sir," Smith-Jenkins said and hurried off.

"How long *have* you had him on a lead?" Noel asked as he and Fitzhugh strolled toward the broad marble stairs that let one into the ballroom from the street. They bowed politely to acquaintances but did not stop to converse.

"He stepped into the collar himself, and there was no lead attached."

"Whatever prompted that?" Noel asked, trying to

resist the notion that he had stepped into something he had never intended.

"He has a profound respect for my wife," Fitzhugh said.

"Do I ask whether you keep him close to better observe him or to employ him?"

"Neither. Between us, we do enough in that department."

"Such modesty on your part is not called for, surely."

Fitzhugh smiled, then grew serious again. "I hope he may be developing a decided preference for Dorrie."

"Oh." Noel swiped a glass of Madeira from a circulating footman, gestured to ask if Fitzhugh would like one, too, and took one for him. "Do you see any sign of her returning the feeling?"

Fitzhugh drained his Madeira in one impressive gulp.

"I will take that as a no," Noel said.

"I had hoped," Fitzhugh said, twirling his empty wine glass, "that if I could spend some time with her before Esme came down, she would resign herself. It seems to have had the opposite effect. Esme feared it would."

"Lady Fitzhugh is a wise woman."

Fitzhugh nodded. "I wonder what she will say when she sees you in that monocle. Do not glare at me. It was your idea."

"I am beginning to feel that I have made several tactical errors in my dealings with Mrs. Grantham. She seized on your coming onto the balcony to shake me off for the length of the next dance or two."

"She is still running you a pretty game?" Fitzhugh

asked, too casually. "I thought you had solved her problem and would get your prize."

"It appears," Noel said, watching the dancers exert themselves so he would not be tempted to look at Mrs. Grantham, "she made no actual promises."

"You just took them as promises."

"I have been gulled."

"By a master, if she could get past you."

"Do not try to make me feel better. No ray of sunshine, remember?"

Fitzhugh snorted, and gave up his empty glass to the same circulating footman. He balled and extended his fingers.

"You should have kept your glass," Noel said.

"So what are you going to do about this secret? Drop it?"

"I'll be damned first," Noel said with a cheerfulness he did not feel. He knew it would not fool Fitzhugh, but forcing the tone kept him from a complete black study. Appearances must be maintained, after all.

They stood together, Noel wondering with reluctance and intense curiosity to know what further mischief Mrs. Grantham had in store for him. Would that he could puzzle out another way to appeal to her.

Fitzhugh prodded him. "I think the seventh is next."

"It is but eleven-thirty," Noel said. "Surely midnight is the proper time for torture." He stepped forward a few paces and bowed to the two matrons there. "I beg your pardon, but could you tell me if this is the sixth or seventh dance?"

"This is the end of the sixth," one of them said in

a tone that also said he should have been paying attention.

Noel thanked her, bowed, and stepped back with Fitzhugh.

From before him, however, he heard the matron say to her friend, "These young bucks! If dances were horses, they would never forget."

"If they were," Noel muttered to Fitzhugh, "they might be trained not to bite." No, best not to follow that thought. Confounding woman, this Mrs. Grantham, mixing up all proper feelings.

Fitzhugh gave him a look, which prompted Noel to ask, "Are you promised to someone this dance?"

"Yes, Miss Tunbridge. She will speak nicely of where I might purchase what in millinery. I will speak nicely of what horses to watch for a year from now at Tatt's or the best carriage equipment, and we will walk away from it educated and unentangled."

"Glad you have a plan of sorts."

Fitzhugh said, "Do make sure that monocle stays in."

"Wretched dreadful thing is giving me the headache."

Fitzhugh grimaced his sympathy, and Noel set off across the ballroom to find Mrs. Grantham, his contradictory, uncomfortable feelings stowed, he hoped, underneath his eminently respectable, if slightly foppish, exterior.

She stood between her brother- and sister-in-law, turning first to one and gesturing, then to the other. Sir George was nodding as though he understood, but Noel suspected he did not. Lady Grantham just appeared bewildered.

The hawk educating the puffing pigeon and the dim pigeon.

The jay contemplated murder beneath dark curls and lace.

There was no sign of either Smith-Jenkins or Miss Bourre.

Mrs. Grantham spotted him, and spoke a few quick words to the pigeons. They looked up with alarm.

The jay folded her arms.

Noel bowed, made excruciating, pointless, but polite conversation with the pigeons, then took Mrs. Grantham's hand to lead her onto the dance floor. As her fingers closed around his, though, he lost his head for a moment. At least, that was how he explained to himself his kissing her hand.

"My lord," she said, protesting and blushing.

"Ooooh," Miss Grantham said, and promptly tripped. Over her own feet, no less.

"Steady there," Noel said, putting out his hand.

She yanked her arm away.

Noel chucked her under the chin. "Charming, m'dear, charming. Do make your bows to the Patronesses just that way."

There was a squeak behind him from Lady Grantham. Miss Grantham's jaw dropped.

"You will catch flies," Noel said with pleasant deadliness.

"My lord," Mrs. Grantham said, and he almost jumped as if she were a general officer and had issued an order.

Resenting that, resenting the whole miserable situation, Noel strolled and seethed. When they had gone halfway onto the floor, he said, "Do tell me that miserable chit will not show up on the dance floor with me again."

"Never tell me you have a temper, my lord."

"Quite the most lovely one you will ever lay eyes on. I enjoy starting it over a slow flame, which gives one plenty of time to adjust the seasonings before it comes to a full boil."

"Temper as ragout?"

"Nothing so very fancy. Stew suffices."

They took their places in the line forming. The orchestra began playing the entry notes of "Barley Mow."

"Well?" he asked.

"I beg your pardon?"

"Will the chit be dancing?"

"No," she replied.

Noel sighed. "You have not asked me why I am in a temper."

"I know it already," she said and did honors.

"Is there an ounce of sympathy in your frame?"

"That is frustration speaking, my lord."

Which, Noel understood, was no answer at all.

"Besides, it is improper for you to discuss my frame," she said.

That made him assess it again. He might just be able to fit his hands around her waist, not . . . no, he should not be thinking that way.

"Next you will be explaining why I should not be frustrated," he said. The dance required them close together, hands clasped to waists. Noel was almost accustomed to the feeling of Mrs. Grantham's firm hand and the feelings it provoked within him. Feeling her hand higher upon his arm released an entirely new set of sensations he should not have. He really should not have started thinking about her figure.

She must have glimpsed something in his expression—dashed monocle—that caused her to speak.

"You should not be frustrated, because I was entirely clear with you in Leicestershire that I will not share Annie's secret. The notion of a test was your idea."

"Do I get nothing for accomplishing it?"

"My thanks, sir."

"Your thanks?"

"Temper, temper. Do calm yourself," she said, "or we shall attract unwanted attention."

Noel eyed the other couples surrounding them. They had progressed a few times, but no one had spoken to them.

"That is better," she said. "Now, there is nothing to be done, so you may as well take your frustration elsewhere."

"Is that what you were doing, out on the patio, General?"

"I beg your pardon?"

"Were you volunteering poor Smith-Jenkins, whipping him up so he might consider giving me a challenge?"

"You have no great opinion of me, do you, sir?" She said it almost like she was pleased.

"Have I not called you the most amazing woman I have met?"

"Amazing is a two-edged sword. Be careful you do not cut yourself on it."

"Touché, but you will not get rid of me that easily. Oh, I have it. Is this another test?"

"I do wish you would stop talking about tests," she said.

"Indeed we shall not. I want another test. I crave another test. Indeed, I plan to adopt the name Hercules."

"Is that an improvement over your current name, my lord?"

"You do not know it? Honestly? It is Noel."

"You were born on Christmas?"

"July."

"Christmas in July," Mrs. Grantham said dubiously. "Very droll."

"My mother had a sense of humor. She had to. You may as well not leave me in suspense."

"She had to?"

"No, no, ma'am, we are not bargaining for my secrets."

"I am amazed you have any."

"Why?" he asked.

"Because you are what you are."

And, Noel thought, she did not think much of that. He tapped his monocle before he had to pass behind the next couple.

"That is a lie," Mrs. Grantham said, "not a secret."

"But some secrets are lies."

She inclined her head as they faced each other across the line of dancers. "Shall we indulge in logic diagrams? All Greeks are men, but not all men are Greeks?"

Noel bet that she regularly drew them in her head. "I think you like Greeks too well."

"I never met one, my lord."

She had to be the most opaque woman he had ever met. "Oh, I have it," Noel said, frustrated into banter. "You would rather I be known as Atlas, more strength than native wit?"

"Are you strong, sir?" she asked, gaze intent and pointed. "I inquire because you would pass on bulls and duels."

"Who wouldn't pass on a duel?" he asked insouciantly, blessed if he would give in and descend into primitive displays. "So sorry, old man, but since neither of us really wants to die this fine morning, let's see who can spit a cherry pit the farthest and call it quits, eh? And bulls, well, it isn't in the course of normal events for a man to fight bulls."

"The Plaza de Toros, in Spain, my lord, became so popular because a man jumped into a bull ring when some aristocrat fell off his horse."

"You don't say."

"He waved his cap at the bull, and to hear the story told, everyone thought him so funny and yet so brave that he transformed bullfighting."

"How nice for him," Noel said. "Did he live a short but romantic life? He deserves it."

"I begin to understand you. You are a cynic."

"I prefer thinking of myself as a well-punctuated realist."

Mrs. Grantham actually smiled.

"You are quite pretty when you do that," Noel said. "Now don't be tiresome and scowl."

"I have no intention of doing so. I am merely surprised to find a thread of commonality between us."

"I suppose a General Grantham would have to be a realist. I must beg your pardon for my momentary surprise. Putting your niece on the market seems the height of rosy-eyed optimism."

"No more than your notion of obtaining my secret as easily as putting a pianoforte on a barge. But I will tell you something, sir, if you must speak of common threads, there is one running between you and my niece."

"A fine dislike of each other?"

"No, sir. Loyalty. I am loyal to Anne, and I am come to be loyal to my late husband's family."

"And your expression tells me that you see nothing of such finer feelings in me. I am sorry, but whatever your view of me, I see little in that family to merit loyalty."

She smiled again, but it was not the pretty smile of before. This smile put him on full alert.

"What?"

"You wished a test, sir, and you want to share my loyalties. Well, here is your test. Share my loyalty and help me see Lizzie successfully through her come-out."

Chapter Five

She had surprised him. He was the one catching flies now. Meg took a grim delight in shaking his sangfroid. Wretched man thought he was so superior, but she had tricked him into getting her to leave her alone once, and she would do it again.

"Oh, no. No. Not on any account," Lord Reversby said.

"It would be a challenge worthy of Hercules, do you not think?"

"Ma'am, it would take the entire pantheon."

"Lizzie can be quite lovely," Meg said. "Charming, even."

Reversby snorted.

"But she does not have the experience of age to inform her that not everyone will judge her on her poise."

"You mean whether she trips over them or into them? That could make a difference, to a great many men," he replied tersely. "One does think about what one must face over the breakfast table, or, in her case, whether one will have one's breakfast in one's lap."

"That would be a shock," Meg said.

"Especially without the comfort of considering her fine connections and extensive fortune."

"Your attempts at humor leave something to be desired."

"So do Miss Grantham's."

"If you stood up with her on a regular basis," she said, "perhaps the breakfast table would appear a sunnier place."

"Please, ma'am, I will gladly fight a duel instead."

"I do not understand duels," Meg said. "Wellington was right about them. They are a waste of time and men."

"But you think bullfighting admirable?" he asked.

"I never called bullfighting admirable."

"Really, Reversby," he said, "you ought to pay more attention to the lady's words, as she is exceptionally precise, for all she leaves you to interpret what you will." He twisted his lips. "Very well, ma'am, you have me over the proverbial barrel. I will do your little job for you, if you will promise me that at the end of it, I will get to learn your secret."

"A successful end, my lord," Meg said.

"Define success."

"She is having her banns read."

"Not saying her vows?"

"Banns, then vows."

"So no elopement for her?"

"No," Meg said, proud that she held herself together. The wretched man had almost caught her.

Reversby heaved a sigh. "Very well. If I have to marry the chit myself."

Meg felt as if he had reached across the line and stabbed her with his monocle.

"I am quite an excellent catch," he said.

"To be sure. But I hope it will not come to that."

"Maybe there is an ounce of sympathy in your frame, Mrs. Grantham."

Meg forced herself to push back her black mood and stay on top of Lord Reversby's conversation. "For what am I to feel sympathy?" she asked.

"It is in your head, not your heart. Isn't it?"

She did not want to understand the question. She had, instead, an inexplicable desire to throw herself upon his broad chest and cry. Not for pardon, but for freedom. If only the world could leave her be. She had not felt like that for a long time, she realized. She had spent too much time being the one cried upon that she had forgotten the indulgence.

But to choose Reversby to cry upon? There was that odd attraction between them, but that was merely a thing of the flesh, to say nothing of impossible.

"She really does have some excellent qualities," Meg said.

"A diamond in the rough?" he asked.

"The right husband would steady her."

"What was she so angry about before?"

"I scolded her for the yoo-hooing, and for stepping on your foot."

"Oh-h," Reversby said as they progressed up the line.

"Truly, she only began to be this way within the last month or so."

They did their final bows as the music ended. With the lines of dancers now a crowd, Reversby took her hand and drew her toward him, to a place free of buffeting. "You know that this is an impossible task?"

"I hope it is not," Meg said softly.

"Your hand, on my arm, if you please."

She rested her hand on his arm, felt its strength. Her insides turned into water.

"Even if it's not an impossible task, it is distasteful."

"That may be," she said, resisting the pull of his attraction. She held her chin up. "But it is what you have before you."

An angry glint robbed his face of his usual irony, leaving only arrogance. "When I have done it, Mrs. Grantham, I will have not only your secret, but a kiss as well."

Appalled by how she wanted his kiss, Meg pulled away from him.

"Hello," Mr. Smith-Jenkins said, suddenly before her. "What have we here?"

"A woman who is beginning to think well of dueling," she said.

Mr. Smith-Jenkins frowned, looked over Meg's head to Reversby, who said, "You should ask her about bullfighting, too. Fare thee well, sir." He bowed to Meg. "Madam, we have a deal."

Meg walked. She did not know precisely where she walked, but she figured if she continued down the streets of the West End, eventually she would find Hyde Park.

She wore a dark, soberly cut blue dress and a straw hat with a large brim, but her unfashionable dress did not prevent merchants and street vendors from calling out to her as she passed. She exchanged good mornings with a kindly woman street vendor, and promised she would buy a sticky bun with currants and cinnamon glaze when she came back. Her spirit needed to walk more than her body needed sustenance.

Hyde Park soon stretched before her, with its gravel walkways, gentle hills, and streams and ponds. As she stood, surveying it, trees bent to a stiffening breeze. Meg turned her face into it and walked.

She had made a bargain she did not intend to keep.

When had miserable bargains become such a theme in her life? It was as if having made the first mistake, she had set her feet upon a path that led farther and farther into the valley, never over the mountains.

The path had started full of adventure. As girls of eighteen, Meg and Anne had giggled with abandon over the local regimental officers. Anne had inclined her head to courtesies from a young ensign named Wilkes. After several visits and a dance, she declared she liked him very much.

Meg had liked Lieutenant John Grantham from the start. Brash and broad, he could paint pictures with his words that she could almost touch.

When news came that the regiment would be taking ship for the Peninsula, Meg and Anne had succumbed to the grand notion Lieutenant Grantham had of them following. But that could be done only if the couples married.

So Meg, Anne and their two officers had traveled north. Had Meg eyes for anything but Lieutenant Grantham, she would have realized that Wilkes came along for the scheme, and nothing else. A thread of disdain ran through his deference to a superior officer.

The two couples married by so declaring their intentions before witnesses. They then retired to an inn a few miles south and made merry. Meg came down the next morning before her new husband to find Anne agitatedly sipping what passed for coffee that far north.

Anne embraced Meg with all fervor under the suspicious eye of the inn owner, and pulled her against a table by the wall where they might not be overheard.

"Did you?" she asked. When Meg nodded, Anne closed her eyes briefly before saying, "Meggie, listen. We never made it to Scotland last night."

"But those people—"

"They played a trick on us. We are not married at all."

The enormity of what she had done crashed upon Meg. There was no time for another trip to Scotland. The officers had to report in two days to their embarkation point. Meg could not go with him now, and she thought he would feel the stain on his honor and hers most keenly. "My God, what do I tell Lieutenant Grantham? This will devastate him."

"You will tell him you are married, if that is what you want," Anne said. "Ensign Wilkes and I decided we should not suit. I am as unmarried in body as I am in law. I plan to remain in England. But we will keep your secret. Ensign Wilkes swore on his honor. We will travel with you to Portsmouth and have my brother Xavier meet me, as though he had come along with me to see you off. And we will pretend I decided not to go. On the docks, if necessary. That will be my secret, for no one will believe otherwise."

And that was what they did. Anne waited with Meg through the dreadful lottery, which selected which wives could accompany their husbands. Meg had drawn a no, but Anne drew a yes and gave it to her. Meg held it, dumbfounded, as others holding no's wept and carried on. Should she not pass her card on to the poor villager with four children?

Perhaps Anne had glimpsed this thought in Meg's expression, for she closed Meg's hand around the card and said to Lieutenant Grantham, "See, you two have luck."

Lieutenant Grantham had taken Meg's hand and said, "You will be my luck in this war, Mrs. Grantham. You will get me home."

If only luck had been what Lieutenant Grantham had needed. Instead, from the new colonel shipping out with the regiment, Meg found out her husband required a spine.

Colonel the Honorable Phineas Seward. Second son to the Earl of Wyetoncliffe and resentful of the necessity of being placed among the riffraff. He thought he should have been able to get into the Guards, not some deuced regiment of foot.

Meg could still hear his bored, high-handed accents, smell the two small dogs he expected everyone to give all deference to, their stink made worse by the sweltering heat of that August day in 1808, when she had entered his tent to return some sewing, and he had suddenly set his hand upon her breast.

Meg knew better than to slap her husband's commanding officer, but she had stepped back, only to run into the damp tent side.

"Startle you, my dear? Imagine that, a woman grown and married and all. You must know you are quite the brightest jewel in this sorry little crown, and I mean to admire your sparkle. Why did you think I asked you to do my sewing instead of some sergeant's wife?"

"I did not suppose to presume to question your motives, sir," Meg said.

Then he had stood, casting aside the shirt she had stayed up late repairing for him by the light of a single candle. He wore his regimentals and a sly smile. "Do you mean to tell me Lieutenant Grantham has not told you why I asked you and only you to do and deliver the sewing?"

Meg had noted the distance in her husband's manner that morning, but she had ascribed it to the heat and the common knowledge that a French general, Delaborde, waited for them a day's march south at Obidos, and that the order to march would come any minute. Their first battle would follow.

"Oh, this is too perfect," Seward said in his haughty tones. "I had teased and tormented myself wondering what you would look like when he told you. Now I may see myself."

Her heart beat fast enough to choke her. Nothing could be good here. "When he told me what?"

Seward picked up his sword, held the hilt in one hand and bounced the scabbard end against the other. "Do take note, my dear. To every sword there is a business end and a hilt to protect the hand. In every regiment there are companies that go faster into the heat of battle, and then there are the ones that hang back." He separated his last words with swaggering affectation.

Even then Meg did not understand.

"Come, woman," he said with a sigh, "show the native wit I have found so scintillating in this dreary place."

"You must be plainer with me, sir."

"Your husband, Mrs. Grantham, has made a bargain with me. The pleasure of your company. To the hilt. My hilt. For the hilt." He slapped the sword hilt into his palm.

Meg started as though he had slapped her.

"I am not lying."

"I am an honest woman," she choked out. "How can he—" She blinked, as a dreadful notion occurred to her. Had the lieutenant learned their marriage was fictitious?

"Yes, exactly that way," Seward said, "although the venue was over cards last night. Oh, but I am quite remiss. I have told you none of the benefits to your lovely self, have I? There will be benefits to you, my dear, and not just keeping your husband alive."

Meg made an effort to stop shaking and put her chin up. "I am an honest woman. I pay for nothing in base coin."

Seward flushed and his mouth twisted. Then he said, as though he had merely asked her for a drink of water, "I will give you until we march to change your mind."

She took that as dismissal and fled the tent, only to halt immediately lest she run into the green-coated, silver-buttoned chest of an officer of the 5/60th, who stood looking dark and dangerous between two sentries.

"Steady, ma'am," he said. "Are you all right?"

Meg pushed back a sob by covering her mouth with her fist.

"What is this, sir?" asked Seward from behind her.

The rifleman came to attention. "Lieutenant Sandeford, sir, 5/60th, with a message from General Fane, sir."

"Well, get in here and tell it to me, then."

The rifleman gave Meg a look that gave her the courage to put her chin up again. She nodded.

"Now, Lieutenant."

Meg went back to her own tent, to find no evidence of Lieutenant Grantham. She sat on a log while other women and soldiers bustled about her. Finally he came.

"No," she said to her unlawful husband.

Mindful of the others around them, he did not protest.

The order to march came in the next half hour.

Later Meg learned, although not from him, that his company stood in the forefront of the fifth brigade and watched two assaults on the hill west of Roliça fail before charging and failing and charging again.

They never spoke of it or any other personal matter beyond the needs of the day. Nor did they discuss how Colonel Seward came to take a bullet in the shoulder that necessitated his replacement when the Frenchmen were well out of musket range. Rifles, Meg learned, had a much longer range.

She never allowed Lieutenant Grantham to touch her again, but she heard every cry he made in his pillow before each intimation of battle. After the first year, the disastrous retreat to Corunna, and their redeployment, it was as if he came to resent her for his weakness. Meg would never forget the way he had looked at her before Buçaco, as though he had become both afraid and contemptuous of her.

But by that time, she did not fear he would ever lay a hand on her, whether a Lieutenant Sandeford was about or not. The fiction of her marriage might be complete, but Meg had come into her own.

Meg had quickly learned, as other wives had, that one could not depend upon the Army to obtain proper provisions, not for themselves, their children, or their soldier husbands. With others, she scoured the countryside for them, moving far in advance of the marching soldiers. The practice became so prevalent that Wellington issued a proclamation prohibiting wives buying bread.

So laughable did the proclamation appear to the wives that Meg organized them into a shadow quartermaster's band. Rarely speaking to the local men, she and her band would appeal instead to their womenfolk. Women, whatever their spoken language, understood first the language of children's hunger.

It was this organization and the way Meg shortly organized most of the other workings of her husband's company—for their captain had no wife and was content to leave such matters to Meg—that she earned the sobriquet of General Grantham. She did not even know it until the day an exploring officer of the 43rd, Major Lord Thomas Dashley, had sought her out for information about the locals around Ciudad Rodrigo. Upon learning as much as she had to tell, he had bowed very nicely to her and

Glenda Garland

said he would have expected no less thorough a report from "General Grantham."

The name had pleased her immensely, but also saddened her. She regretted that she needed the protection her abilities gave her, and that she lived with the shame of wishing she had never "married" Lieutenant Grantham.

She lived like that until Vittoria, where a French carronade ended Lieutenant Grantham's battle with cowardice. Meg found herself needing to come home, but to what? Her parents' death had led her to live with the Nevilles. Anne had died, but Meg had no idea what Anne had told her brother about why Meg was married and Anne was not. From Anne, Meg had learned everything there was to know about being slippery on fine details. She could no longer live on false pretenses, at least, not with Xavier Neville. As to marriage, she could not contemplate giving herself to another man without being honest about her past, and who would want her then?

Then along had come Lord Reversby with his arrogant chasing after secrets that had nothing to do with him. He pushed her down again as surely as Seward had.

What good would it do him to know her and Anne's secret?

Worse, the feelings he had made her experience last night could only be described as dangerous. Desire had led her to war, shame, suffering, and death.

She did not think he would give up, though, despite the daunting task she had allotted him. He had a determined way about him, for all his easy irony and clever remarks.

"It will be your problem, sir, not mine," she said, and realized she had spoken aloud when a sober businessman passing her blinked and dropped the hat he had raised to her.

Meg apologized to him, declined a kind offer of assistance, and asked if he had the time.

It was ten o'clock. She was needed back for a modiste appointment at noon. She wished she could have walked all day, as she was used to do, and arrive so spent she could plead fatigue and fall into oblivion.

But instead Meg turned back. She stopped long enough to buy the currant and cinnamon sticky bun. She ate it while walking, breaking it up piece by piece and licking the glaze from her fingers, then using her handkerchief to wipe away the last.

There is more than an ounce of comfort in sticky buns, my lord, she thought.

Meg had no sooner stepped inside the fair-sized house Sir George had rented for the Season than she heard Lizzie cry out, "There she is. Aunt Meg!"

Lizzie rounded the drawing room door into the foyer, hitting her shoulder slightly on the door frame. With her mouth screwed into a knot and her red ribbons sticking up, she presented the very picture of frustrated indignation. The source of her frustration followed her.

At not eleven in the morning, Lord Reversby looked as fresh as if he had slept two days and then spent another on his toilet. His monocle had acquired a dark green ribbon that matched his coat. He bowed before continuing in Lizzie's wake.

Tessa emerged from the drawing room, wringing her hands, her lace cap gently hitting her cheeks.

"Aunt Meg, at last. Why must you be gone when I have express need of you? Lord Reversby has come with the most bizarre and unacceptable proclamation. He says you have enjoined him to help with my come-out. You must tell him it is not true. Not true, I say!"

Meg sighed. "Lizzie, do be still."

"But he is unkind to me!"

"Do. Be. Still."

This time Lizzie obeyed, but not happily. She took turns glaring at Meg and Reversby, who pretended to be contemplating a sickeningly coy painting of cherubs. He had his monocle away from his face, and was adjusting the distance between it and the painting as though plumbing for details.

"Sister-in-law," Meg said to Tessa, "would you please permit me to converse privately with Lord Reversby? We will meet you in the drawing room."

"Yes, of course," Tessa replied.

Meg met Lizzie's glare, and the girl again bowed to Meg's will. As it should be.

When they had retreated, Reversby held up his monocle to Meg's face. "You have a smear of something upon your cheek."

Horrified, Meg touched it, felt a sticky spot that was likely brown with cinnamon. She fumbled for her handkerchief, but he was faster with his. Gently he wiped at her cheek near her mouth. Their gazes locked with painful intensity. Meg stood as still as one does when one feels an intense pain and hopes that by taking not even a breath, one might make it go away.

You fool, she thought. *This is indeed your problem, too.*

He pulled away first and watched himself fold the handkerchief. "And what have you been about this fine morning, Mrs. Grantham? Walking and eating sticky buns?"

"There is much sympathy in sticky buns," she said, and cursed herself for such a stupid remark.

"More than an ounce?"

Meg nodded.

"And did you fancy yourself in need of some?" he asked.

Meg did not want what might pass for sympathy from him. Likely it would have an edge of condescension. "You are here very early. Did you believe we had an appointment?"

"I believed we should have an appointment," he replied. "Lady Grantham mentioned that you three ladies were going to the modiste's today. If I must be involved in putting the chit on the market, I should be involved in packaging the goods, so to speak, don't you think?"

He had a point. Blast him.

"I will not make you admit I am right. You see it already, and 'twould be ungentlemanly. Now, shall we discuss why the chit has no notion of my magnanimity in assisting her?"

"You are asking too many questions at once."

"I am asking two questions at once."

He could make her heart race with a look, but he could be insufferable, too. "She has no notion because we arrived home too late last night to begin the conversation, and I left walking too early this morning."

"That answers the first question."

"The second answers itself in the need for someone of your stature."

"She does not like me," he said with feigned reproach.

"You do not like her. That makes you even."

"No, because she does not like me because I do not like her. That makes it all decidedly uneven. She will have to work much harder at not disliking me so much."

He had too many valid points.

"Very well," Reversby said, "we understand each other."

No, we do not, my lord, Meg thought.

He sighed. "At least on this subject. Go upstairs and change your clothes, as, no doubt, you were intending to do. Take the chit with you and explain the matter."

"Are you giving me orders, sir?"

His mouth hardened. Then he collected himself. "I would never believe for a moment that General Grantham would delegate everything to the lower ranks and not at least present her strategy."

"Clever, sir."

"I must remind myself constantly that this is not a job for brute strength," he said. "Much as I should like to employ it."

"Your restraint touches me," she replied.

His eyes took on a smoky expression. "Clever, but it would not be my restraint touching you."

It had grown entirely too warm in the foyer. Meg tore her gaze from him, marched to the drawing room, and motioned sharply with her head for Lizzie to come with her. Lizzie did, with mouth mutinously set. Meg stopped her at the stair.

"Turn and curtsy to his lordship, Lizzie."

Lizzie's mouth set more mutinously.

"Now," Meg said, lowering her voice, "or so help me, you will buy one and only one ball gown this afternoon and wear it to every dance we attend this season."

"Papa and Mama would never let—"

"Try me," Meg said. "Curtsy and then come."

The girl turned, her head high, and curtsied.

Reversby surveyed her, monocle back in, and said, in that languid First Cousin voice, "She must try to smile, you know. Can't have them unless they smile."

The girl forced a smile.

"Better, but without the curl to the lip next time, eh?"

"Make yourself to home, my lord," Meg said, and then, "Come with me," to Lizzie before she could protest. Lizzie decided that following Meg lay along the path of least resistance. "Not a word, until we are upstairs."

In her own room, Meg pulled the call bell and waited only a second before Lizzie exploded. She called Meg every name she could think of, expostulated mightily on Meg's total lack of judgment, bemoaned Meg's sway with her parents, and then began her long list of objections to Lord Reversby, beginning with, "He said I would catch flies!" and ending with, "He does not even appear impressed by my looks, which as you know were regarded as being the best in western Leicestershire."

Meg let Lizzie run down, which coincided with

the arrival of her maid Hemmie, who had the misfortune of being now well used to Lizzie's tirades. "The pink figured muslin, please." The maid bobbed and went to get it.

Then Meg said to Lizzie, "I have told you time and again that your looks, while pleasing, would not be sufficient to attract anyone in London. Here there are many young ladies with more beauty, greater wealth, and higher consequence. More to the point, they are gracious and dance divinely."

Lizzie frowned. "But they don't play the way I do."

"You don't know that." Meg paused to let that sink in. "You would not believe me, but Lord Reversby's opinion was fair. He had no stake in your future. To him you were as any of the hundreds of girls he has seen come up to London."

If Lizzie noticed Meg's artful use of tenses, she passed on it. "But why him of all people?"

"I don't understand," Meg said, spying Hemmie returning with the muslin. She began untying her laces.

"If he is such a fine and mighty lord, why does he stoop to taking me under his wing?"

"It has been my experience that gentlemen do odd things for odd reasons." *Yes*, Meg thought, *that understated the matter.*

Lizzie sank down on Meg's bed and propped her arms against the red-and-blue patterned coverlet. "Maybe I am the subject of a bet," she said in a dreamy voice. "I should like above all things to be the subject of a bet."

"If you are, your family will writhe in shame."

"Mama and Papa would not care if I were the subject of a bet. Mama would merely hope it involved something that has never been bet on before. Papa just wants me married."

Lizzie probably had her parents aright. "I will not speculate on your parents' good feelings, but prospective husbands do not like wives touched by scandal."

"Not all prospective husbands," Lizzie said. "Why, Fitzhugh fought a duel over Lady Notorious before he married her."

"Ladies do not discuss duels."

"I will bet that lady does."

"You will not."

"Maybe that is why he wishes to help," Lizzie mused.

Hemmie slipped the pink figured muslin dress over Meg's head and tied the laces around the back.

"What do you mean?" Meg asked.

"He knows I am the subject of a bet, and wants me to have a good name." Lizzie screwed up her lips and bounced her foot rhythmically against the bed. "No, Lord Languid would not give a care about my good name."

"Lord Languid?" No matter that Meg had thought of his tone in just that way, she could never dream of calling him Lord Languid, not after she had once been the object of that heated gaze. "Lizzie, you must not say such things in public. It is very unladylike."

Lizzie held out the foot she had been bouncing, ruched up her skirt, admired the ribbons on her shoes, and went back to bouncing. "But it might make me a wit, which I hear is the very thing." Her shoe became decidedly loose.

"Maybe when you are better established," Meg

said, fighting the urge to laugh. "In the meantime, act properly."

"Lord Languid would like a wit, I think, or a very silly chit of a girl. What? Are you surprised that I might have figured out another reason for him to take such interest in me?"

Now Meg fought both the urge to laugh and to cry. She could not fence with Lizzie anymore, though, until she had some time to adjust herself to Lizzie's bizarre thoughts. "Tie your shoe. Go downstairs. Be gracious. Be a lady."

"Oh, very well," Lizzie said. She retied her shoe and flounced from the room.

"Your hair needs redoing, ma'am," Hemmie said.

"Bother my hair," Meg said. She smiled an apology. "Thank you, Hemmie. Whatever style appeals to you."

Hemmie had the sense to be quick, though artful. Years ago Meg had stopped thinking of her looks as anything to remark upon. They were not her, really, not the way Anne's beauty had contributed to her fortunes. Meg had long thought that Seward had favored her because Lieutenant Grantham had offered her, not because she possessed any great beauty.

But as Hemmie gathered her blond hair into braids and wound them around and about, Meg realized that the shape of her hair affected how she viewed her face. Its oval lines, down to her pointed chin, softened, and her nose looked more proportionate.

"Have I never given you free rein before, Hemmie?"

"No, ma'am." And Hemmie smiled.

"We will consider your judgment far superior to mine in these matters from now on."

"Thank you, ma'am. And, if I may be so bold, ma'am, did you have matching ribbons for your hair, I could achieve a lovely effect."

Meg stood, twitched one last fold of her dress, and marveled over the transformation and how it gave her an unexpected confidence. She tried to picture how Lord Reversby would look when he saw her. "I shall have to do something about that, then." It was important, after all, to select the proper equipment for battle, and what would all interactions with Lord Reversby be but battles?

Meg descended the stairs as quickly as she could but still being silent. She wanted to know how matters progressed before she joined the other three. Silence greeted her. Meg's shoulders slumped. Tessa was not even trying to keep a conversation alive. Why, why, why did everyone conspire to make life difficult?

Meg took a deep breath, squared her shoulders, and breezed into the smallish drawing room. It felt smaller, the atmosphere so charged, but not because of Tessa. Tessa sat wide-eyed upon a small white chair and seemed to want to shrink smaller could she but manage the feat. Lizzie wore an expression that suggested she was annoyed and so happy to stay that way that the least provocation would suffice.

Reversby did not sprawl, exactly. He had arranged himself into the corner of a white-and-blue striped settee, one booted ankle resting on the other buff knee, arms folded, chin sunk to such a degree he was in danger of crushing his cravat, his expression an interesting mix of indolence and impudence.

Did it change when Meg entered, or did he simply move his head, and the light from the windows flashing off his monocle led her to believe he was startled?

It was the reaction Meg had spent the past ten minutes hoping for, but now that she had it, she had no idea what to do with it. Fool, she told herself.

His expression—again? still?—calm, he rose and waited for her to sit—on a chair quite far away from his, thank you!—before wedging himself back into the settee's corner.

"I am still quite at a loss as to why you are here, my lord," Lizzie said.

"It was your aunt's judgment that I should assist you." He had said it at least once already, if the resignation in his tone was anything to go by.

At least, Meg thought, Lizzie was no longer saying how much she disliked Reversby.

"My aunt is no better than we," Lizzie said. "She has no experience with this sort of thing. She has been following the drum these last six years."

"Thank you, Lizzie, for that glowing endorsement," Meg said, stung and amused.

"Your aunt is a Neville, and raised in the home of Mr. Richard Neville," said Reversby at his most pompous. "The family goes back almost to William."

Lizzie turned narrowed eyes on Meg. It was her thinking expression. "What did she die of, your wife?"

"Lizzie!" Meg exclaimed.

But Reversby said, quietly, "We thought it a simple sore throat at first. Then it turned into a fever of the brain. Three days later she was gone."

Meg had learned of it from Xavier, a kind soul, but not given to excesses of emotion or imagination. The news had grieved her, of course, but not as much as it might have, had she been seeing Anne regularly and not been so concerned with survival. Reversby's tone did not bring on fresh grief but the memory of what it might have been. She had the urge to fold him in her arms, as she had comforted many a soldier and widow at the end of a battle, even those she had not much liked.

She could not give in to such an urge. The circumstances differed so greatly. Still she had to say something. "My lord," Meg began but did not know how to finish.

After a silence Reversby said, "That was all sixteen ounces, my dear, was it not?" His voice lacked all its customary irony, leaving Meg painfully aware that there was a wounded soul inside the offhand façade. She tried to say something, but he said, the irony gleaming afresh. "Yes, a pound, pure and entire."

Meg looked out the sheer curtains and flushed. He would take nothing good she could offer. Only what he wanted.

"A pound of what?" Lizzie asked.

"I owe your aunt some chocolates," Reversby said. "After the modiste's, we must stop by Gunter's."

"Do they have caramels?" Lizzie asked.

Mortification adding to her hurt and anger, Meg kept looking out the window.

"Would they call themselves a confectioners without caramels?" Reversby asked.

Chapter Six

Mrs. Grantham did not meet his gaze while the ladies gathered their bonnets and reticules and gewgaws in preparation to leave for the modiste's, nor in his landau on the way through the crowded squares and streets of London's fashionable shopping district, nor when she was whisked away into the back room to have her measurements taken.

She also conversed little, replying only when asked some question by her miserable niece or Lady Grantham. Lady Grantham had the sense—or the lack of courage—not to prod her husband's sister-in-law.

Possessing a fine social tin ear, Miss Grantham continued talking about sweets until she latched on to the subject of the poor driving skills of draymen and hackney drivers.

Noel thus had limited capacity to determine Mrs. Grantham's feelings. He supposed her embarrassed, but by what mixture of sentiments he hesitated to speculate.

Her voice, as she had said, "My lord," had pulsed with such feeling that he had felt as though she had hugged him to herself. He had been profoundly startled, and said the first stupid thing that entered his mouth. He wished he could take it back. Whatever she kept from him, she had not deserved to have such feelings trampled by what Anne had so often called his badminton response.

"You do keep your feelings in the air like a shuttlecock, Noel, adjusting to whatever breeze takes them up or racquet whacks them. It's very wearying, dearest."

But Anne had been angry with him whenever she said it, so Noel had not regarded it as anything he should heed. Now that he could no longer regard Mrs. Grantham as lacking in sympathy—indeed he began to believe that her calm, competent demeanor hid a wealth of emotion—he puzzled over how she managed to hold so much in check. No shuttlecock her, but a firework or a flare, which suddenly blazed brightly against a monochrome background.

Noel tried to remember her letters to Anne. Had any of them hinted at this depth? There had been descriptions of the Portuguese and Spanish landscapes, the kinds of people Mrs. Grantham had met, stories of triumphs about obtaining food or shelter, but nothing of great travail or suffering.

Had Mrs. Grantham thought to spare Anne stories of unpleasantness, or had Anne kept only the letters of victory? Although Anne had readily given sympathy or comfort to those who needed it, she had never liked unpleasantness. She had been a coaxer, not a bargainer or an organizer, like Mrs. Grantham.

To be fair, however, Anne had never needed to do more than coax, for she was a beautiful woman who could wheedle her way through any human obstacle. *And I loved you,* Noel thought, *because you could, and you took me with you.*

Now that Noel thought about it, though, as he cooled his heels in Madame Dastier's elegantly appointed Bond Street waiting room with its swathes and swatches of muslins, silks, and cottons, he could not identify anything that he and Anne had accomplished, except the odd grand party. She had taken him with her but where Noel could not say. It occurred to him that he might be missing something.

The incident, in short, provoked vague but definite unsettled feelings. Noel did not like feeling unsettled. He had been feeling unsettled since he had found Anne's cache of letters from Mrs. Grantham. What unsettled him even more, though, was that these unsettled feelings were different in kind.

Being near Miss Grantham would not contribute to his puzzling the matter out, either. Despite the walls and corridors separating him from them, he could hear her. A woman cried out, and then the exclamations began again, and apologies, too, from which Noel gathered Miss Grantham had managed to clock a seamstress on the cheek.

Miss Grantham was a challenge, but it seemed she had accepted Mrs. Grantham's relation to Anne as sufficient motivation for his involvement in her affairs, although she still did not like him.

"No, I tell you, I do not like it!"

Someone murmured, and Miss Grantham continued, "Yes, why don't we ask the great and mighty?"

That was Noel's warning to stop fingering the muslins and silks before four women surged through the corridor leading to the fitting areas. He bowed.

"At your service, ladies. Viscount Reversby, the soothing emolument of resolution."

Now Mrs. Grantham did look at him. He gave her the slightest of nods, more an inclination than anything else, and her expression firmed. She was accepting something, and he suspected he would not like whatever it was. "Here he is," said Mrs. Grantham. "Do explain the trouble, Lizzie."

"This—the demi-train," Miss Grantham said. "I want it. My aunt says not. That is the trouble."

With her chin high and her dignity wrapped tight, Miss Grantham acquired some measure of attractiveness.

"May I see?" Noel asked. "Turn."

Miss Grantham turned. No mishaps.

"Walk."

"Why? I walked out here, did I not?"

"You came out here like you were being chased by hounds. Walk like a lady, down to that wall, turn, and come back."

Miss Grantham managed to get as far as her turn before she stepped on the demi-train. It ripped, fortunately at a basted seam. Miss Grantham flushed. Lady Grantham fluttered. Mrs. Grantham and Madame Dastier winced.

"There is nothing for it," Noel said. "We shall have to make an accommodation."

Mrs. Grantham looked stern. Did she not know he was being deliberately provocative?

"Perhaps there is some way we can suggest the train without having it flow out so much. We shall set a new style, Madame."

Miss Grantham agreed that this was a fine idea, and Noel's cachet increased to such an extent with

Madame Dastier that she insisted he review some of the fabric choices for Mrs. Grantham.

Mrs. Grantham did not like being under his judgment any more than her niece had. If anything, she liked it less. To tease her a little, he murmured, "Are we not all slaves to fashion?" before indicating to Madame Dastier to show him the swatches.

While Madame turned to get the swatches, Mrs. Grantham shot him a glance of pure exasperation.

One swatch was the dark blue Mrs. Grantham often favored. The other was a sky blue. The difference in colors on her was startling. The sky blue made her eyes beam like torches. But it never did to let on. "I must agree with Madame on the lighter blue, Mrs. Grantham," he said. "The darker color makes you look like a jay." No hawks wore blue, either, but it might be time to stop thinking of her that way.

Then he ruled on several shades of yellow and peach.

Noel could not wait until he could see her in the dress made from that blue. He had to take several breaths before he felt his composure would not suffer when she returned.

He wondered if he fooled anyone but himself when he said, "Gunter's, ladies?"

They strolled down Bond Street, Miss Grantham now chatting happily about her choices to her mother. Noel's driver followed in the street with the carriage.

"She talks as if she had come up with the idea,"

Noel said in a low voice to Mrs. Grantham as they walked ahead.

"It is her way. I compliment you, my lord, on handling her."

"I suppose I do have a few uses," Noel said. "The occasional skill."

She frowned a little. "Why can't you just say thank you?"

"Why," said an officer of the dragoons, who appeared as if by magic upon the street, "if it is not Mrs. Grantham."

"Major Black," Mrs. Grantham said.

It was indeed. In his uniform, he looked much more substantial, and he had shed some of the confused air he had worn in Oxford. Black, it appeared, had more cunning than Noel had credited him with.

"In the very flesh," Black said. "I made it to London, and I told you I would shortly call upon you. I had planned to call tomorrow, but how much nicer is the chance meeting, eh?"

"Much nicer, certainly," Mrs. Grantham said, her expression at once warmer and more wary.

Noel puzzled over her expression, but had no time to form a hypothesis. Major Black said, "Why, if it isn't Mr. Dodd. How do you do, sir?"

"How funny, Mr. Black," said Miss Grantham, giggling. "You have mistaken Lord Reversby for Mr. Dodd."

Noel was tempted to remind her she had made the same "mistake." Instead he squinted around his monocle and said, "We are first cousins, sir. Common error when we're not standing right next to each other. How do you do, sir?"

"Dashed strong resemblance. Dashed strong."

"Mothers," Noel said. "Twins."

Black grunted at the novelty, a surprisingly loud noise for someone with such a slight frame. "Hunh. Well, tell me, Mrs. Grantham, did the pianoforte come?"

Their group of five began to become a nuisance to passers-by. Mrs. Grantham signaled to Lady Grantham that they should all step off the curb. When she did, however, Black quickly put out an arm to draw her up. He pointed down with his chin to where some luckless shop boy had failed to sweep his allotted part of the street.

"Why, even in Bond Street!" Miss Grantham exclaimed.

But Mrs. Grantham and the major grinned at each other. A curl of anger twisted through Noel, and he recognized its source as jealousy. Amazing, but there it was. The major had done the task, he deserved the credit and the smiles. Insane, Noel thought, to expect anything of the kind from Mrs. Grantham, who so clearly and irritatingly disliked him.

But an idea came to him. "We were off to Gunter's, Major Black. Do you join us?"

Mrs. Grantham looked warily at Noel.

"Oh yes, do," Miss Grantham said, and smothered a giggle.

"I should like that," Black replied, very much on his dignity.

"Excellent," Noel said. "Shall we, ladies?"

They proceeded along the street. The major asked Mrs. Grantham again about the pianoforte. "Devilish tricky situation, there. Why, I thought I would have to hire a conveyance and bring the dashed thing right back myself."

"I am glad you and m'cousin were able to solve the problem, sir," Noel said. "I had the pleasure to hear Miss Grantham play it this morning."

He spoke nothing but the truth. Despite her rather sticky temper and her clumsiness, she played the instrument with heart and feeling and skill. Noel would have been far happier were all his interactions with her to be over the pianoforte. *Hmmm,* he thought, struck.

"Your cousin is a right useful gentleman," Black said, and if he implied any comparison, perhaps Noel just imagined it.

Arriving at the store with its sign of the pineapple overhead, Noel watched Mrs. Grantham survey the offerings. She took her confection-buying seriously, for she studied each case with its glistening offerings as though she desired to ask the proprietor all his secrets, from where he imported his chocolate and vanilla beans, to his exact recipe for marzipan.

Then suddenly she met Major Black's gaze and said, "Did you hear about the caravan along the road to Valladolid? What a far cry from that this is!"

The major laughed. "I never saw it, but Sandeford described it to me. Dashed proud of himself, he was, when he stopped being embarrassed."

Taking pride in his control if not his temper, Noel said, "Order what you like, and we may eat an ice from the carriage. The waiters will bring them out. Do look, Mrs. Grantham, chocolate-dipped fruit as well as chocolate-covered cherries. Or wait, did you not mention you disliked chocolates?"

"I have decided to take your advice, sir, and acquire new habits," she said, reining in her merriment and glancing at the major, who turned away, doubtless to hide his contempt for such an obvious play for her attention.

Noel felt like a cad. She smiled so rarely.

But he began a regular simmer over Black. He had not had much use for Black in Oxford. He had resented being lumped into the same category as Black: Persons Whom Mrs. Grantham Wished From Sight. He had equally resented Black's stratagem for regaining her attention, as it had necessitated Noel's being dispatched to Oxford and frustrated his pursuit of her secret.

Now Noel was again in the same category as Black.

Nor could he quite rid himself of the feeling that by using a pianoforte as a stratagem, rather than fruit dipped in chocolate, Black had trumped him.

It was the blasted Army. Black shared that connection with her and ever would.

There was not enough room in the carriage for all five of them. By tacit agreement, Noel and Black stood and leaned against the open sides. Interspersed with admonishments from Mrs. Grantham to keep her voice low, Miss Grantham rhapsodized about how fine the square was, how fine the other members of the *ton* appeared in their carriages and walking clothes, and how absolutely stunning she herself would be in her new gowns. She did not cease until the waiters brought the ices and wrapped confections.

Mrs. Grantham set the beribboned box of chocolate-dipped fruit on the seat next to her.

"Do you share the story, ma'am?" Noel asked.

"Which story, my lord?"

"Of the caravan on the road to Valladolid."

Miss Grantham sighed.

Mrs. Grantham hesitated, then said, "It was a silly thing, really. An officer with the Rifles—"

"The 5/60th," Black said, as if that should mean something.

"Yes," Mrs. Grantham said.

Black flushed slightly, and Noel repressed a grin.

"His name is Sandeford, Captain Sandeford now, and he is known as something of a devil-take-all," Mrs. Grantham said.

"You have news of him?" Black asked.

"Thank God, yes, his name was in the lists of those returning," Mrs. Grantham said. "He was wounded a little while ago, but I understand 'twas not serious. As I said, he is a rifleman, so it was in the normal course of duty for his company to scout and raid any French caravan or supply line they could find. One day, while escorting Lieutenant Grantham's regiment and others, they happened along a small French caravan, only about five wagons. The French went quite mad defending it, which convinced Captain Sandeford he must have had quite a find."

"Idiots," Black said.

Mrs. Grantham ignored him. "When our ranks came upon him, oh, probably about a quarter hour after the skirmish was done—we had heard the muskets and rifles firing—there were chests after chests of chocolates open on the road."

"Chocolates?" Miss Grantham asked.

"Fine Belgian chocolates," Black said.

"Captain Sandeford had found orders of lading," Mrs. Grantham said. "Marshall Marmont had ordered the chocolate, whether for his troops or himself we never knew. Captain Sandeford had everyone take a piece, right then and there. Then everyone feasted again that night in camp."

"Why was he embarrassed?" Noel asked. The picture he had in his head of chocolates sitting in chests at the roadside struck him as poignant, not embarrassing.

Mrs. Grantham smiled. "Captain Sandeford is one of those gentlemen who tan deeply, and one of the younger children asked him if he had taken a bath in the chocolate first. And so for a few weeks afterward, he endured the nickname of . . ." She looked at Black, and they said together, "'The Belgian Bather.'"

Miss Grantham laughed.

Smiling wistfully Mrs. Grantham said, "Not quite the image the dashing captain appreciated."

So, Noel thought, she had thought this captain dashing. What opinion had the captain had of General Grantham?

Black was wondering the same thing, Noel realized, judging from his frown.

"Dashing?" Miss Grantham asked on a sigh. "How dashing?"

Mrs. Grantham looked wary again, then said, easily enough, "He is an exceptionally handsome man. Something like Lord Reversby. Their coloring is the same."

Noel bowed, but could not decide whether she had truly given him a compliment. It satisfied him some, though, that she had not compared the dashing captain to Major Black.

"If such a man is back in England, why have you not introduced me to him?" Miss Grantham asked.

Because she likes him too well, Noel thought, and spooned some ice lest his thoughts show and provoke trouble.

"He is back in England because the 5/60th was returned, but he may have duties that keep him from London, unlike Major Black."

Now it was Black's turn to bow and wonder whether he had been complimented.

"Besides, I cannot imagine the woman who could domesticate Captain Sandeford. Does she exist, I wish her all luck."

"Is not luck needed in all marriages?" Noel asked.

"Yes," she said soberly, "I suppose it is."

"That and timing," Black said, breaking in, "don't you think? And speaking of timing, I wanted to invite you ladies to accompany me to Astley's Amphitheater tomorrow evening." He puffed out his chest a little. "Astley was in the 15th, you know, and has called himself 'The English Hussar.' The performances are an amazing blend of show and horsemanship. Would he could have taught us all."

Now who appealed blatantly for attention? Noel thought.

"How I should love to see it," Miss Grantham said. "Please may we, Aunt?"

Please?

Black harrumphed. "You are welcome to join us, my lord, of course."

"Have you a box?" Noel asked.

"I had intended to secure one," Black replied.

Which you will do this afternoon, Noel thought, not entirely pleasantly. "Nothing like a box to give an outing that touch of *je ne sais quois*. I accept, with thanks. Are you ladies done with your ices? I will escort you home. Black, do you join us?"

Chapter Seven

The chandelier at Astley's alone made it worth the trip. It held fifty lanterns and descended from the ceiling over the center of the large oval amphitheater. Reversby and Major Black vied over seating Meg at the front of the second-tier box Black had secured, and then which should precede the other from the box.

At least Major Black was vying. Whether Reversby considered it vying or just teasing Black, Meg did not know. She suspected the latter, though, for how could a man of Reversby's stature feel the need to vie with Major Black's?

Either way, the situation had a faintly comedic, and therefore disturbing, feel.

Meg had known Major Black a long time but had never dreamed of his having any interest in her until he had found her a bare three months ago after returning from France. Then his attentions had become marked. The notion of marrying Beanpole Black was absurd, but Meg wanted to count him a friend. Would he turn his back on her when she rejected his inevitable proposal? The prospect depressed her.

Reversby's presence would accclcratc Black's proposal. Major Black had all the twitchiness of a soldier who realizes he must fight much sooner than he had been given to believe. Impossible to tell Black that Reversby thought it well within his rights to tease and be high-handed. Impossible to tell him Reversby wanted not marriage but a secret she could never tell.

The desire Reversby had professed for her . . . she could account for it only by Seward's logic: that she was the most interesting thing in his small, confined sphere. Seward had geography limiting him, Reversby his desire for her. That sort of compliment was the very antithesis of a compliment.

What then to explain the way her heart raced on seeing him, how his touch affected her? His good looks and the length of time since she had let a man satisfy her? Fear? A stupid yearning after what could be, had she lived her life differently?

"When will the performance begin?" Lizzie asked, leaning over the box's railing. Her gloved arm slipped on the railing, her bosom thumped it, and she dropped her fan.

"Ow," came a male voice below them.

"Do sit back," Meg said, but Lizzie was already doing that.

The box door opened. "Of course you must join us," Major Black said with too much bonhomie. "I insist."

"We should be very pleased, thank you," Lord Fitzhugh said.

Meg turned and beheld him and Miss Bourre, followed closely by Reversby, who raised his brows, then winced because of the showy, extensive bruising around his left eye. Meg did not want to think about that.

"Miss Bourre, how lovely," Meg said. "Reversby, do pull up a chair for Miss Bourre next to mine."

He bowed very nicely, although not without irony. The dratted man probably understood exactly what she was about—keeping distance between herself, and him and Black.

"How kind," Miss Bourre said. She looked fetching in an off-white frock with dark red ribbons.

Reversby said, "We shall have to squeeze a bit."

"Squeeze?" Lizzie asked.

"You are very kind to put up with us," Fitzhugh said, making a bow. "I had reserved a box, but it turns out a mistake was made and the box given away."

Reversby arranged the chairs so that the women would be in front and the gentlemen seated behind. Meg told herself not to feel all shivery when his hands were upon her chair while seating her, but she did anyway. She looked from his hands up to his bruised face, murmured "Thank you," and knew herself a hopeless fraud.

"Your shawl, Mrs. Grantham," he said, picking it up. He settled it around her shoulders.

"My lord," she replied a little breathlessly.

He smiled, a smile of acknowledgement. *Blasted man.* Then he backed up and stumbled over Major Black, who had seated himself directly behind Meg. Reversby begged Black's pardon, rolled his eyes once Black's back turned, and sat down in the middle seat. He and his friend Fitzhugh began talking quietly.

"I do not think Mr. Astley Junior will have an earful tomorrow about this mistake," Miss Bourre said to Major Black in a low voice, as though continuing a conversation. "Fitzhugh will never breathe a word. He does not like fusses."

"I hate to disagree with a lady," Major Black said, leaning forward between their chairs, "but what with Fitzhugh's reputation in the horse world and the number of people seeing him turned away, Astley is bound to learn of it."

"Major Black," Fitzhugh said, "do I understand that you are a member of the 15th?"

Lizzie sighed mightily.

Miss Bourre's blue eyes sparkled as Major Black was forced to converse with the gentlemen. Reversby, too, looked like a cat that had lapped his proper cream.

"You see? No fusses," Miss Bourre said.

"You have known Lord Fitzhugh all your life?" Meg asked.

"Yes, we are neighbors. He spent so much time in my parents' house, I thought of him like the brother I never had." Miss Bourre then looked out at the crowd and said, "I am glad Reversby found us and brought us here. I felt certain you would be a sympathetic person. You know I am in love with him."

Meg's amazement over this expression of feeling stifled her smile over being called sympathetic, which Reversby had made her far too sensitive to. "Yes. It must be very hard."

"The worst part is that I am starting to like Lady Fitzhugh," Miss Bourre said, meeting Meg's eye. "I would far prefer to hate her."

Meg had to smile. "I have felt that way myself about others. It is the very devil."

"I felt certain you had. It is in your expression when you look at Reversby."

"He has not sent you with reel and tackle, has he?"

"Oh, no. Never. But do you know how he came by the black eye? He muttered to Fitzhugh not to ask."

"He is a casualty of dancing," Meg replied.

At this, Miss Bourre could not resist looking behind her at the gentlemen. Meg did likewise to see what mischief there would be. Reversby looked alarmed, then smiled at her in the way she had come to recognize as his demanding something from her later. A blush started in her belly and threatened to work its way up.

Mischief aplenty.

Fitzhugh's brows rose, then he nudged Reversby and they reengaged Major Black in conversation.

"Do tell," Miss Bourre said.

"This afternoon he asked my niece, Miss Grantham, and Major Black to demonstrate the very latest steps. The room, you must understand, is not large. Lord Reversby was sitting down when the couple turned, my niece kicked out, and her pretty little shoe flew off her foot and smacked him squarely in the eye."

"Oh!" Miss Bourre said, hiding a smile with her hand. "Oh, I should not laugh."

"Is news of my embarrassment complete?" Reversby asked. He leaned forward by Miss Bourre.

"Look, sir," Black said, "the performance is about to start."

Meg noted the man in formal wear in the wings, then said, "Your bruise will fade in a day or two."

"Do you hear Mrs. Grantham?" Reversby asked Miss Bourre. "She would have you think I suffer from an excess of vanity."

Miss Bourre giggled. "But you do, sir."

"I am wounded, sore wounded."

For a second, the ironic light left his eyes. Meg noticed, although she did not think Miss Bourre did. And he noticed her noticing.

"How shall I recover?" Reversby asked, causing another warm flush of feeling within Meg.

Miss Bourre tapped him with her fan. "One must get right back up on the horse, sir. Is that not what you Corinthians all say?"

"You suggest I proffer my other eye at shoe level? You see, it is a difficult metaphor to employ in this situation."

"It is not difficult at all. You must merely get yourself to a ball sometime soon," Miss Bourre said.

"Only if you will dance with me," he said. "And you, Mrs. Grantham."

"Reversby," Fitzhugh said, "the show begins."

Reversby sat back, but there was something caressing in the movement that made Meg wriggle her shoulders within the shawl he had placed there.

Dratted man, she thought. Why, after having planted himself firmly in her life, did he seek to uproot her?

Or, and here was a novel thought, did he seek to distract her with himself as he had accused her of doing? *Well, two could play at that game, my lord.*

Lizzie leaned around Miss Bourre and whispered to Meg, "Does no one care at all that I was very sorry?"

"Lord Reversby knows that. You apologized."

"Well, at least he does not ask *me* to dance. He is not a comfortable sort of person. He will tease me and tease me, and I will forget my steps and step on him again. I far preferred dancing with Major Black."

This amazing speech diverted Meg to such a degree that she missed the entrance of the horses. Soon, however, she was following the story of a horse race enacted in the circle below. The animals were exquisitely trained. Meg found herself rooting for the bay, her hands clenched across her lap.

Immediately following it, a clown emerged, made up as a thief with a painted-on mask. On the other side of the ring, a well-armed traveler puffed about as though making camp. The clown thief made much of trying to find a way to sneak up on the traveler. The audience's laughter turned to surprised squeals when a man dressed as a lion suddenly jumped from the sidelines and wrestled the clown thief. The orchestra accompanied the action with a piece so fraught with drama that it was funny.

The struggle attracted the well-armed traveler, who came to watch as the clown thief finally rendered the beast senseless. The traveler heartily congratulated the clown thief and pulled a heavy bag from his coat pocket, and pressed it into the thief's hand. With a cheerful wave, the traveler returned to his camp.

The clown thief pointed to the purse, and then the lion, and shrugged, as though wrestling the lion had been the easier way of getting the money. Then his eyes widened and he fell backward flat onto the dirt.

He arose to cheering and applause, kissed his hands to the crowd, and took his bows with his hitherto enemy, the lion, and the well-armed traveler. The announcer said intermission would begin.

A whiff of lemon was Meg's warning that Lord Reversby leaned toward her again. "I shall have to ask that gentleman where he obtained his lion skin. Tell me, do you think he is a more or less likely Hercules?"

"Hercules?" Miss Bourre said. "Good heavens, Reversby, one little battle with a shoe has you spinning grandiose delusions? Were you concussed?"

Reversby looked pained. "It is just likely, given my current painted state, that I am sympathizing with the clown."

"You are too ridiculous," Miss Bourre said.

"Yes," Meg said.

Reversby smiled sardonically.

"Major Black," said Lizzie, "would you be so kind and fetch me some refreshment? I declare I never laughed so hard! It has made me quite parched."

Miss Bourre seconded this, and before Meg quite knew what had happened, Lord Fitzhugh had gathered all the party except her and Reversby from the box in pursuit of refreshment.

Meg stood to allow the others to pass by her, and when Reversby indicated the chairs, she said, "I would prefer to keep standing, if you do not mind. I feel as if I have spent too much time sitting today."

For answer he let his monocle drop, leaned against the side of the box by the purple curtain, and folded his arms. "Did you not leave me with your relatives this morning while you were out walking?"

She answered carefully, "I did not know you were coming so early."

"That does not quite answer the question."

"I turned back early," Meg said, a little defensively.

"This walking, from what your niece says, you do it regularly."

"I was used to it."

"In the Peninsula, you mean?"

"Yes."

"I do try, you know," he said, twirling the monocle on its ribbon, "to remember that you have had a much different life."

"What is that supposed to mean?"

"I cannot imagine another woman asking me to do what you are asking me to do."

"You are upset because the day has not worn easily on you. I might have expected Lizzie to trip and fall into your lap, but I never expected her shoe to come off and clout you in the face. Your eye looks a little better, though. I think."

"Buck up, old thing, is that it?"

She did not quite know how to read him. His humor seemed strained, overpointed. An answering tension rose in Meg, although she could not pin it on any one emotion. "Are we reopening the subject of sympathy?"

"No, merely nibbling around its edges."

"I cannot quite picture you as a mouse, my lord."

"But not someone who would wrestle bulls or lions, either, I daresay."

"I never asked you to do that, my lord. The bull was your idea. And cursorily dismissed."

He considered that. "True, although one could hardly miss the association."

"You may ascribe it to your being better educated than I."

"A mere soldier's wife? No, ma'am, that will not do. So, you cannot picture me as a mouse. A rat, perhaps?"

"No," Meg said, with more emotion than she had intended.

"I must be thankful for that, I suppose."

"And your eye does look better," Meg said.

"I am in the shadows of a purple curtain. That is why my eye looks better."

"I *am* sorry about that, my lord."

"Is that impatience, Mrs. Grantham? You may be sorry, but sorry the way a general who knows he must lose troops to take the fort is sorry."

"I meant I was sorry about Miss Bourre's teasing you so."

He shrugged, drawing attention to the broad line of his shoulders. Meg flirted with the notion of casting herself upon them. Then she remembered Anne, her Anne.

"Miss Bourre has known me for a year. You, on the other hand, have known me a week. You have a decided advantage."

"You are speaking nonsense again."

"Again? Do you mean to tell me you think everything I say is nonsense?"

"Part nonsense, all manipulation."

"A compliment from the master, so to speak," he said.

"We understand each other."

"Do we?"

Meg swallowed. "I begin to conclude that tonight you do not want sympathy."

"No," he replied.

What he wanted fairly glowed in his eyes, despite, or maybe heightened by, their being shadowed by the bruise and the curtain. Meg did not, however, think of backing away. She resented him for putting her continually to the test and had no inclination to perform such an undignified maneuver again.

"You set your payment yourself, sir, last night,"

she said, tossing her head. "You cannot collect it until you have earned it. Otherwise you are a thief."

"Did not the performance just now convince you that there is more than one way to skin a cat?"

"You did say you sympathized with the clown."

"There is nothing funny about the way I feel about you."

Meg shivered from wanting his hands caressing her. "There is nothing funny about the way I feel about you, either, my lord. That is because we have an arrangement, you and I. Did you break your part of it, what holds me?"

"It was a corollary."

"I beg your pardon?" she asked.

"The kiss. It was something extra I added to the bargain. At base our bargain remains the same. Banns and vows for a secret."

"But I accepted it."

"Yes," he said, "and I wonder why."

"Perhaps I am too honest to take advantage. And kissing you, my lord, would be to my advantage." Meg held her breath. It was a risky thing to say, provoking and feeding his arrogance all at once.

"You give yourself too little credit," he said, his voice so pure liquid pomegranate that Meg wanted to dip herself in it.

"I may have been raised in Mr. Neville's household, but none of my family is left."

"I do not care for connections. I do not need them. You may have your advantage."

"Is it wise to complicate our interactions?"

"Our relationship is already complicated."

"Anne," Meg said.

He looked downright dangerous. "So you abandon your appeals to logic."

But even as she disliked him for showing his true nature, she said, "My feelings do not follow logic. Did they—"

He straightened, reached out with one hand. Mesmerized, she allowed him to run it along her cheek. "You are the oddest creature. No honesty is too little for you."

She flinched. Living the lie she did, she could not bear even his conditional approval of her. Nor did she trust it.

"I cannot account for how you have seized hold of me so," he said.

"Blame it on the monocle," she said shakily.

"I would if I could. I am not wearing it. No, there is no accounting for it, however unflattering that may be. Your mentioning Anne should have made me impervious to all other beauty. I find I cannot be, for yours is so different in kind."

He sounded sincere but was he? No, he could not possibly be sincere, and Meg forced herself to resist, saying the first thing that popped into her head. "You though . . . you are as she described you."

"Am I?" he asked.

"More or less."

"More or less? Do I dare ask?"

This sort of exchange with him Meg understood. She relaxed into it, even as she chose her words with care. "She thought you amusing and handsome."

"And to you I am less handsome and more amusing?"

"More handsome and less amusing."

He tucked in his chin, so the shadow of the curtain obscured his blackened eye. "How droll that you can say that."

"You are a handsome man, my lord. That is no news to you."

"Modesty does not permit me to say."

"What is modesty between us?"

"Your secret," he replied immediately.

"No, that is my life," she said. The moment that the quick, hot words were from her lips, she regretted them. Foolish Meg, for thinking she could relax a moment with him.

He registered her mistake with a nod. "Could it be anything less, my dear, and you would have found me more amusing."

"Did you set out to trick me, or did you see an opportunity and take it?"

"I have been waiting upon opportunity, but have suspected Anne's secret touched you. How deeply, I do not know."

"Then it is you who thinks me amusing," she said, and felt ashamed at the bitterness she heard in her voice.

He straightened, the light from the grand chandelier falling full on his bruised eye. "No, I am not laughing at you. I enjoy laughing with you too well, when, that is, you remember how to laugh."

The sudden turn in conversation struck Meg deeply, even though she did not believe him. "Life is more than laughter."

"I have heard so," he said.

What note in his tone caused her to do what she next did, she would spend hours that night puzzling.

She stepped forward so that she pressed him back into the shadow. The rich lemon, masculine scent of him filled her. He realized her intentions at the last moment before she kissed him.

Standing so close to the hard length of a man thrilled Meg in ways she had forgotten. Reversby embraced her as he deepened their kiss, drawing her deeper into feeling. His mouth chased hers in dizzying darts as, feeling the slight roughness of his skin, she changed the angle of her face. Before she knew it, she had twined her fingers in his thick dark hair.

Finally, both of them breathless, they separated. Meg took her hands from him, one at a time.

"Why did you do that?" he asked, looking a trifle wild.

"Because we needed to rid ourselves of that complication," she replied, lying. How stupid of her to think she could compete with him on this front, for she would be fighting not only him, but herself.

"You were right the first time. This adds complication."

She forced herself to shrug and take a step back. "There will be no more corollaries. Our bargain remains as it was. Banns for a secret."

"And if, like that clown down there, I fall straight backward, will you let me hit the floor?"

"You will survive," Meg replied. "He did."

The door handle to the box rattled. Meg jumped aside, toward the balcony edge, before the door fully opened. Reversby refixed his monocle.

And anyone who thought they portrayed the picture of two people who had barely conversed had the sensitivity of a block of wood, Meg thought.

Fitzhugh took in the situation right away, raised

his brows at Reversby. Miss Bourre, too, looked all too knowing. Major Black quivered, and suddenly appeared ratlike, but that was merely the notion Reversby had planted in Meg's mind. Lizzie had the sense to look puzzled. Only Tessa's pretty face registered no expression other than serenity.

"I still think it a good idea," Reversby said to Meg. She frowned but before she could ask what he was talking about, he continued, addressing Lizzie.

"I proposed to your aunt that we have a musicale to introduce you to Society. You do play beautifully, Miss Grantham. But your aunt feared you would lose your nerve."

You sly devil, Meg thought.

"I should most certainly not," said Lizzie.

In for a penny . . . "You are quite certain?" Meg asked. "It would mean playing before more people than those you are accustomed to. You may also be asked to share the instrument."

Lizzie looked a little martinet-eyed at that but said, "Whatever my lord thinks best."

Reversby's brows lifted a little before he could control them. Then he said, looking at Meg, "There, did I not tell you?"

"Reversby," Miss Bourre said in protest.

"My apologies, Mrs. Grantham," Reversby said. "I should have said, 'See?'"

Now even Miss Bourre's lips twitched.

"Apology accepted, sir," Meg said. "I should be glad to be proved wrong. That is up to you, Lizzie."

Lizzie smoothed her hair.

Like a cat after it has eaten a mouse, Meg thought and upbraided herself for continuing with rodent images.

"Now all we have to do is set a date," Reversby said.

"You will all be invited, is that not correct, sister-in-law?" Meg asked Tessa.

Tessa started and said, "Yes, of course. Of course. Yes."

"The show is starting again," Major Black said. "We should all take our seats."

"Certainly," Reversby said, his irony in full gleam. "We may discuss details tomorrow. What say you, Mrs. Grantham?"

"Do let my aunt have her walk first," Lizzie said.

Meg was surprised at Lizzie's kindness.

"She will be the veriest bear does she not walk tomorrow," Lizzie said, ruining the impression.

"I could not have that," Reversby said. "Not after the lions I have seen this evening. Do permit me to hand you ladies to your seats." He neatly cut Major Black from all possibility of enjoying that privilege.

His hand firmly on hers, Meg sat down. When he did not let go, she looked up at him.

He whispered, "And the lioness. I will not forget the lioness."

Chapter Eight

When Noel reached White's after escorting the Grantham ladies home, he found Fitzhugh playing cards with a decidedly odd mix of gentlemen. Smith-Jenkins could be counted upon to gravitate toward Fitzhugh. Fitzhugh and Sommers, however, had never been friends. Any pretense of camaraderie they might have enjoyed over fencing had vanished when Fitzhugh learned Sommers had delighted in some ugly rumors about Lady Fitzhugh. Indeed Fitzhugh must be feeling magnanimous in the extreme to have him at the same table.

But the most amazing addition was the Duke of Breshirewood. Shortly before Fitzhugh and Lady Fitzhugh's wedding, the duke had put about his opinion, in excessively grandiloquent terms, that Fitzhugh had treated Dorrie Bourre poorly. Noel did not know whether Breshirewood still harbored a tendre for Miss Bourre. His statements might have been resentment over Miss Bourre refusing his proposal. Noel did not know and did not ask. But to see him with Fitzhugh and Smith-Jenkins— who made little pretense about his feelings for Miss Bourre—piqued Noel's curiosity.

Noel greeted the unlikely foursome and placed his hands on the backs of Sommers and Breshirewood's chairs.

"Good Lord, sir," Breshirewood said, "what the devil happened to turn your eye that effusive shade of purple?"

"A disagreement with a lady's shoe," Noel said.

Smith-Jenkins laid a card upon the green baize-covered table. They were playing whist, which explained why Fitzhugh had a pile of coins near him. Fitzhugh was adept at calculating which cards were likely out and which not.

Sommers smirked.

"Now," Breshirewood said, "how the devil did you manage that?"

"It was far easier than you might expect. No, Sommers, that one." Noel pointed to the king.

Fitzhugh gave him such a look. Sommers was not his partner.

Sommers, however, lay down a jack. As expected.

"Details, sir, I beg you," Breshirewood said. "You must not leave us in thrall to our imaginations."

Noel did not want to imagine Breshirewood's imagination.

Fitzhugh took the trick with a queen and a basilisk smile. "He was helping a young lady improve her dancing."

"Her dancing, eh?" Sommers asked.

"Her dancing," Fitzhugh replied, and Sommers lost his smirk. "This young lady is come for her first Season."

"What is this fine specimen of womanhood to you, Reversby?" Breshirewood asked.

"She is a relation of a relation," Noel said.

"I do believe," Fitzhugh said, glancing at Noel for confirmation, "she is holding a musical evening in a week. She plays the pianoforte quite wonderfully, I understand."

"Indeed," Breshirewood said. "I like music."

"I am sure you gentlemen will receive invitations," Noel said.

"Will the chit be dancing, too?" Sommers asked. "I mean, she will have to control both her hands and her—"

"Offer your face as target, Sommers, and maybe we will see greater effort at coordination," Smith-Jenkins said, and then smiled to indicate he meant no offense. Noel did not believe for a second Smith-Jenkins did not mean at least a little offense, but he had an openness to him that did not make one believe so automatically.

The others, except Sommers, grinned. "Heard your brother's due in Town, Reversby," he said.

"Quite," Noel replied, although he had not heard anything about Malcolm coming, and would be more than pleased not to see him. Was it not just like Sommers to be friendly with Malcolm?

"Trick and rubber," Fitzhugh said.

"If you will excuse Fitzhugh, gentlemen," Noel said, "I do believe I must have his help to secure a drink."

"Going rather blind, are you?" Sommers asked. "That's why the monocle?"

Noel picked up the thing, pretended to inspect it, and then let it drop back on its ribbon. "Not at all, sir."

"I told him it makes him look exceptionally bang up to the mark," Fitzhugh said in his calm manner. "Do you not agree?"

Sommers elected to agree.

Noel and Fitzhugh strolled away from the card tables and toward the various groupings of leather chairs and heavy side tables. Conscientious waiters had set up silver trays of crystal glasses and decanters of brandies, ports, and cordials. Fitzhugh poured them both some port and looked deep into his glass while waiting for Noel to come to the point.

Now that he was come to it, though, Noel had no idea of how to proceed. He could not speak of Mrs. Grantham kissing him. Not yet. The sensations that had coursed through him had left him feeling as if he'd been shaved hard with a dull razor. He had thought his desire for her had been a residual effect of his wanting her secret. Now he could not be at all certain.

He needed another subject.

"How did you come to be escorting Miss Bourre this evening?" Noel asked. "I had thought you had decided to put paid to that as unproductive."

Fitzhugh glanced sharply at him. "Not quite what I expected you wanted to talk to me about, but, as it turns out, my father appealed to me when I returned from Kent this afternoon."

"He has not reconciled to your marriage?" Noel asked.

"He has accepted it," Fitzhugh said. "I would not go so far as reconciled. He has abandoned my marrying Dorrie, at least. But last night, he wanted Mrs. Bourre all to himself."

"Oh. The wind blows in that direction?"

"From my father's direction, certainly."

Noel shared Fitzhugh's grin, and then his own faded. "I am beset, Benedict."

Fitzhugh did not joke, but refilled Noel's glass and said, "I am at your service."

So Noel told Fitzhugh about Mrs. Grantham's latest test and his suspicion that Anne's secret involved Mrs. Grantham as well.

"I had wondered about your taking such an interest in the chit's progress," Fitzhugh said. "I was inclined to believe, though, that you had jumped in because you found the widow attractive."

"All protests to the contrary."

"You protest a lot of things. That aside for now . . ." Fitzhugh paused to gauge Noel. "Do you believe she will keep her end of the bargain?"

"She wriggled around the last test, but we have achieved clarity this time. Her secret for banns and vows."

"So we need to induce some poor idiot to marry Miss Grantham," Fitzhugh said.

"That is my gloomy fate. It need not be yours. I was merely looking for advice."

"You did not abandon me last year. Could this be worse?"

Noel pointed to his eye.

"That does look damned painful."

"The devil of it is, I have no notion of how to conduct a dancing school—or a Learn-How-to-Use-One's-Limbs-Properly school—or how long the process takes."

"On that score, I am not your best judge. Is it only you and Mrs. Grantham who would be actively involved?"

Noel nodded, hoping he did not betray the agitation that the notion caused. Fitzhugh had illuminated one of the problems Noel had not quite realized he feared: that after being with Mrs. Grantham day in and day out, one fit of Miss Grant-ham's temper could leave them totally to their own devices and prey to passions they had no business having for each other.

His dear Anne may have considered him capable of batting away any unwanted feelings like a shuttlecock, but Noel no longer had such optimism about doing it with Mrs. Grantham. This evening had taught him that. Her comments had tossed him from anger to hurt to amusement to frustration, sometimes within the space of a heartbeat. And lust—no, more than lust, a yearning—had overmastered him, just as it swelled within him now.

Oh, Anne, he thought.

"Do you think the process would be facilitated by having more than one teacher?" Fitzhugh asked.

"Well—" Noel shrugged. "I don't know. But you promised your lady you would finish your business while she was finishing hers. The last thing in the world I want is Esme Fitzhugh angry at me."

Fitzhugh smiled. "Nor I. What about Aunt Bourre?"

Hope leapt within Noel. If anyone could help and apply a bandage of respectability, it would be Mrs. Bourre, who was so kind and charming and implacable. "She could not possibly ask for such duty."

"No, but I could ask her." Fitzhugh tapped his knuckles against his lips. "In fact, that might solve my problem with Dorrie."

"This port must be addling my wits. Either that or mention of Malcolm coming to Town."

"Still haven't patched up your difficulties?"

"Did I but know what to patch, and how large to

make it. And then there would be the sewing of it. Hopeless there."

Fitzhugh nodded. "Dorrie and Mrs. Grantham were thick as thieves at Astley's. Nor have I seen Dorrie so interested in making a new friend. Aunt Bourre will hear of it and maybe that will make her—"

"Want to push Dorrie and Mrs. Grantham together."

"Especially since it sounds as if Mrs. Grantham will not be available for casual conversation until Miss Grantham officially comes out."

Noel closed his eyes and sighed. "In a week's time."

"That is ambitious."

"Ambitious, maybe. Practical?" Noel shrugged. "Our little chick has to get on the market if she is going to sell, even if she trips getting into the yard."

Fitzhugh shook his head in commiseration. "I will send a note to Aunt Bourre tonight. What time are you going to get started tomorrow?"

"Twelve. Mrs. Grantham needs to walk first, I understand."

"Walk?"

"She says she got used to walking while following the drum."

"Surprised her husband didn't get her a horse."

Noel smiled. From Fitzhugh that was condemnation indeed. "Maybe he did not have your eye and all the nags had expired." *Or were shot out from under her,* he thought suddenly.

"I saw the sweetest goer this afternoon," Fitzhugh said. "Pretty little mare with an intelligent eye. But you don't want to know about that tonight."

"I'm sorry. I promise I will not be so outré as to mope."

Fitzhugh took him by the shoulder so they could look back toward the card table. Sommers glowered. Breshirewood held his neck as stiffly as only Breshirewood could. Smith-Jenkins appeared to be debating whether he should laugh or run away in horror.

"Don't promise anything yet, Reversby."

"Aw," Noel said, "rescuing Smith-Jenkins may provide some entertainment."

Of one accord and in charity with each other, Noel and Fitzhugh crossed the room to do battle.

Miss Bourre played the last bars of Grimstock. Mrs. Grantham was pretending to be the gentleman to Miss Grantham in a series of dances so that Noel and Mrs. Bourre could see if there was any pattern to Miss Grantham's clumsiness. As yet, no, and Noel had ducked more than once.

"No, Miss Grantham, you turn the other way," Mrs. Bourre said.

"I know that. I am not stupid."

"True," Mrs. Grantham said, "but for some reason you do not feel the music in your feet the same way you do when you play it with your fingers."

"What do you know?" Lizzie asked. "You have spent the last six years around a campfire."

The Bourres tried to appear blank as they had whenever Lizzie had been pointedly rude. Noel wondered if Mrs. Bourre was allowing Lizzie enough rope to hang herself.

"We were not always as rough as that."

But a twitch of Mrs. Grantham's lovely mouth told Noel they were sometimes as rough as that. He could not decide if he wanted to call out the late Lieutenant Grantham or envy him his ability to give his wife such interesting experiences. Either way, he recognized his thoughts as ridiculous.

"Then you show me," Lizzie said.

Noel said, "Here, Miss Grantham, sit down in my seat, where you may observe. Your aunt and I will demonstrate. Play Grimstock again, please, Miss Bourre, a little more slowly."

He rose to stand across from Mrs. Grantham.

"Is this necessary?" she asked.

Noel understood from the uncertain edge to her voice that she had meant never to touch him again. To know that the general had made an interesting tactical error thrilled him as if he were racing. "Very."

As they danced to the spirited music, Noel admired the ease with which she moved, the graceful curve of her arm, the tilt to her head, and the way a wheat-colored curl had worked its way loose from her chignon and bounced about her shoulder. She lost more and more of her reserve as they moved up and down the floor they had cleared for the purpose. Now she met his gaze, not with either wariness or defensive boldness but as a woman breathtakingly alive.

He found her transformation more thrilling than her error, and when the dance ended almost made the mistake of kissing her for the sheer joy of it.

"You dance very well, my lord," she said.

It was such a commonplace thing to say that it endeared her to him, and, realizing what he was doing, he said, "Come, come, my dear, the boy was taught something."

"Yes," she said, "I see." But some of the joy left her.

"Now watch again, Miss Grantham," Noel said, putting on his best First Cousin voice. "Miss Bourre? If you would?"

Miss Bourre began the piece again. Then Noel leaned forward, and said quietly to Mrs. Grantham, "I want you to stumble so you can show her a good way to recover."

She gave him a hard look.

"Trust me," he said, and like that, they were off.

She nodded, danced a few steps, and then tripped herself. The others gasped, Miss Bourre stopped playing, but Noel caught Mrs. Grantham, held her upper back against his chest for an intoxicating second, then spun her away.

Mrs. Grantham laughed—a deep, throaty sound— going through the figures of the dance as though Miss Bourre had never stopped.

"Again," Lizzie said. "Again!"

Miss Bourre caught up to them, grinning. And Mrs. Grantham pretended to fall backward, transforming the movement into a turn, and Noel was there to catch her hand as though she had merely added an expected flourish.

Two more times she played at stumbling or stepping wrong. The first time she again looked like she would flatten Noel, but she recovered herself and made it look like she would pass around his back. The second time, he caught her around the waist and spun her about, their faces inches from each other, her eyes sparkling, her color high, her red lips parted.

I have kissed that mouth, Noel thought. *I will taste it again. I will.*

"Excellent," Mrs. Bourre said, "excellent."

"A variation," Miss Grantham said, "a variation on a theme." She was frowning, but it was a thinking frown.

Observing it, Mrs. Bourre rose and said, "That will be enough for today, Miss Grantham."

Miss Grantham wasted no time bobbing a curtsy and fleeing the room.

Noel realized he was still holding Mrs. Grantham. He cleared his throat and released her.

She was working on recovering her poise, taking deep breaths and whisking at her skirts. She said to Mrs. Bourre, "Thank you. I am not certain Lizzie would have stayed as long as she did had she not feared being embarrassed before you and Miss Bourre."

"Oh, she would have cheerfully been embarrassed before me," Miss Bourre said. "'Tis mother that quite frightens one into compliance."

"Do name a time when I ever frightened you," Mrs. Bourre said with good humor.

"I cannot. It seems you no longer frighten her, Reversby," Miss Bourre said.

Noel bowed. "I am more suited to the prancing clown than the roaring lion, do you not think?"

Mrs. Grantham looked sober again.

"Certainly with that monocle in, Reversby," Mrs. Bourre said.

"Will you wear it tonight?" Miss Bourre asked. "Oh, Mother, would it not be lovely if Mrs. Grantham could join us this evening? We are having a small dinner party, Mrs. Grantham, with Reversby here and Fitzhugh, and his father, the Earl of Hadley, and my cousins, the Tunbridges. Do say you are free to come. We have had no chance to talk this afternoon."

Mrs. Grantham waited the polite beat necessary for Mrs. Bourre to add her delight before saying, "Your offer is very kind, but I visited the modiste only yesterday."

And then, despite all his cautions to himself, Noel said, "True, but you needn't stand on such ceremony this evening."

"Yes, heed Reversby," Miss Bourre said. "At least on this point."

"Eudora!" her mother said. Then, to Mrs. Grantham, "You would be most welcome, and Reversby is correct. We are none of us high sticklers, although we could start behaving that way."

Miss Bourre pretended to look reprimanded, but Noel caught her eyes twinkling. So did Mrs. Grantham.

"Please do say you will come," Mrs. Bourre concluded.

"I should be honored," Mrs. Grantham said.

"There, then, that's settled. Would you bring her by around eight o'clock, Reversby?"

Mrs. Grantham looked faintly dismayed, which made Noel more than faintly annoyed. He said, "Will that be at all acceptable to you, ma'am?"

"I am certain traveling with you will leave me with no permanent damage, my lord," she said.

"Oh, Reversby's carriage is excellently sprung, and he's a fine whip," Miss Bourre said.

"To be sure," Mrs. Bourre said, back to appearing serene.

"And there is no wild livestock in this part of London," Noel added.

"Wild livestock? What do you go on about?" Miss Bourre asked.

"Lord Reversby has been amusing himself with a joke since I met him," Mrs. Grantham said. "I believe it is growing wings and flying away."

"Now that I should like to see," Noel said, amused.

"Do you know," Mrs. Grantham said, smiling, "I should as well."

Ah, Noel thought. *Is this progress?*

Chapter Nine

The party was so intimate—only nine including Meg—that the hostess encouraged general conversation. Thus Meg felt as if she gained a real knowledge of others in a way she had not since leaving Lizzie's maligned campfires.

With the ease that bespoke custom, bluff Lord Hadley placed his portly frame at the head of Mrs. Bourre's table and signaled to the footman for wine.

"The Hadleys and the Bourres are neighbors back in Somersetshire," Reversby said in an undertone as he seated Meg.

"Did I give away any ill-bred surprise?" she asked.

He had leaned down so that he could continue speaking discreetly, and, as it had that afternoon while they were dancing, his lemon-warm, masculine scent invaded her senses. During the drive to Mrs. Bourre's charming town house she had tried to sit far enough away from him to avoid its intoxicating effect on her.

She had confirmed the Bourres' claim that Viscount Reversby had a sure touch on the reins. Meg was as susceptible to a sure touch on the reins as she was to fruit. She reminded herself, however, that she knew wife beaters in the Army who were sure touches on the reins.

But . . . Anne's husband would never be a wife beater.

Anne's husband.

"Only to someone who knows you," he replied.

"That's as well, then," she said, and hoped he did not detect the lie in her voice.

"No, Reversby," Mrs. Bourre said, "do not sit down next to Mrs. Grantham. You are on the other side."

Reversby caught Meg's gaze and gave a sardonic smile before taking himself around the table. When he sat down, an epergne of flowers, although low, obscured his mouth and nose. The flowers, lavender and blue and yellow, highlighted his bruised eye, which now showed tinges of green along with the purple.

And Meg was struck by how handsome he was, even bruised, without the other side of his face scrunched up to wear his monocle. He had left it off this evening, and no one had remarked upon it. *An intimate group indeed,* Meg thought.

Her immediate dinner partners were Mr. Edmund Tunbridge—a pleasant young gentleman who sat between her and Lord Hadley—and Lord Fitzhugh, who sat between her and Mrs. Bourre. Miss Bourre, Reversby, Miss Tunbridge, and Lady Tunbridge took the opposite side.

And that, Meg decided, had to measure a hostess's true generosity—inviting someone who made her party have an odd number.

Mrs. Bourre, Meg soon learned, knew how to stoke a discussion by asking someone who had not much stake in his answer to volunteer a point of view. Thus she did not ask Meg, Reversby, Miss Tunbridge, or her daughter about how they found the Season, but instead Mr. Tunbridge, who showed absolutely no interest in marriage.

"There are too many pretty girls on the wall," he said. "I dance with them to keep them happy."

"It is kind of you," Meg said.

"He is a fraud, ma'am," his sister said.

"Emma," protested their mother.

"It is true, Mama," Mr. Tunbridge said. "It is common knowledge that I am not looking to marry now."

"Still, I am certain that the invitation to dance itself lifts their spirits," Meg said.

"I hope only that more of those who have been serving will come home to even the numbers," Mr. Tunbridge said, "now that the Peace is signed."

"Except that you want to go off," Miss Tunbridge said, "and that will reduce the complement again by one. Eventually, brother, you will count."

Mrs. Bourre said, "My nephew anticipates that there will be extensive negotiations over the peace, and wishes to partake."

"That is a noble goal, sir," Meg said warmly.

"You young things," said Lord Hadley, "seem so fixed upon proving your worth. Tunbridge there has an estate he must learn to manage, not run off to meddle in the affairs of other countries. Look at Reversby here, he does not hie off at the littlest thing."

"Lack of imagination, sir, 'tis merely lack of imagination. Now, did I have something that interested me, and at which I excelled, I might be the worst landlord in England."

Between the too-easy speech and Fitzhugh's hands stilling upon his fork, Meg came on the alert. Perhaps she had gone too long without sufficient challenge, or perhaps she needed to be on the offensive rather than the defensive, but she said, "We are not all so fortunate, begging your pardon, my lord, to both know our duty clearly and have the ability to act upon it."

The table appeared to be holding its collective breath. Mrs. Bourre still looked serene, except for a certain tenseness about her mouth. The Tunbridges were wide-eyed. Miss Bourre appeared both excited and apprehensive, and looked pointedly at Lord Fitzhugh, who appeared quite, quite blank. Reversby had on his catchall ironic gaze.

Lord Hadley raised his brows and cut his meat. "I do not know you well enough, ma'am, to know what demands are put upon you, or determine whether you have ability to do anything."

"I was not proffering myself as an example, my lord," Meg said.

"Then what was your point?"

"My point was this. I bemoaned and resented the loss of those trained for other occupations, most notably those lords who held landed title. They should never have been allowed to take their chances under cannon that cared not one whit if its victims had so many dependent upon them at home. Mr. Tunbridge's father is yet alive, and Mr. Tunbridge appears to have a level enough head that I am certain he could take over the reins were he called upon to do so."

Mr. Tunbridge was nodding.

"In the meantime, why should he not pursue some useful occupation that he enjoys?" Meg asked.

Lord Hadley put down his fork. "Do you mean to tell me, ma'am, that you were over in the infernal war?"

Mrs. Bourre said gently, "Do you not remember my telling you of the lady we met who had followed the drum?"

"You are she?"

Meg nodded.

"Then you could use yourself as an example, could you not?"

There were too many memories, of success and loss. Meg could neither conceive of sharing any of those stories around Mrs. Bourre's dinner table, nor of choosing which one to bring forth. "All of us here could, my lord."

Hadley would have protested further, but Reversby said quietly, "I would wager Mrs. Grantham has seen things she would either wish never to have seen, or never to relive."

Amazed that he could sympathize, he who wanted to wrest whatever he could from her, Meg sat riveted, her gaze locked with his in painful intensity. Who was Lord Reversby? Could she but understand his character, she could . . . what?

"Miserable French," Hadley said, breaking the spell.

"Miserable the impulses to go to war," Meg said.

"You do seem to insist upon arguing with me," Hadley said.

"No, my lord, not argue. Disagree."

That brought smothered smiles around the table. Mrs. Bourre so far forgot herself that she patted her mouth with her napkin.

Hadley assessed the others and decided to play along. "Then you do not blame the French?"

"I blame certain Frenchmen," Meg said readily. "But at the level of the soldier in the field, there was little to choose between us. At least, in our relations to each other. Some of the soldiers in our camp learned a little French from washing their clothes alongside French chasseurs. We traded necessities. The Spanish were another issue."

"Spaniards," Hadley said. "Why we fought for the Spaniards, I will never understand."

"That was not my meaning. Unlike Mr. Tunbridge, I have no political leanings."

Reversby's expression had returned to mocking her. "None?"

"Perhaps a few. I meant that while our soldiers and the French treated each other with some modicum of decency, they both treated the Spanish very ill. I do believe we have seen the end of civility in war."

"You draw very broad conclusions for someone in your position," Lord Hadley said.

Fitzhugh sighed. But Meg understood that Hadley implied a question as much as attempted to put her in her place. She opened her mouth to respond.

"Begging your pardon, my lord," Reversby said, "but Mrs. Grantham's position may not be what it appears."

Meg flashed him a warning glance, but he pretended not to see it.

"I have learned that within the Army, Mrs. Grantham was known as—"

"My lord!"

"General Grantham."

Meg blushed fiercely.

"You have embarrassed my guest, Reversby," Mrs. Bourre said, even as Hadley leaned forward and said, "Indeed? How interesting. Do tell me how that came about."

"Yes, please, Mrs. Grantham," Miss Bourre said, "unless the memory is too painful."

"Yes, please," Miss Tunbridge and her brother said at once, then looked at each other as only siblings can do.

"You are not obligated," Mrs. Bourre said gently.

Meg disliked the position Reversby had placed her in. She had not intended to monopolize the conversation, or appear as though she were bragging about what she had done, although she would do what she had done again if necessary. Still, she could not take unadulterated pleasure in her accomplishments. Since they had protected her, they were tainted with shame.

But maybe it was time to overcome that shame.

"It is all right, ma'am," Meg said. "Thank you, but it is no secret."

Reversby scrunched up his mouth a little at that.

"The truth, my lord," Meg said to Hadley, "is that I do not know who gave me the nickname. It came about, I believe, because I became a de facto quartermaster."

The earl frowned.

Fitzhugh said, with a nod to Meg, "A quartermaster is responsible for securing supplies, shelter, and food. When the Army marches, he goes ahead and negotiates for these items with the local population. When encamped, he ensures supplies continue to flow."

"Yes," Mr. Tunbridge said, "and Wellington had strict instructions about taking what could not be negotiated. He wanted the Spanish population as his willing allies." He flushed under Hadley's pointed glance.

"How did this duty fall to you, a woman?" Hadley asked.

"We were unfortunate, back in '10, to have an exceptionally poor quartermaster assigned to our division. He could not negotiate his way out of this room if you all pointed him toward the door. We had children marching with us, my lord, and nursing mothers along with other women, not just soldiers."

"Did you negotiate with the same people who had refused your quartermaster's offers?" Fitzhugh asked.

"No, my lord. I went first to the local women."

Lady Tunbridge said, "Brava."

"The women worked with me. They drove hard but fair bargains, and we fed our people."

"With your own money?" Fitzhugh asked.

Meg smiled. "The quartermaster desired to eat, too, my lord."

That brought chuckles around the table.

Then Lord Hadley asked, "Did your system never fail you?"

"When the whole Army had to fall back behind the Lines again, over the winter of '11—"

"The Lines?" Miss Tunbridge asked.

"Of Torres Vedras," her brother replied. "An elaborate series of fortifications to protect Lisbon." He flushed. "I do beg your pardon, Mrs. Grantham."

"Not at all, sir. The Lines performed excellently, but conditions did become a bit crowded. As I was about to despair, I met the most remarkable woman, who had come up from Lisbon to look us over. We were something of a tourist attraction."

"Good gracious," Miss Tunbridge said, "I would never regard an army as a tourist attraction."

"She was an Englishwoman," Meg said.

"But what was she about, being there?" Miss Bourre asked.

"She said she was arranging some matters for her husband."

"Still," Miss Bourre said, "to go down there."

"She was perfectly safe, I do assure you. She had as escort a Portuguese general, and, as she was a very beautiful lady, he showed her every attention."

"Was she titled?" Miss Bourre asked lightly.

Reversby came to attention. He did not do anything so overt as to sit up in his chair with metaphorical whiskers aquiver. Instead he tightened his mouth, and cocked his head toward Miss Bourre, although he glanced toward Fitzhugh. Fitzhugh, Meg noted, wagged his hand parallel to the table, close to his plate. A small gesture, subtle.

"No," Meg said, "a plain Mrs."

"At first, when you spoke of her as being remarkable," Miss Tunbridge said, "I had quite another picture in my mind. Certainly not a beautiful young woman."

"Do describe her," Miss Bourre said.

"It would be a useless endeavor, I am afraid," Meg replied, "for did I say she had striking eyebrows and a fine nose, we would all picture something different."

"How true," Mrs. Bourre said.

"Her hair? What color was that?" Miss Bourre asked.

"Eudora," her mother said.

Meg wondered why Miss Bourre pressed but smiled and said, "She had it covered in Iberian style, by a mantilla. I think that was a concession to the Portuguese general."

"Who was helping her arrange matters for her husband, no less," Hadley said, attacking his meat again. "What was the clod's name?"

Meg did not need to meet Reversby's gaze to understand the question was significant. Why it was significant had her burning with curiosity, but she sensed prevarication was called upon.

Later she wanted to ask Reversby some extensive questions. She also wanted to ponder how well she knew what he wanted from her, and why she felt inclined to do it.

"I have forgotten it, I am sorry to say," Meg replied. "It was three long years ago. But as to your point, my lord, the general merely served as escort—pleased escort, to be sure. The lady made her own decisions. One of them, fortunately for me, was to introduce me to a circle of acquaintances who proved useful in provisioning us. We were not to see the like again."

Reversby smiled, and Meg felt relieved.

"Your experiences are quite amazing," Mr. Tunbridge said.

"I would not label them so," Meg said. "They were born of exigency, which is the reason I disagreed with you earlier, Lord Hadley, that to know one's duty automatically enables the means of performing it."

"You make me regret my earlier statement," Hadley said.

This time no one bothered to hide astonishment.

"You are very kind, sir." Then Meg met Reversby's intent gaze. The memory of kissing those chiseled lips wiped away her pride. How could she be proud of herself and still have these improper thoughts?

Fortunately Mrs. Bourre chose that moment to stand and have the ladies withdraw. "Do carry on, Hadley," she said.

When they reached the drawing room, comfortably decorated with mellow beige walls, jewel tone cushions on the divans and chairs, and vases of flowers, Miss Bourre took Meg by the arm and said, "What an interesting evening it has been. I have never seen Hadley so taken by a new notion. Have you, Mama?"

"Never," Mrs. Bourre said, and began pouring tea from a silver service on a table set between two divans.

"And to listen to an idea from a mere female, why, I am amazed."

"Now you are overstating the matter," Lady Tunbridge said, although she smiled.

"He has certainly become more open to the possibility within the last couple of years," Mrs. Bourre said, "even from mere females. We do not want Mrs. Grantham to think our circle composed of rigid thinkers, Eudora."

"I am in no danger of that, ma'am," Meg said, accepting a cup of tea and sitting down next to Miss

Bourre, with her back to the door. "There is a matter that presses me, however, that I would appreciate an opinion on from good friends. Would you tell me, do I stand in any danger of stirring up gossip because of Lord Reversby's assistance with my niece?"

"I have heard nothing," Mrs. Bourre said. "Sister?"

"I have heard a few people wonder why he has been seen thrice with you. I have not heard more than that."

"But it will cause more talk as we go on," Mrs. Bourre said. "Last season, Reversby had an air about him that said quite plainly, 'do not touch.'"

"It is amusing, Aunt, that you use those words," Miss Tunbridge said, "for I myself had thought of him as a fine article under glass."

"You would," Miss Bourre said, "since you are forever shopping."

Miss Tunbridge grinned. "Do you invite me to tell you what I found today in the most charming little—"

"Cease now!" Miss Bourre said, holding up her hands.

"This year, however," Mrs. Bourre said, "there has been a decided change to him, and the young ladies—"

"Can sniff it like a banker an investment," Miss Tunbridge said.

"Emma," her mother said with exasperation.

"Sorry. It's true, however, despite his sporting that monocle this year. What is that all about?"

Mrs. Bourre shrugged. "Perhaps it is a test to see if a young woman will see him and not his title and fortune."

Meg hoped her expression remained calm. When apart from the gentlemen, these ladies of balance and humor spoke of Reversby with fondness. Had her gropings toward understanding his character missed the mark entirely? Or did he merely show her his most determined, arrogant side? That was not a comfortable realization. The kiss in the box at Astley's continued shimmering in her memory.

Miss Tunbridge tossed her head. "It is a silly way to do it, but typical for a gentleman, I suppose."

"Who said gentlemen are rational?" Mrs. Bourre replied.

The women shared conspiratorial smiles.

"Mrs. Grantham, Fitzhugh told me that you and Lady Reversby were childhood friends," Miss Bourre said.

"We were second cousins," said Meg, "and almost of age, although I was older. I lived in her father's house after my parents died, from when I was about ten years. We were not enthusiastic about each other at first. Anne enjoyed being the littlest and petted by one and all. She was beautiful, too, which helped."

"Yes," Miss Bourre said, "I have noticed that."

Her aunt and cousin looked away. Her mother gave her a rather sharp look. "It sounds as if you managed to get on eventually."

Meg smiled. "I remember the day we took each other's measure and found each other not as wanting as we thought. It had rained that morning and was threatening to do so again. Do you know that smell of rain that lingers in the air? But Aunt Neville wished us to get some exercise outdoors. I do not remember what nonsense Anne decided to prattle on about. She was often, at that time, prattling on about something ridiculous. But she came round to the subject of her fine dress. It was a beautiful yellow, and she was quite inordinately fond of it, not the least bit because it was a color I could not wear, not having the same brilliance in my hair color."

Lady Tunbridge and Mrs. Bourre smiled at each other, possibly remembering their own childhood.

"I admit I threw the first handful of mud. Smack into the front of her dress. It made a rather horrible squishing sound before falling onto the grass and leaving a dripping mess."

Miss Bourre said, "And then what?"

"We stared at each other, both horrified and both furious. Then Anne scooped up some mud and dashed it at me before I fully comprehended her intent. Well, that settled that. We slung squelching, smelly mud at each other with cheerful abandon, me yelling at her how much I hated all her airs, and her screeching that I was no better than I should be to think I could take an equal place in her house."

"Who broke up the fight?"

"Anne's brother Xavier. He was just there one moment, and picked us up under our arms. Well, we wanted none of that. How dare he involve himself in our fight! When he asked Anne what she thought she was doing, brawling with a guest, she stuck her tongue out at him, and a glob of mud fell off her nose right upon it."

"Oh, how foul," Miss Bourre said, screwing up her mouth.

Meg nodded. "She started trying to spit it out, and that had me laughing, I am sorry to say. Xavier gave her his kerchief, and when she had the taste mostly out, she started laughing, too. When he asked us who had started the fight, I was about to confess, but then Anne chimed in. I will never forget what she said: 'I called her dress so ugly that mud would improve it, and added some to show her I was right.' I could see I would not convince Xavier she was fibbing through her muddy nose."

Even dripping mud, her dress streaked beyond repair and stinking, Anne had retained the hauteur she could never quench, Meg recalled. Anne had much the same look to her then as she had the morning after their false weddings. Meg had not thought of it that way, but however she and Anne had drifted apart during Meg's years in the Peninsula, those years of shared childhood still counted for something.

"That," Meg said, freshly warmed, "was the true worth of my friend Anne Neville Reversby."

Mrs. Bourre smiled, but her gaze shifted from Meg to the doorway behind her. "What a wonderful story."

"Were you friends right away?" Miss Bourre asked.

"Not immediately," Meg replied, suspecting who Mrs. Bourre had seen and choosing her words carefully.

"But why not right away?" Miss Tunbridge asked.

"Anne was punished harshly for initiating the fight. At least, the punishment was harsh from her perspective. Her father had never punished her before, and she had to endure three days alone in her room and nights without supper. I, it seems, was not considered sufficiently schooled to understand that a lady does not brawl in the mud. It may be that I never learned the lesson, either, considering the way I have spent the last seven years but one."

Meg looked brightly at the others, because she would not look behind her. "I have talked rather a lot this evening. I am not usually such a chatterbox."

"We enjoyed hearing your stories," Miss Bourre said.

"Yes," added Miss Tunbridge. "Our own company, while comfortable, can be predictable as well. It is like going into the same shop day after day. You are a fresh shipment from an exotic port."

Her mother and cousin looked on her with mock despair.

"Yet you have made me feel very much at home," Meg said. "All of you. Thank you."

"You must come back frequently," Mrs. Bourre said. "Reversby, do you think you could arrange that?"

Chapter Ten

Miss Tunbridge and Miss Bourre, who also had their backs to the drawing room door, startled and turned to gawp at Noel—as though Mrs. Bourre had announced he had stripped off all his clothes and intended to go bathing in the teapot.

Mrs. Grantham did not so much as twitch. Noel wondered if she had received some signal from Mrs. Bourre that the younger women had failed to recognize, or if her senses had been sharpened by her time following the drum.

Certainly the conversation over the dinner table had again reminded him of how alien her life had been. The story of the chocolates upon the road had been so extraordinary that when Noel had not been annoyed at its refreshing Black's connections to Mrs. Grantham, he had half-regarded it as a fairy tale.

But when she had spoken of riding ahead of the Army to bargain with the native women, and when she had described the beautiful Englishwoman who had solved her procurement problems, a different tone had crept into her voice—powerful, authoritative. Like the Bible, which had long fascinated Noel for its deceptive simplicity, what she had men-

tioned obtaining conjured images of what she had
been deprived of, how hard she had struggled.

Perhaps he imagined more struggle than she had
endured, but he did not think so. What did it all
mean for him and for learning her secret?

Hadley had distracted Noel by asking more about
her. Noel spoke of what he knew from Anne. Anne,
he realized, had not said much, and about facts
rather than feelings.

Then, to overhear Mrs. Grantham describe the
fight between her and Anne . . . Noel felt as if she
had reached into his chest with a hot poker and
stirred. He wanted to weep. He also wanted to laugh.

But he could not, so he did not. Would that all sit-
uations give him such opportunity to bat strong
emotions away, and he could withstand anything.
The question was, however, would he want to live
his life that way?

Noel stepped into the room and bowed. "Pleased
to do my part as always, don't you know. Trained
viscount, at your service."

"There, then," Mrs. Bourre said, "that is settled.
Now, Reversby, do tell how you came to be listening
in doorways."

"I have no great excuse for myself," Noel said,
"other than I would never dream of interrupting a
lady. Well, except that the others are coming to join
you, and it is close on midnight. I do believe Mrs.
Grantham mentioned that she must be up at some
ungodly hour of the morning."

She had mentioned no such thing, but he had
deduced as much from knowing her need to walk
and what time they would begin Miss Grantham's
training.

"Lord Reversby is very kind to remember," Mrs. Grantham said to Mrs. Bourre. "I have lost track of the time in congenial company. Are the others coming now, or should I make my good-byes for them to you?"

"They are coming now," Noel said.

Noel concealed his impatience as everyone bid Mrs. Grantham a sincerely regretful good night. He wanted to convince himself that he had passed through childhood and could share approving of her with Hadley and young Tunbridge. But even Fitzhugh's approval tried his patience.

"You have nice friends," Mrs. Grantham said after Noel could finally take the reins and start down the dim, cobbled street.

"You need not gloss over Hadley for my sake," Noel said. "He has always been contentious. Unless, that is, one wishes to do nothing but shoot, manage one's property, or chase widows in London. Oh, I must add one other thing: do nothing until one has come into one's property."

Mrs. Grantham wriggled her shoulders within her dark blue wrap. The movement distracted Noel from his driving. Usually nothing distracted Noel from his driving.

"Some of his comments were rather pointed," she said. "Which of his edicts does Lord Fitzhugh most often break? No, do not tell me. I shall guess. Miss Bourre mentioned that he has quite a reputation as a trader of horses. And someone mentioned that Lord Hadley did not entirely approve of his choice of wife. Miss Bourre also let drop a comment or two about her having a rather bad reputation. What is wrong with her?"

"You do not know?"

"Only the barest outlines."

"You could have asked me," Noel said.

"Am I not now?"

"The general officer tone is in your voice, my dear."

"Do not say that."

Noel could no longer pretend he paid attention to his driving. He pulled over to the side and let a hackney pass him. "To what do you object? 'General Grantham' or 'my dear'?"

"Both, now that you mention it. Why are we not driving?"

"Because we are talking, and I need all my poor mental capacities to converse with you."

"You do not."

"Do," he said. "Dare you."

"You are being absurd again," she said.

Her wistful smile touched him deeply. "Well, it amuses me."

"It makes me forget," she said.

"Forget what?"

"Nothing," she replied.

He studied her long, decided against immediately pursuing that thread. "Now that I can direct all my mental capacities, let us return to the subject at hand."

"Which one was that?" she asked.

"No, Mrs. Grantham, that is my style. Not yours."

"Perhaps your style is infecting me."

"Such a lovely word, infecting. It does make me think of sore throats and rashes."

"Not charming at all," she said.

"No," he replied.

"Influencing? Inducing? Overwhelming?"

"I am sorry, but you will not distract me any more," Noel said. But he liked the overwhelming part.

She made a reproachful moue.

"I thought we had General Grantham behind us," Noel said.

"I don't know what you are talking about."

"It is who you are."

"It is who I was. It may be who I am again, but now . . ." She shook her head.

"What are you thinking about?"

"I have seen and done too many things I would forget. And I cannot believe I would tell you that."

"Why not tell me? Oh, was it the 'my dear'?" he asked.

"It was the 'my dear' on top of that lovely evening. I had forgotten what is between us."

"If that is your objection, I shall not apologize," Noel said, restraining himself from bringing up either her secret or Miss Grantham.

"I would never think you would," she said.

"Bereft of all social niceties?"

"That is a silly thing to say. Far too extreme."

"What standard do you have to judge me by?"

"Hadley approved of you," she said.

"Well, I do fit all his requirements." The flippant words could not quite hide the bitterness in his tone, nor did Noel fully understand why he felt bitter. He was what all Englishmen wanted to be: a man of substance and property, with more freedom than most to do as he pleased. What matter that he had worked hard to get there? What matter that, irrespective of Anne's death, he felt a curious hole in his life, as though the intended goal had been nothing more than an illusion?

"Do you really think so?" she asked.

"Don't you?"

She looked out at the grand houses lining the street. "Not exactly."

"No?"

"No," she said.

"What exactly, then?"

"You may have all the outer trappings, but there is a depth to your character not included in Lord Hadley's requirements."

"Flattery, Mrs. Grantham. Pure flattery."

"Not exactly."

"I sense something familiar about this."

"Did you meet his requirements," she said, "you would not want my memories. You would not care."

Her comment hit a chord within him, but he was dashed if he knew what. He played with the reins in his hands, thinking. His dappled gray geldings stamped their feet. One snorted. Finally he decided he should be angry as only he could be. "Now this is a different approach. You are nothing if not novel."

"I beg your pardon?"

"First you told me there was no secret. Then you told me you would tell me the secret did I round up Miss Grantham's pianoforte. Then you told me you had made no such promise. Then you told me I need only help you marry off Miss Grantham."

"We have already discussed whether I promised you anything about the pianoforte. Must we argue?" she asked.

"Am I arguing?"

"It sounds like it to me," she said with a voice that dripped icicles.

"I was giving a précis of our history," Noel said, "so you would understand how interesting I find your approach. It is unbelievably subtle."

"Too subtle even for me."

"Oh, that will not do, Mrs. Grantham. You are nothing if not an intelligent creature. Anne said so, and all of your parsing and subtlety, not to mention your stories of what you accomplished in the Peninsula, prove the point."

"You would please be kind enough to spell out what you are trying to say."

"That is right. I am a simple landowner. A man about Town. A Corinthian who cannot handle his reins while talking to Mrs. Grantham for fear of missing some important phrase that she will later parse into something entirely advantageous to herself. How laughable is that!"

"I do wish you would stop going on about parsing."

"It was not you who lost half a week of his life conversing with Major Black, nor the time spent traveling to and from Oxford."

"My apologies if you considered him poor company. I have found him a gentleman these last five years," she said.

"There you go again."

"I beg your pardon?" she asked.

"Diverting the conversation. Whatever I think of Major Black, which, admittedly, is not much, the point is that I had no desire to be relegated to Oxford with him."

Her brows rose at his description of Black, but she said, with the same air of high lady that Anne had often employed, "You do understand that I did not much want to see you."

"I could not fail to understand that. So, having taken my mettle, you have tried chipping away at my resolve, first by enticing me with yourself, then by appealing to my sense of myself."

Her lip curled. "You are an attractive man, Lord Reversby, that I will not deny. But the last thing in the world that I want is a husband."

"Nor a lover?"

"I beg your pardon. I misspoke. The last thing in the world I want is a lover. The next to last is a husband."

"When did you become a follower of Madame de Stael and Mrs. Wollstonecraft?"

"I need follow no one to make up my own mind."

"Then why are you so set against men?"

"Who said I was against men? I am against entanglements," Mrs. Grantham said. "Is it my fault that men most often cause them?"

"Let us note that conversational path and choose to follow it some other day. What have you against entanglements? It seems to me you could have gone home to the Nevilles, where there would be few entanglements. Instead you elected to stay with your late husband's people, where entanglements are as thick as the floor polish. As I certainly know." Noel pointed to his blackened eye.

"Take me home," she said, tight-lipped.

"Why?"

"Because you have ruined this perfectly lovely evening with your parsing and arguments. You do not own me, Lord Reversby. You have no more rights or privileges toward my thoughts or feelings than Lord Hadley does toward Mrs. Bourre."

"You will tell me what they have to do with this conversation?"

"I fear I misspoke when I said you were so unlike Lord Hadley, for now I see you do fit all his requirements, including chasing widows in London. You number among a despicable subset, however: those who chase widows who do not wish to be chased."

Noel had not thought he could become any angrier, but that did it.

"Hullo, what's amiss, Reversby?"

Noel cursed under his breath. He had barely registered the few other phaetons and hacks that had passed them while he and Mrs. Grantham had argued by the side of the street. But Sommers, blasted Sommers, would stop and poke his nose in.

Noel turned, beheld not only Sommers but Major Black as well. He muttered another curse, but before he could deny a problem, Major Black tipped his shako and said, "Mrs. Grantham. Is everything quite all right?"

"Major, would you please be so kind as to take me home?"

And before Noel knew it, she had slipped down from his phaeton, high wheels neatly avoided and all, and crossed before his grays.

All solicitation on his face and all triumph in the set of his head and shoulders, Major Black jumped down so he could hand Mrs. Grantham up to Sommers's phaeton. "My pleasure, Mrs. Grantham. Is that not right, Sommers?"

Sommers grinned and agreed.

"Thank you, gentlemen," Mrs. Grantham said.

"Lord Reversby, I do hope your trouble will resolve itself."

Like hell, Noel thought. No one saw through that flimsy excuse.

"Good night," she said.

Sommers flicked his reins, and they were gone.

Noel looked about the deserted street. One of his horses snorted and stamped again, which reminded him that he was about to leave his compassion for poor brutes in his care in the road along with his dignity. Neither loss made him happy.

His foul mood tempted him to go home and begin a systematic progression of drinking. But a prideful impulse made him head for White's. Let it not be said that Reversby hid his head whenever some flibbertigibbet of a widow tried to embarrass him.

Besides, he could get as systematically drunk there as at home. He turned the horses and then checked as a thought occurred to him.

Why had Mrs. Grantham not gone to Xavier Neville? Something about the Granthams must compel her to stay with them, and Noel was going to find out what it was.

Chapter Eleven

Delaying fuming was no fun. On the ride home, Meg forced herself to make polite small talk with Major Black and his cousin, Mr. Sommers. But the larger issue crowding the already crowded phaeton—why Meg was crowding it at all—made it a strenuous activity. Both men's eyes gleamed with greedy interest, but neither would ask; and Meg, who was so used to avoiding volunteering information, did not give herself away.

Upon returning home and apologizing for not being able to offer them hospitality—it being very late and the rest of the family abed—Meg went upstairs and gave into her dark and roiling rage. A porcelain bowl that held her favorite lavender potpourri found its way into her hand. She threw it against the wall papered with light blue flowers. It smashed with a splintering pop.

And yet it did not satisfy.

Nothing had been right in her life since Lord Reversby had come searching her out about that blasted secret.

No, that was not quite true. There had been plenty of things wrong with her life in the Peninsula, but she had at least been capable of some things. Nothing had been right in her life since she had come back to England.

Meg paced about, her hands held tightly under her folded arms, lest she be tempted to throw something else. She had never been a thrower. Her usual style of anger consisted of an aloofness so icy thick that Lieutenant Grantham had said an entire regiment could safely parade upon it.

Why had she ever eloped?

Meg sat down on her bed, its coverlet a match for the dainty wallpaper, her arms still folded. There was no point to feeling sorry for herself. She had indulged enough while the Spanish stars made their slow progression across an inky sky.

Still, she muttered curses toward Lord Reversby. No matter what charming stories she told, the fine people she had met this evening might understand her mistake but not forgive her the covering up of it. She had willingly lived—at least to all appearances— as someone's mistress.

If Reversby learned of it, what would he think of her then?

Meg shook her head. What would it matter? There could be nothing between them, regardless, and after she had abandoned him in such a public fashion, he was unlikely to put himself in her company. She might as well consider their bargain canceled.

That should have made her feel better.

She wished she knew why it did not.

Someone scratched on the door. "'Tis Hemmie, ma'am."

Meg sighed and said, "Come in."

"I heard a noise, ma'am."

Meg pointed to the smashed bowl. "I knocked it down."

"Yes, ma'am," Hemmie said. "Shall I sweep up the pieces now or in the morning?"

"Now, please," Meg said.

She sat on the bed while Hemmie went to get a broom, then took the broom from her, and bent down.

Hemmie clucked and said, "'Tis not right, your doing that."

"It is entirely right. We both know I threw the thing."

Hemmie shrugged and waited for Meg to finish before saying, "Then I'll help you from your dress now, shall I?"

This help Meg accepted, and Hemmie's quick fingers took out pins and undid buttons. When Meg stood in her shift, her hair brushed and neatly rebraided, Hemmie said, "Go to sleep, ma'am. You can make anything out in the morning. Better that way, too."

"Thank you, Hemmie," Meg said. She stood there long after Hemmie had closed the door behind her. An idea was suggesting itself from what Hemmie had said.

Better that way. Better *that* way. Reversby wanted her memories, but would he know true memory from story? If he came around again, could Meg invent something to tell him, something believable enough to explain her resistance?

It was the devil's own idea, and made her feel as if she were abandoning another piece of her honor. Meg resented Reversby for making her think it. He obviously had a bad influence on her, and she on him.

She decided not to think such things or invent stories. Meg climbed into bed. Instead of stars, the blue canopy of her bed stared flatly back at her. Even with her eyes closed she could see it.

With a sigh, she got up, opened the casement window, and let in the night's breeze. It ruffled the canopy, breaking its unblinking gaze. Meg pulled the covers up to her chin and promised herself that tomorrow would be different.

Tomorrow she would not let Lord Reversby bother her. She would not let his words fray her patience. She would not let his presence put her on the defensive. She would not give in to the desire that weakened her.

Tomorrow would be different.

Noel arrived at Mrs. Grantham's house the next day around noon, feeling as though his head were a hot air balloon ready to rise laboriously. He had fulfilled all his plans of getting drunk, but he had not found one damnable officer—or any other damnable personage—who knew anything more about Mrs. Grantham and Lieutenant Grantham than what Noel knew himself.

It was as if they had all gotten themselves killed on purpose to frustrate him.

Black he could not stomach asking, although he had opportunity. Black and Sommers came into White's after dropping off Mrs. Grantham and could barely contain their glee. Despite the club's intimate lighting, Noel noted the whispers and cocked brows and poured himself another brandy.

And another, before Fitzhugh joined him. They both drank.

"She found Esme, you know," Fitzhugh said.

"So thinks Miss Bourre," Noel said. "And Hadley."

"They know her pattern now, so it was not a far-reaching guess. She was in Portugal at the time."

"It seems she assisted the Army nobly," Noel said, not able to bring himself to say Mrs. Grantham.

"Damned Portuguese general," Fitzhugh said, and refilled their glasses. "And do not look at me that way. I know Esme gave him no favors other than a smile, but I hate the way some of those nearest to me will think she did."

"Always willing to be your second, Fitzhugh."

"Be yours if you need me."

"Damn me, but I'm drunk," Noel said.

"Me, too. What's dashed Sommers grinning about?"

In answer, Noel had held out his glass. Then he had managed to convey to Fitzhugh, in a fashion that made complete and succinct sense to two drunken men, that he wanted to find out about Lieutenant Grantham. If anyone could find a person who could tell them, it was Fitzhugh.

So perhaps it was no surprise that Leeds, the badgerlike butler at the Granthams' house, took one look at Noel and said, while taking his hat and gloves, "A masculine refreshment, milord?"

"God, yes," Noel replied, wondering if the damned monocle rendered him more or less the worse for wear. It certainly pinched his face. "Good man."

The man did not so much wink as convey male solidarity. "They are in the drawing room, milord."

Noel could hear them, or rather, he heard Miss Grantham. Mrs. Bourre had decided Miss Grantham would practice conversation today; and although the afternoon would not improve her poise, Noel had to admit that she needed the practice. For someone who could be so musical at the pianoforte, her speaking voice grated on the nerves even on the best, most sober-day-before days.

He steeled himself. Being here had to rank last on his list of preferred things to do. Miss Grantham aside, he had no desire to see Mrs. Grantham shooting sparks at him.

"Are the Bourres here already?"

"Yes, milord."

Noel nodded. That at least was something. He crossed the small foyer to open the drawing room door.

"Very pleased to meet you b—" Miss Grantham's voice stopped as he entered.

Four pairs of feminine eyes greeted him with varying degrees of coolness. The fifth pair, Mrs. Grantham's, were so conspicuously neutral that all Noel's deadened senses came painfully back to life. Shooting sparks would be better. Neutral meant she had made some sort of decision, and a woman who could be called General Grantham making a decision should not be taken lightly.

"Good morning, ladies," he said.

"Good afternoon, Reversby," Mrs. Bourre said.

Noel bowed. Point taken.

The butler brought Noel a large pitcher of

punch and one tall glass. It was lemony, sweet enough, and laced with rum. Very good man.

Despite the punch, however, Noel had to endure listening to Mrs. Bourre and Mrs. Grantham instruct Miss Grantham in the fine art of conversation. She practiced speaking things, and was told repeatedly that she must lower her voice and speak more slowly, until Noel thought his head would burst.

Then Mrs. Bourre said, "Let us take a break for some refreshments, and then you and Reversby can practice together."

Mrs. Grantham rang for refreshments while Noel and Miss Grantham eyed each other with varying measures of reluctance. Then they all went into the back garden, Miss Grantham trailing behind.

Lady Grantham asked the Bourres a question so quietly they paused to hear. That left only Mrs. Grantham.

Having more or less promised himself that she would be the first to broach an apology, Noel surprised himself by saying, "I am sorry you sought alternate transportation last night."

Her mouth twitched, but not in a happy way.

Noel remembered how her smile could transform her face, how much of a cad he felt whenever he had been responsible for dimming that smile. He made himself a promise then and there. Whenever he could he would behave so she could smile more. It was a ridiculous promise. He wanted her secret and would do what he must to get it. But he could not stop himself from wishing to make the process as painless as possible. However bizarre a pairing, she had been Anne's friend.

Noel stepped toward the graveled circle that led

round a pretty stand of cherry and holly trees, forcing her to keep up with him and away from the others. "Black and Sommers were civil, I trust."

"Major Black has always been civil . . . and correct," she said, effortlessly keeping to his pace.

He took her implication. "Of course."

"Mr. Sommers is of a different stripe, but that is of no moment."

Noel opened his mouth to ask her what she meant, but she beat him to it.

"Listening to him speak of you, I realized, my lord, after the fact, how embarrassed you must have been. For that I apologize. I was thinking merely of my own embarrassment at the time, not of punishment."

"Punishment?"

"For your presumption."

Now Noel felt bewildered, and he could not ascribe it to too much lemon rum punch. "Presumption?"

She blinked in exasperation. "We are not friends, sir, whatever our common bonds."

"What about your acknowledging that you know me better than those," he tipped his chin toward Miss Bourre, "who have known me a year."

"Better is a relative term, is it not?"

"Now who is parsing?"

"The fact of the matter is, sir, that we barely know each other."

"And you would prefer to keep it that way," he said, all his resolutions washing away in fresh anger.

"We have an arrangement. That is enough."

"Not entirely."

"I beg your pardon?" she asked.

"There is more between us than your so-called arrangement," he said.

A holly tree's thick leaves separated them from the others' view. Noel touched a smooth curl that rested against her throat, let his hand pass from it to the delicate, pulsing skin beneath.

She stiffened and caught her breath. For a second they were merely a man and a woman recognizing each other. Noel's heart raced, and every fiber of his being sang into life. The world hung, suspended, circumscribed by them and them alone.

Then she stepped back. "The more I see of the world, the more it seems fixed."

"What do you mean?"

"Men will boil everything down to lust and damn the consequences."

"You think me that simple?"

"You would have it so." She backed a few more steps away from him and smiled. "Come, sir, where is your witty comeback?"

He had none.

That was a decided problem.

Meg wished she could say Lord Reversby was going to be trouble. The trouble was, Lord Reversby was already trouble, and getting worse. The issue of Anne aside, she should not feel for him what she felt for him. No matter that when he had touched her hair and her neck she had felt curiously elemental, as though pure water had taken over her knees and her feet were encased in rock. No matter that her skin had seemed on fire, but only the sweetest air filled her lungs.

No, it was no matter. Circumstances and her own choices had made such a connection impossible, and she did neither of them any favors by indulging in such feelings.

But rationalizing did not lessen the pain she felt in leaving him so exposed. She wished she could remember all her anger of the past night, how nicely it had fueled her defenses. But if wishes were kisses . . .

No, best not even look down that road.

She left him by the holly tree, and joined the Bourres and Tessa on the small flagstone patio. "Lord Reversby needed to walk a little farther. Where is Lizzie?"

They found her inside, sitting on a divan with floral cushions, a tray with a pitcher of lemonade and glasses on the low table before her. A used glass stood closest to her.

Meg scolded her for drinking before their guests. Lizzie took the scolding with surprising good nature, apologized, and remained quiet while Tessa poured lemonade for the others. Reversby joined them, declined lemonade by indicating his own pitcher, and sat down, subdued.

Mrs. Bourre noticed. "Reversby, you look worn."

Reversby smiled with his usual self-deprecation. "You are too kind, ma'am."

"I did not mean it that way."

"I was being quite literal, ma'am."

"Do not be so hard on yourself."

He glanced at Meg, while she pretended not to observe. "I shall try not to be, thank you."

Had anyone else noticed the slight emphasis he had placed on *I*? Meg wondered. Dash him, that was not playing fair. Then again, Meg admitted, neither had she when she had left his carriage last night, nor when she had provoked him just now in the garden.

She had promised herself that despite her firm belief in the world's many evils, she would do her part to make it a better place. She would be kind. She would act graciously toward others. She would . . .

Hell.

"If you would, then, my lord," Meg said, gesturing to Lizzie.

He rose to the occasion in full Lord Languid. "My dear Miss Grantham, such weather we are having."

"Indeed, my lord," Lizzie replied.

But was there a trace of a snicker? Or was it vacuity? Lizzie could be short on kindness, not wits. But did she look a little glassy-eyed? Was she merely tired?

"It is entirely fine," Lizzie said.

"Tell me, what comprises your favorite outing when the weather is so fine?"

"Well, I do not care for activities out of doors at all, since bees frighten me and one must make conversation or admire Nature, and there is no pianoforte outside, so what is the point? But when the weather is this fine, my Aunt Grantham takes longer walks than usual, which I like because then I may go into her room and read all her poetry and oh, how I wish she kept a diary, because I bet it would say something pretty interesting because she is moping and brooding, and so I wonder what—or whom—she is moping and brooding about, and then I look at whatever else she might have lying about under lock and key, which makes me wild to try to pick the lock open, but not so she would ever know about it because my Aunt Grantham can be exceptionally severe—"

The others were staring at Lizzie, transfixed.

"Enough, Lizzie," Meg said, standing up. "What are you thinking?"

"He asked," she said, pointing to Reversby with a wobbly finger.

Reversby's lips twitched.

"See? He thinks I am amusing. Me. Am I artless, Lord Reversby? A gamine? An ingénue?"

Meg went over to Lizzie. A decided odor of rum rose from her. "You are not artless, Lizzie. You are drunk."

Tessa gasped, and the Bourres covered their mouths.

"Oh," Lizzie said, round-eyed, "am I?"

Meg picked up Lizzie's glass. "Rum. Definitely."

"But how did she—" Tessa asked.

"Did you drink some of my punch, Miss Grantham?" Reversby asked.

"I was waiting for Leeds to bring the lemonade and there was the pitcher you were using and so I poured some and drank it and it tasted really delicious." She paused, blinked. "So I had a second glass because when I tried the other lemonade that Leeds brought, it did not taste as good."

"That would be a yes," Reversby said. He turned a little to one side, removed his monocle, and polished it. Likely, Meg thought sourly, because he was containing a smile.

At least Tessa required no prodding to take Lizzie directly upstairs. But Meg, the Bourres, and Lord Reversby could still hear her as she ascended the stair.

"I still don't know why the great Lord Languid is doing this for Aunt Grantham. He cannot like her.

Her coloring is not striking like mine, and she's old and cranky. She doesn't play music. That's the doorbell at the back entrance. Leeds, are you there? Have someone get the door. Is there no one back there? Does my aunt not line them all up each morning for inspection, just like she were yet in the Army?"

Lizzie tittered, and her mother must have remonstrated with her, for she said, "All right, she sings nicely, and she knows some interesting Spanish tunes and when to turn the page, but I do not think the way she runs me around is quite fair, because I am a nice person and well-brought-up—you know that, since you were there—and, oh, Mama, why do the walls tilt so? If this is why men get drunk I do not know if I like it."

Lord Reversby snorted but did not look at either Meg or the Bourres. Did Mrs. Bourre or her daughter know the real reason why Reversby was helping her, or merely the ostensible one of Meg's contention to Anne?

The possibility of embarrassment made Meg want to cringe. But she had not cringed when one of the camp women had remarked that no one ever heard sounds of lovemaking coming from the tent she shared with Lieutenant Grantham. If she could weather that, she could weather this.

"My niece and I do not always agree," Meg said, hoping she sounded composed.

Mrs. Bourre glanced at her daughter. "Whoever stands as a parent experiences such expressions of feelings."

Leeds at the door saved Meg from saying more than she should. "If you would excuse me, ma'am, but that was a delivery from the modiste's. Some evening dresses, I believe he said."

Miss Bourre said, "That is by all things excellent. Mrs. Grantham, it is unlikely your niece will be available the rest of the day, do you not agree, Reversby?"

His monocle ticking back and forth like a clock's pendulum in his hand, Reversby glanced at the size of the glass Lizzie had used. "Quite."

"Mama and I are promised to Lady Whiteforth this evening, and she asked me about you just two days ago during our at home. She would be pleased to have you come."

"Well—"

"Eudora's enthusiasm is not overtaking her manners," Mrs. Bourre said. "Lord Whiteforth holds the rank of colonel for some regiment of foot, and there are always officers in and out of the house. Lady Whiteforth has heard of you from several of them, and only our telling her that you had not yet clothes convinced her you would decline an invitation. What do you think, Reversby?"

"So long as no one speaks of death or dismemberment, I would have to agree," he said, employing the ironic tone that most put Meg's back up.

"Such a subject, my lord," Mrs. Bourre said.

"Indeed, Reversby," Miss Bourre said. "Is it not ironic that you are the one introducing it?"

"Never let it be said I shy away from hard facts," he said.

He did not look at Meg, but she understood the words as directed at her. "There are times, though, when too much can be said, don't you think?" she asked.

"Indeed," Miss Bourre said, "but that aside, you would imply that Mrs. Grantham needed your leave to attend."

He bowed. "You must forgive me did I imply any such thing."

Now he did look at Meg, and monocle or not, she felt as though a warm wind had swept over her entirely exposed skin.

"My sole requirement, if I may be allowed a requirement, is that Mrs. Grantham promises to smile often and frequently."

"Given the company," Miss Bourre began, but did not quite know how to finish.

"Not often, sir," Meg said. "Perhaps a veritable redundancy of smiles?" She willed herself to say nothing else. She had slipped after she had promised herself she would not engage in banter with him. She must guard herself against him.

"Your pardon, ma'am, for assuming. It is a shoddy practice, and no better than leaving lemon rum punch within reach of children," he said.

They all grimaced.

"Do say we may pick you up at nine o'clock, Mrs. Grantham?" Miss Bourre asked.

"I would be very pleased, thank you."

Reversby did not speak to Meg again until she stood at the door to say good-bye. Then, as he bowed over her hand, he said, "Wear the apricot, if it is among those finished."

Then he and the Bourres were gone. Meg shut the door behind them, wondering if, overall, she had succeeded in treating him with the necessary distance. She felt, obscurely, as though she had failed and that the world remained off-center.

A burst of off-key, muffled singing sailed down the stairs. Lizzie played divinely, but she could not have sung along if her life depended on it. It was one of life's many mysteries.

Meg snorted. The world remained off-center for a good many people, it seemed.

Chapter Twelve

"Do you know what I absolutely hate? Noel asked, surveying a veritable sea of bright uniforms talking and laughing with Mrs. Grantham in depressingly disorderly fashion in Lady Whiteforth's ballroom.

"I feel certain I am about to," Fitzhugh replied.

"Are you joking with me? No, of course you are not joking with me. You are the best friend I have, and friends do not make such jokes. Well, not unless they are I."

Fitzhugh grimaced.

"Doesn't sound right, does it? But it is grammatically correct."

"You have been fixed on grammar lately."

"I do feel as if I have been returned to school."

"Are we discussing what you refused to discuss before?"

"We most certainly are not," Noel said.

"Then do not leave me in suspense about what you absolutely hate."

"It is this: two gentlemen wearing black in the midst of all this color. It is ludicrous. What was Brummel thinking? Did he intend to counter nature entirely by setting such a fashion?"

"Esme adores men in black," Fitzhugh said.

Noel screwed up his lips then said, "The peacock has his tail, the lion his mane—"

"You have also been muttering much about lions and bulls."

"Why do we fine, upstanding English gentlemen think it a good idea to let ourselves appear as drab as peahens and yet allow so many others to dress like peacocks?"

"Esme adores men in black."

"Well, she has you to look at in black, doesn't she? All settled." Noel looked at Fitzhugh, away from the cluster of uniforms around Mrs. Grantham, and resented each and every one of them. "You are joking with me."

"If I read Mrs. Grantham correctly, I believe she will measure a man by what he is worth, not by what he wears."

"That, my dear Fitzhugh, is what I am afraid of. At least did I have claim to better plumage, I might be ahead in one category of two."

"We are discussing something you refused to discuss."

Noel sighed. "I have been up and down this ballroom doing my best imitation of Reversby-is-a-simpleton-and-you-can-tell-him-anything in the hopes of learning more about Lieutenant Grantham."

"You would know the competition? The man's dead, Reversby."

"So?"

Fitzhugh looked sympathetic.

"Fine, but Mrs. Grantham remains with his family, and is subjecting herself and me to the ordeal of Miss Elizabeth Grantham, when all she would need to do to secure herself a place in this world is appeal to Neville."

Fitzhugh started tapping his knuckle against his lips, a sure sign that he was thinking hard. "She does not strike me as someone who would easily accept charity."

"He is like a brother to her," Noel said. "And as far as I know, the only service she provides to the Granthams is her schooling the terrible miss, which duty she has admitted to being serious about only this past week."

"Perhaps that is enough," Fitzhugh said.

"Were it enough, it would have required advance thought."

"Hmmm?"

"She came to live with them almost a year ago. Can you imagine Sir George, not to mention Lady Grantham, encouraging Mrs. Grantham to live with them for the sole purpose of some task a year away? No, Fitzhugh, I think Mrs. Grantham has some reason for staying there that has nothing to do with a reluctance to accept charity. Mrs. Grantham has become the most shocking realist."

"Has become?"

"I reread some of her letters last night, to confirm my first impression."

"Which was?"

"That they start out very wide-eyed and optimistic. Now she barely smiles."

"Her face does not lack animation." Fitzhugh glanced over at her, and Noel followed his glance. "True, she appears excited but there is no joy apparent in her."

"Good man," Noel said.

"There is no call to be patting me on the head."

"True, but 'tis amusing."

"Esme was like that until we married, and sometimes she goes back to it whenever we meet some wretched, sniffing old biddy or some lackbrain who has forgotten that she is married."

"There are gentlemen in this world who forget your sword arm?" Noel asked, diverted.

"Did I not label them lackbrains?"

Noel bowed. "You did. My mistake. Were the solution to Mrs. Grantham's lack of joy as simple."

"I do not follow you."

"You cannot marry Mrs. Grantham and make her as happy as you do Lady Fitzhugh."

Fitzhugh smiled. "Do I need to say it?"

"No, because it makes no difference," Noel said, and the irritation in his voice annoyed him. "She would not have me, even if I wanted her. But she was Anne's friend, and I do not like the notion of her fighting her way through the lonely world."

"So," Fitzhugh said after a skeptical beat, "what does your research show?"

"This is what I do appreciate about you, friend. You know when to stop arguing."

"You may mention that point to Esme one day."

"Subtly, of course."

"Of course," Fitzhugh said.

The music for one dance ended, and a blue-coated Hussar officer approached Mrs. Grantham. She curtsied prettily and accepted his hand for the next dance. Noel set his teeth, then said, "When I mention her, there is nothing but glowing admiration. Mrs. Grantham did this, or Mrs. Grantham did that. When I inquire, subtly, of course, what Lieutenant Grantham thought of her enterprising spirit, I receive the most guarded of looks and a variety of mumbled replies."

"Do they point toward any consistent pattern?"

"Do you remember the elaborate scheme we devised for sloughing off our Latin tutor's exercises?"

"I remember feeling certain we did more work avoiding him than he would have given us," Fitzhugh said. "I also remember that it was your idea."

"Well," Noel said, "it was fun."

"Fatiguing, though. Are you saying the lieutenant is like our Latin tutor?"

"No. He was either a saint or much more accomplished than we were at keeping himself well away from work or other peril."

"Interesting trait for a soldier."

"Quite."

"Toward which category do you incline?" Fitzhugh asked. "No, wait, do not tell me, you being so favorably disposed toward anyone who would be Mrs. Grantham's husband."

"She worked very hard in the Peninsula. That much is certain."

"Because he did not?"

"A possibility," Noel said.

"Or because he was a saint, and she ascribed to some notion that she must aspire to his greatness."

Noel shook his head. "Those guarded looks, remember?"

"Hmmm," Fitzhugh said. "Then why would she settle with her husband's family?"

"It is a puzzle, isn't it?"

"You could sound more cheerful if you tried."

"Dash it all, I suppose I could. Will you look at

that wretched Hussar? He does not need to swing her around quite so quickly to prove that he can, despite all those dashed buttons."

"Why are you not dancing with her?"

"Because she would as like to spit in my face," Noel said.

"Faint heart never won fair lady," Fitzhugh said.

"Whoever wrote that should be shot."

"I think he's well safe from you."

"Damn. And damn again."

"What?" Fitzhugh asked.

"There is wretched Black, just waiting for her to come off the floor. Is that a smirk on his damned face, which is pointed in this direction, or has this monocle made me blind?"

"He is definitely smirking at you. What a novelty. Tell me, Reversby, why does he think he has any right to smirk at you?"

"Such nice loyalty. Do you often indulge in this sort of no-one-but-me-may-say-an-ill-word-about-him?"

"Are you not going to answer the question?"

"I find myself in no great hurry to," Noel said.

"You tried to kiss her, and she slapped you?"

"What do you think I am?"

"I wonder sometimes," Fitzhugh said with perfect candor.

"So if I do not color in my words, you will."

"With bordello red."

Noel considered. "We argued on the way home from Mrs. Bourre's dinner party. About what, it does not matter. When she saw Major Black and Sommers come by, she promptly jumped ship and asked them to take her home."

"That is not good," Fitzhugh said.

"No."

"Come with me over there."

"No, no, no," Noel said. "You are not going to go over there and make nice in the way you usually make nice when your eyes get that particular glint."

"I am the most inoffensive of creatures," Fitzhugh said.

Noel rolled his eyes. "You are as transparent as water."

"What of it? You will be able to ask Mrs. Grantham to dance. She looks to enjoy the exercise, and maybe she will have softened toward you."

Noel could not help but remember the way she had felt in his arms the last time they danced, and how she had made him feel: protective and tender, joyous and aroused. So he elected to be swayed.

As Fitzhugh renewed his acquaintance with Black, Noel envied Fitzhugh. Noel had worked just as hard on his property as Fitzhugh had to become both a master swordsman and a knowledgeable dealer in horses, but for some reason, Noel felt himself as considerably less impressive.

Fitzhugh moved in a gradual semicircle, so that by the time the music stopped and the dancers started back to the edges, Black had his back to the floor. Noel stepped forward to greet Mrs. Grantham.

"Would you dance with me, ma'am?"

She took in what was happening in a trice. "I will admit to admiring a good plan."

"It was Fitzhugh's, and finely executed."

She paused. "Then out of respect for his effort, I accept." She took Noel's arm, and he led her onto the dance floor.

Wearing black or not, Noel suddenly felt as color-ful as any of the officers. It was a transitory feeling. He knew that. Likely it would last only as long as they continued silent. He promised himself, as the music started and couples formed a line around them, that he would not be the one to break it.

He lasted the first round of figures before saying, "You did wear the apricot."

"Yes," she replied.

"Did you take my recommendation on it, or did you choose on your own?"

"I balanced your recommendation against my in-clination."

"And?" he asked.

"And I remembered all the reasons why I thought you would bc an assct to Lizzic."

"Too kind."

"My lord." She looked away, then back, wistful. "Perhaps it would be better did we not talk?"

Even though Noel had thought that himself, it hurt to hear her say it. "You have said all you would say, certainly. I am not as certain that I have."

"Are you going to say it now?"

She seemed half-fearful, half-annoyed, so he said, "No, I have to do some more thinking on it."

She nodded, smiled, and responded to some sally that an officer passing by made to her.

They moved through the dance figures. Noel watched her, and she seemed to be watching him, not quite as intently as two fighters sizing each other up, but . . .

"You are looking at me very oddly," she said.

"Am I?"

"Yes. I am fancying myself as some dangerous

animal that you half-expect to reach over and bite you at any moment."

"Did you not tell me I should discontinue all reference to wild animals?" Noel asked.

"I made no such stipulation for myself."

"True," he replied, feeling himself back on ground that, if not solid, at least he understood.

"May I inquire why you regard me in such a fashion?" she asked.

"Because," he replied, seeking as light a tone as he could manage, "you have told me we are not friends."

"Not friends is not enemies, either."

"True," Noel said, "but do you not think Hercules looked at lions differently before he slay the Nemean?"

"I am not sure what you mean by that, but I would insist that whatever the reputation, no two lions are alike."

"Not alike, perhaps, but they do share similarities."

"I think, by speaking so figuratively in our endeavor to be civil," she said, "we are speaking of very different things. Perhaps we could just dance?"

Noel assented and forced himself to be content with watching her. The apricot dress highlighted the color in her cheeks and rendered her skin as pale honey, freshly taken from the comb. Her hair did not glow like Lady Fitzhugh's coppery locks, nor his own dear Anne's golden ones, but there was a depth to it—as it was lighter on top than bottom—that struck Noel deeply. For fun he followed one streaky strand as it wove through her coiffure.

She spun lightly on her feet, one delicate ankle and then the next showing its outline in a pale stocking, and seemed in utter harmony with the music. He tried to picture her dancing in Spain and failed. He had not backdrop and no costume for her. Besides, her new dress made her look completely natural to London, although natural in reference to London strained credulity.

As they progressed down the line, she returned sallies from a steady stream of officers, some of whom Noel had observed her talking to before. He deplored their continuing to ask her about idle matters, or worse, reminding her of some conversational thread that did not need to be unwound.

He had never minded Anne's having friends, even gentlemen friends. He had recognized how alive society made Anne. But here, with Mrs. Grantham, he did not want to be reminded of her life in the Army, nor of the information he had learned about the man who had married her. Both or either had caused her heart to turn so cold, and that fact tore at him as much as the notion of Anne's secret did.

For some reason, the fact that her hand was so warm made him feel worse. *Had I been the one to take you to the Peninsula,* he thought, *you would not have come back with such a cold heart.*

Which was silly, really, although not as silly as his wishing to be—somehow, someway—more. Doubtless Mrs. Grantham regarded him as some idler, who, having too much time on his hands, worried the notion of her secret like a child wiggles a loose tooth.

Perhaps he was. Perhaps he did.

She did not know of the shockingly poor condition of Noel's estate when he had inherited it shortly after university, or the unpleasant truth about Noel's father and his need to gamble.

What point in telling her? Much of the work had been done, and Noel had regarded himself as coasting through the world according to one of Sir Isaac Newton's principles of motion: a body in motion tended to stay in motion, along its original trajectory, until some force acted upon it to alter its course or speed.

At least he had felt that way until he had found Mrs. Grantham's letters. Between them and the lady herself, he had certainly taken a push from true. But to where, to what end, and for what purpose?

"You are looking at me oddly again," she said.

"Hmmm? What? Oh, sorry."

"You have been in some faraway place this last quarter hour."

"I aim to serve, ma'am."

"I do not recall asking you to retreat entirely."

"That would be my mistake, then."

She frowned. "Why do I feel as if I have been reprimanded?"

"I do not know. I did not intend to."

"I wish I understood you."

"That makes two of us," Noel said, recalling Fitzhugh's earlier comment. He was indulging in entirely too much self-reflection this evening. Did he but know some of the answers to some of the questions he was asking, it was entirely likely that it would be an easier process.

Not to mention a shorter one.

"If you are out of sorts, you might try walking," Mrs. Grantham said.

"Does it really work for you?"

"I could not be here, among so many people, did I not."

"It is something to consider."

"I shall go out tomorrow morning for quite a ways," she said. "I doubt Lizzie will be up to anything before one o'clock."

"That is good to know."

"I am sorry you are out of sorts," she said.

"Never worry about me. It would not do you any good."

The look she gave him, bewilderment mixed with a curious gratitude, struck him deeply.

The dance ended. Before they could finish bowing and curtsying to each other, ten or so officers clustered about. Noel bowed again, almost striking his forehead against an epaulette that suddenly moved before him.

The Fates' way of telling him he needed another black eye?

He rubbed his temple, forced a polite smile, and retreated to find Fitzhugh.

Fitzhugh was still talking to Black. Oh, joy.

Chapter Thirteen

The next morning Meg left the West End by way of the Islington Road. The miles passed so quickly beneath Meg's steady feet that she could scarce believe her eyes when she saw the sign over the wide brick building reading "Angel." The famous posting inn that served as gateway to the entire North of England was bustling with ostlers leading horses, carriages of all pretensions or lack thereof, and glassy-eyed travelers. Meg stood and watched the ebb and flow from across the broad thoroughfare until she had the sensation, as she had often had in Spain, of what remained constant and predictable and steady, and the sudden random elements that provided color and drama.

A clock down the street chimed once. Meg shaded her eyes with her hand. It was a quarter to eleven. She would go inside and get herself a scone and maybe a glass of cold milk, then head back for the daily afternoon session of torture. Lizzie had begun to smooth out some of her clumsiness, but would she ever wrap her mind around the notion that not every social situation was a forum for her to display acidic comments? Did she not understand that no person of taste or breeding would find attractive such temper in a chit barely out of the schoolroom?

Had Lizzie any sense of what she had said yesterday or of how large her gaffe had been?

Meg wished she could blame all her complicated feelings for Reversby on what Lizzie had said. Lizzie had merely indicated the cracks in the story Meg and Reversby had put about to explain his assistance. And like an army desperately trying to hold a line of defense, one whisper of scandal would force Meg's retreat.

The fact was, however, that with every afternoon or evening spent in Lord Reversby's presence, she wished to stay firmly within his world. It did not even matter whether he had angered her, or how many times she reminded herself that he had been Anne's husband, or what Xavier would think of her.

She did not understand Reversby, but he was starting to appeal to her, as a person and not just as a handsome man. Desire, she told herself, she could and would conquer. But she was beginning to suspect that what she had taken as arrogance stood as façade for a great many other emotions. There was still arrogance there—she could never forget that— but there was more to it, from his silly jests about wild animals to the rather disconsolate way he had concluded their dance.

His comment last night that she should not worry about him had surprised her. Such a sentiment seemed so at odds with her normal experience of men. Lieutenant Grantham's horrible attempts at protecting himself aside, she would have merely needed to listen to the women who followed the regiment complain of their men's neediness or lack of basic survival skills.

Meg would never forget Tall Mary tossing her blond braids across her thin, young shoulders and saying, "Me man could shoot a Frenchman were he so called on, I suppose, but he'd starve by yon river full of fish."

They had called her Tall Mary because she stood no higher than Meg's shoulder. She had not the weight to stay upon her horse crossing "yon river," a tributary of the Douro. Her husband had dived after her, only to need rescuing himself. His panic had not given him the ability to swim. Meg's last view of Tall Mary had been her blond head disappearing through narrow canyon walls.

A scream rent the air. Meg looked about her, disoriented. A stone bridge rose gently before her, breaking the undulating, sharp-smelling wildflowers and grasses beside her. Trees along the riverbank had screened it from view, but Meg could tell from the rushing that it ran high and fast.

She must have started walking again.

A young woman ran up from the left bank, screaming and wringing her hands. She seized upon Meg, then pushed her. "The child! My little boy! My Jim! The river! Get help!"

"Where is he? I'll go down. I can swim."

The woman pointed.

"You go, go get help," Meg said, but the woman just blinked. Having done what she thought she could do, and passed on the only message she thought would be effective, shock had taken her. Meg had seen it too many times to argue with it. She weighed the option of running for help herself against trying to do something now, and pulled off her bonnet, pelisse, and shoes.

The river stretched about forty angry yards and

met the bank not two feet below the level of the bridge. Meg cast about, yelling above the din of water, "Jim! Jimmy! Your mum sent me. Call to me, there's a good lad."

She sighted a tow-headed boy, likely no more than six, clinging to a fallen branch that had wedged itself between two rocks fifteen feet upstream of the bridge. Too close to the bridge. Too far from the bank.

The water churned all around him and from the frozen fright upon his face, Meg did not know if he had heard her.

"Good Lord," a male voice said next to her.

Meg jumped, beheld Reversby. "What—? How?"

Reversby hopped a little as he removed a tall, polished boot, let it drop on the grassy bank, and then he put a hand on Meg's shoulder to balance himself while removing its mate. "I was driving over the bridge and saw the woman." He stripped off his blue jacket and dropped it beside the boots. "I was looking for you." He cupped his hands around his mouth. "Hey, boy! Hold on, lad."

He started forward, but Meg caught his arm. "You cannot, my lord. There is no way of getting to him."

"Trust me," he said. He squeezed her hand and tore himself away. The rapid current pushed against his legs, and he jerked his body upstream. Torn with rage and fear, Meg shoved her fist against her mouth. Arms out, he waded, keeping his shoulder and side to the current so it would have less to push against. He slipped, making Meg gasp, but he recovered and pressed on.

The water was halfway up his chest, and he seemed permanently kilted upstream, but he was only a few yards away from the boy. Meg could hear that he was saying something but not what.

The current gushed around the rocks surrounding the boy, causing Reversby to lose his footing. Meg gasped again as his head went under, then he was up, arm extended, to catch a rock. He shook his head, tossing drops that sparkled in the sun.

Reversby pulled himself up to the rock and atop it. From there, sluices of water draining from him, he jumped to the next rock and the next until he could hunch down and grasp the boy's branch. The stricken boy took Reversby's outstretched hand and let go the branch.

Reversby pulled the boy onto the rock, which seemed to get much smaller than it should have. Water streamed off the boy, and he clung to Reversby, who tousled his hair, miraculously mostly dry.

There was no way the boy could come back the way Reversby had gone. Did Reversby understand that? Was he trying to figure out some way to extricate them, and was that why he continued to stand there?

Meg stamped her foot with frustrated impotence. She made a move to go down herself. Surely she could get as far as the rocks and serve as a bridge back to the riverbank. But with some uncanny knowledge, Reversby turned his head and saw her. He made a sharp slashing movement with his hand.

No.

She nodded furiously at him, and he shook his head emphatically at her.

Then, as she was about to put her foot into the churning water, she heard a voice call from the top of the bridge, "Milord! Milord! Here, catch!"

It was Reversby's tiger, Jack. He cast a rope from the head of the bridge. Reversby missed it. The tiger pulled it in. Meg assured herself that Reversby caught the second throw before she dashed up the embankment. She looked around, saw Jimmy's mother wringing her hands and jumping up and down practically on top of Reversby's tiger, who was pulling on the rope.

Reversby's tiger gave the mother an agonized look that questioned whether she would be a help or a hindrance.

Meg stepped in. "Let this man help your Jimmy." She interposed herself between the tiger and the woman, and slowly backed her up.

The tiger shot her a grateful look and heaved on the rope. He had tied it to an abutment of stone on the bridge's opposite rail, and had wound it from his palm to his elbow and was drawing backward.

Meg leaned over and looked down the bridge wall. Reversby had tied a loop into the rope and fixed it around the boy. "Use your legs, Jim," Meg said, "and climb like you're climbing a castle."

He turned big wet brown eyes at her but did not understand. Meg pantomimed pushing against the bridge wall. Then he seemed to understand.

The woman shouted encouragement to him, and after what felt like only half a year, he had bumped and climbed and been pulled his way up. Before they could detach the rope from him, his mother drew him, shivering, tightly to her, then began telling him how naughty he was to have disobeyed her by going so close to the river. Since she kept firm hold of him, Meg let her run her course. She had seen this reaction, too, and there was no stopping it.

Reversby cupped his hands around his mouth and shouted up, "Bring the rope." Then he pointed toward the embankment. Meg and his tiger understood, and Meg approached the woman and managed to get the wet rope from Jimmy. It was thick and rough and heavy.

"Here, ma'am," the tiger said. He hoisted the dripping rope over his shoulder and headed for the embankment.

Meg followed, accepted his apologetic, "Would you, ma'am?" along with the end of the coiled rope, and gave him plenty of room to heave the other end toward Reversby.

The rope's looped end fell against one of the rocks Reversby had stepped over. He nodded and picked his way back across the rocks. Once he wobbled and windmilled his arms for balance. Meg held her breath and tried not to look at the foaming water on the downstream side of the rock. Reversby righted himself and grabbed the rope. He looped the end over his head and opposing arm so that it settled on his shoulder like a soldier's crosspiece.

Then, with both hands on the rope, he jumped from the rock into the current and battled its push. The tiger began looping the slack around his palm and elbow as he had for Jimmy. Behind Meg, Jimmy's mother said, "Cor, did he do that to go out there?"

Meg nodded but did not look away. Each painful foot that Reversby made, she made.

Then he was upon the embankment itself and ducking his head to lift off the rope. It hit the embankment with a sodden thump. Meg did not know what possessed her at that moment, but she cast herself upon his chest, heedless of his dripping shirt and trousers. She hugged him fiercely, then ran her hands over his collar bone, down his shoulders and arms.

Before she could check any further, however, he

caught her hands between his. "I have not broken anything, my dear. I am hale and whole."

Again she wrapped her arms around his waist, slid them up his back. Now that she knew the strength he possessed, she wanted nothing more than to lose herself in it. She had been denied it so long.

Then, angrily, she pushed away from him. "Do you know how many people I have lost to rivers? Do you?" She turned and knelt down to Jimmy. "I want you to listen to your mother and obey her, do you hear me? That river could kill a grown man."

"Yes'm," the boy said, but he grinned. He was looking over her shoulder at Lord Reversby, who had probably winked at him.

The wretch.

"May I know your name, sir?" Jimmy's mother said.

"He told me his name is Mr. Dodd," Jimmy said.

"Thank you, Mr. Dodd, to you and your groom, more than I can say, sir. And thank you, Mrs. Dodd, for your husband's help."

Meg choked and nodded. Reversby helpfully chucked her on the back. Then to Jimmy's mother he said, "Can my man get you somewhere, ma'am?"

"No, sir, thank you. We live over the rise there. Just came down to see if there were any early strawberries, but there was not." She looked upstream. "There's my basket, there."

And it was, too, under a willow that cast its fresh shade over the rushing water.

With a tip of his head, Reversby indicated to his tiger to get the woman and her errant son situated. "Just let me fetch it for you," the tiger said.

Having thanked him and Meg, the woman found herself with nothing to say. They all waited, silently,

Meg and the woman wrapped in embarrassment, while the tiger retrieved the empty basket.

"Do let me walk you and your boy up the rise," Reversby's tiger said after another silent communication with his master.

"Please, Mama," the boy said.

That settled the matter, for tears formed in the woman's eyes. The three of them walked slowly away, up the embankment and over the rise.

If the silence waiting for Reversby's tiger to retrieve the basket had felt uncomfortable, this silence felt downright thorny and awkward. Meg could not look at Reversby.

She should not have touched him like that. She knew she should not have. Why had she not listened to that part of her that had screamed *do not touch!* instead of the other part of her that forgot whom she was with?

Oh, but she had reveled in every hard plane of his body! Would there be no end to this torment she felt whenever she was near him?

"You are soaking wet and probably cold," she said.

"I have a change of clothes in a box under the phaeton. As a hedge, so I never drop myself in a ditch. So to speak."

She could not respond to his jest and let herself be pulled in. "Let us go get them. You will catch your death." She picked up his jacket from the grass, brushed it off, then grabbed his boots, and handed them all to him. "Here."

She looked at him and instantly knew her mistake. His shirt had dried enough so that the light wind caught at his sleeves, but there was no gainsaying the rest of him. The wet shirt limned every muscle and curve, forcing her eyes to see what her fingers had felt, as though she had taken off a blindfold.

"I will change on the other side of the bridge," he said gruffly.

She could only nod. Had he seen what had been in her thoughts? Meg blushed and turned her back to remove all possibility of her indulging her temptation. The assumption Jimmy's mother had made, that she and Reversby were man and wife, suddenly hit Meg with all its full force.

Had she not declared herself by her actions, by her touching him with such abandon, as she had with her words when she had "married" Lieutenant Grantham?

General Grantham, indeed. When it came to the crisis, she lost her head like any other fool. How inclined would she be to do something so stupid again? Had she learned nothing?

Thank God he had had the sense to call himself Mr. Dodd again.

Meg remembered she had left her own half boots and hat in the other direction, and went to retrieve them. Reversby's footsteps sounded loud on the gravel road.

While Meg struggled with her half boots, lost in self-reproach, she did not hear him come up behind her.

"Tell me," he said gently, "how many people have you lost to rivers?"

Chapter Fourteen

He had left his portmanteau and wet clothes upon the bridge. He had not put his coat back on, however, and the wind blew his cravat against his chin and ruffled his shirtsleeves. Dark brown trousers had replaced his sodden buff ones, but his change of clothes could no longer conceal what he was.

The question, as much as her new knowledge of him and her own weakness, struck her deeply. "Fourteen," Meg said. "At least, fourteen that I witnessed myself."

"I am sorry."

"I was thinking of one of them as I walked over. Maybe I heard Jimmy's mother calling and thought about her: Tall Mary. Her pony slipped in the Douro, cast her in, and she was gone before any of us could do anything."

"You never wrote of any of that in your letters."

"Anne wrote me of parties and fashions and you. I did not think she wanted to hear anything of poor Tall Mary." It had been an odd way to grow apart, missed detail by missed detail. What details, if any, had Anne omitted from her letters? Meg wondered with an uncomfortable feeling in her stomach.

Meg would give him a few more details. "She was just a good-humored girl, nothing special, the daughter of a baker in Taunton, swept away by something that never asked her permission or cared."

Reversby flinched.

"I am sorry," Meg said. "I get bitter sometimes and I have no right to take it out on you. You are a hero today."

"You would have gone in there," he replied.

"And how foolhardy would that have been? I saw how the current pushed at you. I should have been swept away."

"I would not have liked that," he said, and there was nothing of the ironic about him.

"Nor would I," Meg said. "I have not a change of clothing."

"That will not do, you know. You may not use my peculiar gift."

And Meg understood what she had missed before, what she had been trying to puzzle out: he joked when he was at his most serious. So many things he had said that she had misinterpreted. She had compared him to Seward on manner alone, believing that his quest after her secret equated to Seward's criminal venality. But a man who would rescue a boy like that . . . there was much more to him.

Even as she accepted that, Meg recognized the fresh challenge she faced. A simple dislike she could maintain. She had even thought she could resist the pull of attraction. But a complicated man like Reversby, who seemed to desire her, in addition to her secret . . .

"What are we to do?" Meg asked. "What am I to do?"

"I do not know, my dear. This is new territory for me, too."

"I have misjudged you."

"Don't be too sure," he replied. "Things do look different from some angles, but they're still the same thing."

Meg did not want to think about that. "Why did you say you were looking for me?"

"Because I was looking for you. I stopped by your house this morning, to ask if you would like to eschew your walk for a drive. When I found out you intended to walk this far, I decided to drive in this direction and offer you a ride home in the phaeton."

"I would have declined."

"I considered that very likely. But, as you like to walk, I like to drive, and my bay has been getting fat since coming down from Oxford."

"Do you always carry rope in your phaeton?"

"It is another hedge against hubris, don't you know? I cannot be stuck in a ditch when I have rope with which to pull myself out."

"You are an odd man," Meg blurted.

"Am I?"

"Do not be amused at me. Last night I heard, from no fewer than five officers who were vastly impressed, that you turned down membership in the Four-in-Hand Club. You are not like to be turned into a ditch."

"My dear, were I a member of the Four-in-Hand Club, I would be one of the most likely candidates to be turned into a ditch. I could not carry a rope or a change of clothing without enduring much scorn and ridicule, for they do make one conform to a standard. No hedge, no lack of ditches. *C'est la vie.*"

"I have thought of you as the most conventional of men."

Something clouded passed over his expression. "Although last night certainly taught me that you are acquainted with many men, somehow I fear that you have seen many of them being conventional."

Two weeks ago the correction would have bothered Meg more than she could bear. "Perhaps you are right. Perhaps I should start carrying rope, too."

"No, my dear. You walk in the very center of the road. There are no ditches in the very center of the road."

"Potholes?"

"The occasional one, but potholes are not ditches. They might twist the ankle, but they will not break the back."

"You have said some of this to me before," Meg said slowly, "but in other words."

"True."

"Do you think so very badly of me?"

"I think you have been in some pretty deep ditches and had to learn to live without rope."

"That is not an answer."

"It is a fine answer. Until I have seen the ditch, how can I know how difficult it was for you to get yourself out of it?"

They had arrived back where they had begun with each other. They both understood that. But Meg had learned something more about the man who was Lord Reversby.

"I had planned to have a light repast at the Angel," she said, "and then I kept walking for some reason. No matter. Would you join me?"

"I should be pleased. Would you permit me to drive you home afterward?"

"I should be pleased," she replied. "It will be a nice respite before we reenter the fray."

He offered her his arm. "We will laugh and tell each other amusing anecdotes."

She took his arm, understood what the hard muscle underneath his jacket meant, and tried not to lose herself in imaging what other uses she might employ it. She said, lightly, "Do you have amusing anecdotes to tell me?"

"My dear, I have at least an even hundred. It will be you keeping up."

"Oh? Do not be too sure."

"Put like that, how can I fail to rise to the test?"

If anyone noticed the greater amity between her and Lord Reversby that afternoon, no one commented upon it. Meg attributed it to Tessa's lack of sensitivity entirely, Mrs. Bourre's good manners, Miss Bourre's generally subdued air, and Lizzie's frustration at Mrs. Bourre's insistence she express the proper sentiments in the proper form.

The weather was, "Fine enough, I suppose, although my father's servants take too long to light a fire in the music room, and the morning chill does take away something from my playing. I swear there is no shred of musical feeling in any of the beasts."

At which point, Meg and Reversby shared a decidedly amused glance before Meg blushed and changed the sentiment to, "Fine enough, Lizzie, although you will be most pleased to see it turn warmer earlier in the morning. You feel your playing benefits greatly from warmer weather."

"Oh, I suppose," Lizzie said.

They went on and on, with Reversby volunteering conversational openings and Meg steering Lizzie into more polite responses, until Meg called a halt around five o'clock.

Lizzie promptly escaped into the music room, and Meg said, "Would you excuse Miss Bourre and me, please? I promised to show her something I brought back from Spain."

Miss Bourre took quick advantage of Meg's offer to escape, and followed Meg upstairs after receiving a look of permission from her mother.

All Meg needed to do was close the door to her room before Miss Bourre sank into a chair and said, "I have made the worst fool of myself imaginable."

Meg sat down next to her. "The worst?"

"I said something, last night, to Fitzhugh. He said he was not dancing, and when I teased him and said, 'Not even with me?' he just gave me a look that said I would be the last person he would be dancing with. And that's when I said it." Tears started dripping down Miss Bourre's face, the big fat kind that some women could produce as if from nowhere.

"What did you say?" Meg asked.

"I asked him whether he thought that by remaining so scrupulously faithful, he would raise its average in his marriage." More tears, and a gulp. "I should not have. I know that. It was petty and mean, and he is very angry with me."

Meg went to a drawer, pulled out two handkerchiefs, and pressed them into Miss Bourre's hands. Then Meg sat down and waited for Miss Bourre to finish.

Reversby had shared two stories over lunch about

his friend. One had been about how no fewer than five gentlemen had challenged Fitzhugh to sword matches. The second had made Reversby's ironic tone more pronounced. "There were those who put some rather nasty words out about Lady Iddesford, as was, and I do not think anyone but myself understood how very firmly Fitzhugh held in his rage. Do not, I beg you, believe I claim greater discernment than my fellow man. I must attribute it to my years of experience with him."

"Is Lady Fitzhugh worth it?" Meg had asked.

"You do ask the most interestingly blunt questions, my dear."

"Who better to ask? Well?"

"Fitzhugh would fight as many duels for her as he needed to, in whatever forum called upon."

"That does not answer my question. That could as easily reflect his honor, not her worth."

Reversby had put down his mug of small beer and steepled his fingers. "I have long wondered if God intended there to be only one person in all the world for each of us. Have you ever wondered that?"

"No," Meg said, too quickly.

Those dark eyes of his saw more than she cared to have him see. But he did not press. "If it is true, then Fitzhugh and his lady have each found that one person. Which is why, were Fitzhugh to fight another duel, I would happily be his second again."

Meg had not thought of Reversby as a romantic. It had been her second surprise of the day.

Miss Bourre gulped a few more times and blew her nose. "Thank you," she said.

"Today someone told me that I tend to avoid risks," Meg said. "I am not convinced of the degree to which I trust this person, but I think the assessment has merit. I mention this so you may better assess the worth of what I am about to tell you."

"I have a high respect for your opinion."

Meg had no idea where Miss Bourre might have developed such a high opinion of her, but, if that was the case . . . "It *was* wrong of you," Meg said.

Miss Bourre had expected another response.

"Do not think I have no sympathy for your position," Meg continued. "I have more than you can guess. But what is done is done. You cannot undo his marriage, nor can you control his feelings. You can only control your own, and your tongue."

Miss Bourre was quite wide-eyed, and she resembled more a young girl fresh from the schoolroom than a young lady of Town. "What do I do now?"

A child's question that demanded an adult answer. "Do you not wish him to snub you the next time he sees you—and he would be justified, in my opinion—you will write him a nice note of apology and crave his pardon." Meg pointed to the escritoire in the corner. "There is paper and pen and ink."

"Why does he believe her when so many people say the opposite?"

"It is impossible to know what goes on in a marriage unless you're one of the two in it," Meg said, hoping her voice did not tremble as she said it.

"I think she blinded him with lust."

"That has happened to many a man and women, too." Oh, how well Meg could remember her first sight of Lieutenant Grantham in his bright red regimentals, the sun on his hair, the broad shoulders that seemed capable of holding up the very sky. The lust that had snared her then had more threads than she could have untangled at that tender age. Experience had yanked at each one in turn, fraying and twisting and shredding.

She was back to rope. She would not rid herself this day of the image of the rope held taut across unforgiving water, or the rope of fear that had braided itself in her stomach. She did not think she would rid herself of it anytime soon. But there was a more immediate matter before her. "Whatever your theories, they are not germane to your need to apologize."

"You are right," Miss Bourre said, the tears coming again. "But I shall never love anyone like I love him." Miss Bourre blotted her eyes and with an unsteady hand began to write.

Meg sat down again, listened to the irregular scratching of pen against paper, and, with her face averted, stared out the window, where the tops of the trees behind the house lifted and bowed in gentle response to the breeze.

Love was out there at the edge of the road, waiting for someone to come along and have a spectacular accident. Certainly it seemed as if Miss Bourre had had one.

Love, or at least what had passed for love at the tender age of eighteen, had taken Meg to the Peninsula and caused her own "accident" at Seward's hands. The betrayal, the pain, the anger—they rose in Meg's throat to choke her.

Reversby was right. She did stay in the center of the road now. General Grantham had plowed through potholes and lifted herself one foot at a time from the mud, but she had existed so that Meg never confronted the ditch.

And here was Reversby wanting to coax her to the edge. Was it from some true, good, and noble impulse, or had he seized upon her reaction to his heroism and still planned to wrest her secret from her?

How Meg hated to think such thoughts. How they made her writhe inside! She no longer knew what to think. Who was the true Reversby? And if he was the Reversby she had discovered today, could she persuade him to let her secret go?

Miss Bourre sprinkled sand over her letter and blew it off with a rather gusty sigh. Then she looked her question. Meg pointed to the cubby that held wax and a seal. Miss Bourre fished them out, sealed her letter, and, reluctantly, handed it to Meg.

"I will see it gets to him," Meg said.

"Thank you."

"You are doing the right thing," Meg said. The letter weighed light in her hand. Was *she* doing the right thing?

"I hope so," Miss Bourre said.

Meg tucked the letter into her sleeve and gave Miss Bourre some water to wash her face. Then they went back downstairs to face the others, or, in Meg's case, to face everyone except Lord Reversby. She could not quite look at him again. The strains of Mozart tiptoed in and out of the drawing room. Meg envied Lizzie her escape.

"I am sorry we were such a time," Meg said. "After I showed Miss Bourre the fabric, we got to talking of this and that." She met Miss Bourre's eye. "It will be good to have an evening to be quiet and at home."

"Yes," Miss Bourre said. "It is fortunate we are not promised anywhere."

"I have an answer, then," Lord Reversby said, "to an offer I was about to propose—that you ladies accompany me to the theater this evening."

"Another time, my lord," Mrs. Bourre said.

Meg showed them out. Miss Bourre squeezed her hand in parting, and Meg nodded.

Then, when Reversby bowed over her hand, he said, "I see the fine hand of General Grantham at work."

She made herself smile, but he was not fooled.

"You are all right?" he asked.

"So much excitement, sir, although I am the last person who should complain."

"Complain away. Let the heavens know the minutiae of your discomfort or the full gale of your annoyance."

"Must you always be absurd?"

"He is Reversby," Miss Bourre said from the steps outside.

"And you, Miss Bourre, my greatest admirer."

That also brought a smile to Meg's face. Miss Bourre and her mother waved and finished going down the steps.

"Really, you are quite all right?"

"I am just tired, my lord. I plan to retire with a book."

"Very well," he said. "See that you do."

She curtsied and watched him jog down the steps to his waiting phaeton. Then she closed the door and went upstairs for a fresh walking dress. She had an errand to run.

Chapter Fifteen

"What a great pleasure, ma'am," Lord Fitzhugh said, rising from behind one of two large desks placed front-to-front before a massive white marble fireplace. He took her hand, bowed, and then led her to a grouping of pale yellow divans and chairs with gold-striped cushions.

"It is a surprise, but thank you. I am sorry to ask to meet you so unconventionally."

"I insist on your visit being a pleasure and nothing for which you should apologize."

Meg accepted his reassurance. "Your library is beautiful."

He inclined his head in thanks. "My wife needs more sunshine than most London skies can provide."

"I am afraid I do not know whether I bring sunshine or cloudburst to you," Meg said. She handed him Miss Bourre's letter. "I know I interfere."

He turned the letter over in his hands. "Dorrie—Miss Bourre—has no need to fear retribution from me. We have known each other too long."

"She will be happy to know that. She regrets what she said."

"Who among us has not been guilty of that sin?"

"I am much relieved, sir," Meg said. She put her hand down on the divan as if to stand, but then Fitzhugh's words kept her firmly there.

"I hear from my manservant that my friend Reversby almost got himself killed in a river today."

"You heard aright." Meg chewed her lip. "I believe he wanted to keep that to himself."

"I am safe as houses, I promise you, ma'am."

"You misunderstand me, sir. I do not believe he wanted even you to know of it."

Fitzhugh grimaced. "He might as well try not to breathe. Our grooms have spent too much time waiting around for us, over too many pints of ale, to consider our business separable. But I take your point and will not mention it to him."

"Thank you."

"May I know the details from you, please, since he will not admit anything to me?"

This Meg did, concluding with, "He was magnificent."

"I would expect no less. Reversby has an amazing modesty. I cannot recall him ever believing he deserved anything, no matter how much hard work or effort he put into it."

Meg had hoped and feared Fitzhugh would introduce the subject of his friend. Now that he had, she took a little risk. "He deserved my cousin Anne."

"I think he did."

Meg did not know quite what to say to that, especially since Fitzhugh's warm gray eyes remained steadily on her, as though daring her to introduce the subject they both wanted to discuss, but which the rules of polite conversation demanded they ignore.

But she was not quite ready to take that risk.

Fitzhugh seemed to understand her decision. "It is a great pity she died so young."

Meg took the opening. "I last saw her on the docks at Plymouth, waving good-bye. She wore a red cape, and the hood tipped off in the wind."

"Reversby did not see her to say good-bye. You did not know? He had been away, hunting, when she became ill. I understand she insisted he not be sent for, but a day later the doctor overruled her. By the time a rider could be sent and Reversby return, she had gone."

"I did not know it," Meg said, shaking her head.

"I would speculate that is partially his motive for desiring to pry your confidences from you. I have told him it is not very nice of him."

Again Meg met that level assessment. "Nor is it nice of me to make him pay so highly for it."

"We both know who will pay for it, do we not?"

"It will make no difference," Meg said.

His brows raised, and Meg could almost see the way his thoughts moved. Then he said, "This may seem an unlikely offer, but it is meant sincerely. Do you find yourself in need of someone discreet, you need only appeal to us."

"But your friendship with Lord Reversby—?"

"Reversby has stood with me through thick and thin. There is little I would not do for him. Even, perhaps, protect him from himself." The corners of his mouth curved in a wistful smile, and he patted the letter from Miss Bourre. "I feel the same way about Dorrie."

Meg stood, understanding that this was his way of drawing the conversation around to a close. She thanked him again. Instead of ringing for his butler to show her out, Fitzhugh walked with her.

"I wish my wife were going to be down from Yorkshire by the time of your niece's party on Saturday. I regret some matters yet retain her. But you may count on me."

"Thank you, my lord," Meg said. "For everything."

She stepped outside into the twilight. She had learned more, that was for certain. She could rejoice to know Reversby felt conflicted about pursuing her secret, but she could take no comfort in learning that not even his dear friend could convince him to let it—and her—be.

"You look damned grim," Fitzhugh said as Noel sank inelegantly into a stuffed leather chair at White's.

"I am out of sorts. I am not grim. Madeira, my good man," Noel said to a passing waiter. Never, not in a million years, not even to Fitzhugh, would he admit that his hoisting the boy Jimmy and then keeping him steady in the rushing water had left him sore.

Nor would he admit how lonely he had been this evening out and about Town with no hope of seeing Mrs. Grantham.

He could still feel her hands searching him for injury, the insistence of her breasts pressing against him as she had hugged him, the warmth that had coursed through him despite being wet through. He would never be able to look at rushing water again without recalling those intoxicating moments.

"You look grim, however you want to describe it."

"It's the damned monocle. I was told Sir George Grantham was about here tonight, and I didn't want him to start calling me Dodd in the midst of all this." He spread his hand to indicate the room full of gentlemen, some of whom managed to sleep despite the rather raucous crowd that had gathered in one corner. "Tell me, what is going on over there?"

"Two extremely young men are trying to drink each other senseless. The others, for reasons known only between them and their God, are taking bets on which one will pass out first."

"It is a good thing we British are so civilized," Noel commented, "or someone would shortly get the notion that did we but tie the two opponents down and pour drink down their gullets, we would obtain a quicker result."

"Do go ahead and suggest it."

"Too fatiguing." Noel tried to find a position that made the fewest muscles complain as possible. "At last I have it. This is the basis of civilization: it is far too tiring to be barbaric. All those skins must have been deuced heavy."

"I have always supposed there must be much yelling."

"Bellowing, Fitzhugh, bellowing. Which is also fatiguing."

"My pardon. Bellowing."

The waiter returned with Noel's Madeira. He sipped it while Fitzhugh worked on his brandy. The melee across the room continued unabated.

"The Grantham chit—will she be ready for her party?"

Noel fixed his friend with his best gimlet eye, but as usual Fitzhugh seemed unperturbed. "I would

rather take a bet on whichever young idiot is closer
to me to be the first to pass out than to attempt to
set odds on that. Your Aunt Bourre, Miss Bourre,
Mrs. Grantham, and my humble self do what we
can, but I do not know."

"I told Mrs. Grantham she could count on me to
be there, but Esme is still detained in the North. I
have an exasperated letter from her today that—"

Noel frowned. "When did you speak to Mrs.
Grantham?"

"This evening. She delivered a note."

Noel felt something very much like alarm, and
hid it in his usual way. "Then you know what happened today."

"Not from Mrs. Grantham. No, let me be accurate. I had details from Mrs. Grantham, but I had
the original story from James, who had it from your
tiger. What is his name?"

"Jack."

"Jack. So I knew enough to ask, and she told me.
She also told me I was not to bring it up to you, so
you see, I have not. My conscience and honor are
clear."

All the agitation of the morning returned. "Did
she tell you she would have gone in that river herself if I hadn't come along? With no rope in sight?"

"No," Fitzhugh said, sitting up, "she did not. How
interesting that neither of you would mention what
you did."

"I fail to see how that is interesting," Noel said,
hoping Fitzhugh would drop the subject.

"Evening, Reversby, Fitzhugh," Breshirewood
said. "Good God, what is going on there?"

"It is an act of the profoundest alchemy," Noel

said. "Two young gentlemen are turning themselves into two young sots by the copious addition of magical spirits."

Breshirewood looked down his long ducal nose at Noel. "You are not as amusing as you would think."

"I never think," Noel said. "Too fatiguing."

That earned him looks from both of them, the difference being that Fitzhugh was trying not to smile and Breshirewood was trying to decide whether Noel was serious. That amused Noel.

"They are taking bets," Fitzhugh volunteered.

Breshirewood grunted. "Your eye looks better, Reversby."

"I have not encountered the business end of someone's shoe recently."

"How is the chit? I have an invitation to her musicale."

"She plays like an angel, and she has a smile to match."

"At least you do not extol her character, or I should be worried," Breshirewood said.

Noel's brows lifted. From Breshirewood, that was a joke.

Breshirewood sat down and joined them in watching the melee. After a few minutes, a cheer rang out, and the crowd parted to reveal a head with far too much blond hair upon it flat on a green baize-covered table, and another young man, more tawny than blond, swaying violently.

"We have a winner," Noel said.

"By a matter of seconds, I should think," Fitzhugh said.

"For no other reason than I cannot leave well enough alone and am not required to leave my chair to do it," Noel said, "I will give a hundred that he cannot last two minutes."

"Taken," Breshirewood said.

Fitzhugh took out his watch and nodded, marking the time. "A half minute. A minute."

"He's going," Noel said. "I can see his eyes rolling back from here."

"He might yet make it," Breshirewood said.

"A minute and a quarter."

A well-wisher clapped the winner on his shoulder. The young gentleman's eyes rolled all the way up, and he slid off his chair with a thud. The crowd guffawed.

"Well?" Breshirewood asked.

Fitzhugh held up the watch. "Minute and two thirds."

"Damn. I owe you, Reversby."

"You may redeem your vowels at Miss Grantham's musicale."

Breshirewood laughed. "You are as funny as you think. Very well. I'll do it."

Noel was about to respond in kind when the crowd around the two unconscious contenders disgorged one man known too well to him. His younger brother, Malcolm. Like Noel, Mal had dark hair and eyes and a strong chin. But Noel had long thought that Mal's nose was too short and that it broke his face into awkward chunks. Nevertheless, women considered him handsome. Even his Anne had remarked that but for Noel, she would have thought Mal the handsomest man of her acquaintance.

Mal was as always dressed in the first crack, although how he managed to afford it and his other extravagant habits, Noel never knew. Also as always, he had his customary smirk in place.

"Well met, big brother," Mal said. "I say, are those mottles the remains of a spectacular shiner? Do tell how that occurred."

"I had heard you were due in Town," Noel said, although he had hoped that Sommers had said so just to rile him. "When did you arrive?"

"Just before nine o'clock. Old Fred stashed my things in the front room."

Noel knew just how much his butler, Fredericks, appreciated being called Old Fred, and looked forward to hearing the single dour remark that Fredericks allowed himself during Malcolm's visits. Each time the remark became a little more trenchant. Noel wished to ask Fredericks if he practiced them in advance, but did not wish to offend the man. He was a damned good butler, and loyal.

Would Fredericks take to Mrs. Grantham as easily as he had taken to Anne?

What was Noel doing asking himself such a question?

"Hello, Fitzhugh," Malcolm said.

Fitzhugh nodded.

Malcolm tried again. "You must know how my brother acquired that lovely eye." When Fitzhugh did not answer, and Breshirewood continued to gaze at him, he said, "Splendid sport over there. I was surprised you did not come and bet."

There was a roar of surprise, anger, and laughter from across the room.

"We were quite capable of doing our betting where there was no risk of spoiling our clothes," Fitzhugh said, indicating with his chin.

Noel did not need to ask Malcolm to stand to one side, for he had heard one of the contenders become violently ill.

"Do you know the Duke of Breshirewood?" Fitzhugh asked.

Malcolm and Breshirewood made polite noises.

"Oh no," Fitzhugh said, under his breath.

Sir George Grantham was bearing down on them, shaking his head. He sank into a chair with a sigh so heartfelt it was almost a grunt, picked up the glass on the table, and in a swallow drank the brandy it contained.

Breshirewood raised his brows. It had been his brandy.

"Hello, Reversby, Fitzhugh. Gentlemen, such a commotion," Sir George said. "I had no idea it would turn into that. I do swear I wished to be gone long before the second boy passed out, but there was no passage by which to escape."

"Your Grace," said Noel, "do permit me to introduce Sir George Grantham to you. Sir George, the Duke of Breshirewood, who has accepted your kind invitation to your daughter's musicale. And this is Mr. Malcolm Dodd."

Sir George effused almost as well as Breshirewood was wont to. Then, when he signaled a waiter for more brandy for himself and the good duke— the others declining—Breshirewood astonished Noel by leaning toward him and saying, "I do begin to understand the shoe incident a bit better now."

"But a fine character, nonetheless," Noel said, and this time Breshirewood laughed.

"Please excuse me, gentlemen, I must borrow Reversby and then be for home," Fitzhugh said.

"I believe I will come with you. Long trip," Malcolm said.

Noel squinted at him, realized he was wearing his monocle and why, and thought that he must be entirely too tired. First he had thought odd thoughts about Mrs. Grantham and Fredericks. Now he had forgotten that Malcolm could tell Sir George that there was no cousin Dodd who looked just like Noel, and likely would for the sheer hell of it.

As they stepped outside, Malcolm said, "Are you really for home?"

"Yes," Fitzhugh replied. "I drive early to Hertfordshire."

Malcolm shrugged, sketched a salute, and sloped off down the street.

"That was very easy," Noel said. "I was attempting to find the proper quip." There was no need to comment on how little love was lost between him and Malcolm.

"You should soak in a hot bath," Fitzhugh said. "Being a hero is hard work."

Noel nodded. A bath would ease the ache in his muscles, but what, he wondered, could he soak in that would ease the ache in his heart?

Meg spent the next few days debating the confluence of two conflicting forces: Lord Reversby's desire to know her secret—freshly drawn by Lord Fitzhugh—with Lord Reversby's decency. If he did not resign his quest, how long before Reversby gave up all pretense of fair play and put so much pressure on her that she had to buckle or run?

Meg hated to think of the resources he had at his

disposal. Time, certainly, was on his side. Her connection to Anne could carry them through this Season, but what rumors would start if he continued paying her attention?

Meg tried to walk him out of her thoughts. She even paced the length of the house whenever she needed to oversee some detail of decoration or catering. But when she had to sit across a drawing room from him, her heated thoughts would spin about. She felt as though she fairly buzzed with the heightened self-consciousness of repressed passion, and time served only to increase the pitch of the hum. She must not dwell on the remembrance of his muscled body, outlined by a wet shirt and trousers, nor remember his hunger and how it had excited and increased her own when she had kissed him at Astley's.

She could not even let that line from Anne's letter sound with its ironic notes in her thoughts, because the musicale approached rapidly and so did almost everyone else's agitation. The Bourres masked theirs with excessive politeness, although Meg surprised the occasional deeply sympathetic gaze from them. Tessa began wringing her hands at the slightest provocation. Sir George darted looks about as though he were planning to steal the furniture and make off for the Continent. And Lizzie began playing more Beethoven and other impassioned pieces whenever she was not required in attendance.

Reversby, however, seemed as imperturbable as a mountain in summertime, even while wearing his monocle.

Meg had grown to hate his monocle and all the deception and emotion it represented. At least the bruise around his eye had faded completely, for that had been a truly odd appearance. He had also recovered from the stiffness she had discerned the day after he had pulled young Jim from the river. Reversby did not volunteer a comment, and Meg did not press, but she knew he had caught her studying him when he gave her a faint smile.

It should have shocked her, the way they had grown to know each other so well and yet retain this amazing gulf between them. But in her haphazard life, it made a sort of sense.

The day of the musicale, they broke early to give everyone a chance to rest during the afternoon. But when the others left, Reversby made an excuse to stay behind.

"You do not need to rest," he said. "Come walking about London with me."

Meg could not come up with a good excuse. She gave in to what she wanted to do, and retrieved her bonnet and shawl.

"The city lies before you," Reversby said on the steps outside the house. "Where to?"

"I have to confess I have no direction in mind."

"Mrs. Grantham, you amaze me."

"Amaze you. How do I amaze you?"

"I find your confession very hard to believe."

"Do you indeed? You mean that I have no direction in mind?" Meg asked.

"Yes, for you must be the most directed person I know."

"Really?" Meg smiled. "I do not think of myself that way."

"How can you not," he asked, "after all you have accomplished?"

"I suppose it is because I feel as if I have made only one important decision in my life, and that decision has affected everything else. I have made other decisions, but they have presented themselves to me. I did not go looking for them."

He nodded, considering. "How nice it must be to put one's finger on one defining moment in one's life. A single paragraph, say, in a history. Something coherent. I am a collection of random phrases and bon mots."

He said it very lightly, as lightly as he had spoken after Hadley had criticized Fitzhugh for his business pursuits and held Reversby up as a shining example. Reversby had, apparently, taken that discussion to heart. She did not know his reasons—it was quite likely she would never know his reasons—but she knew that light tone presaged an argument.

Not wanting either to argue or to have to think on that one defining moment, she said, equally lightly, "I should far rather be a collection of random phrases and bon mots. Being coherent is too much work, some of which, I might add, I have rather unfairly passed on to you."

"I volunteered."

"Very well. You volunteered."

"You were supposed to protest again," he said.

"My apologies," Meg said. "I do not know if I hope this evening proves to be one of those defining moments for Lizzie. Although I have done my best to arrange this time for her, I still should not like to be responsible for directing the course of her life."

"Does that not depend more on the person she would marry?" he asked.

"I hope so," Meg replied as lightly. Reversby got cagey when discussing marriage, she had noted. "Just let it be someone who could understand her."

"Dare we dream for understanding? I would settle for toleration."

"Lizzie could be a fine person, even if no one ever filed down her rough edges."

"I know. I have seen . . . glimpses. When one speaks of music, really speaks of it, she argues quite passionately, but she will also listen."

"It is hard . . ." Meg closed her mouth on the ugly words that had wanted to come out, ugly words that told an ugly story.

"What is hard?" he asked.

Meg collected herself. "Making choices, good choices, when one is that age."

"I will never think of you as having rough edges," he said, and a note in his voice made a blush form deep within Meg.

"My edges were not rough. No, my edges had more the shape of cloud cuckooland. Why did you stop?"

He frowned. "I did not stop. We have not begun."

Meg covered her mouth with her hand. "My lord, I have never been on this street. We started walking soon after we started talking. Where are we?"

"But this is my house. Good Lord, of course we did not start out from my house." He grew very still. "Without a direction in my mind, I steered us to my home."

"Surely not so unusual, my lord. I somehow always find my way back."

"But I had been thinking of Gunter's."

"Ho, Noel, where have you been? Oh, hello. I am Malcolm Dodd, the younger brother."

The attribution was barely necessary, there being such a strong resemblance between them. But Mr. Dodd's face did not possess the same appealing symmetry as Lord Reversby's. He also possessed that trace of untested arrogance in his manner Meg had seen on countless young officers—before they learned they were no better than anyone else or were killed.

So Meg merely inclined her head and looked to Lord Reversby, who had reacquired his usual insouçiance and said, "May I present Mrs. Grantham, Malcolm. Mrs. Grantham, my brother Malcolm Dodd."

After they had bowed and curtsied, Mr. Dodd asked, "Are you related to the Miss Grantham whose musicale we attend this evening?"

Meg put on her best bland expression and owned she was.

"Were you coming in? Where is your phaeton, Noel? I am off for Bond Street."

"We are not. We were walking, but not toward Bond Street."

"Is that your polite way of telling me to leave you alone, brother?"

"If you should like to regard it that way, I shall not disabuse you," Reversby replied.

"I do not suppose you would condescend to lend me the phaeton, then?"

Reversby smiled, which Meg understood to mean that Malcolm Dodd would drive his brother's phaeton on a cold day in hell. Meg imagined such an exact scene when they were mere children and the little brother asked to play with the older's toys.

Mr. Dodd bowed and took himself off, a decidedly grumpy set to his shoulders and the swing of his walking stick.

Meg looked her questions, and Reversby sighed. "I was going to tell you about Malcolm. He arrived in Town two days ago."

"He is not much younger than you," Meg said.

"No, only a year and a half."

"He never pursued the Army?"

"The Army did not interest him. Not even the militia. What? What were you going to say?"

Meg said, "That it is as well."

Reversby smiled. "Now that we are here, would you like to see my home? It is not entirely proper, I know, but . . ."

There would be a portrait of Anne inside, Meg thought suddenly, or something else that would remind her of Anne.

She could not do that. She did not want to think about Anne and how much Reversby loved her. Their truce still felt too recent and too fragile. Its footing had its base on a sliver of time and a few sentences. She would not erode it before its time. She did not really deserve it. She did not think it wise. But she wanted it as long as she could have it.

"May we walk instead, sir? Now that you have mentioned Gunter's, I find myself wishing for something sweet."

"A direction, ma'am?"

"A whim," she replied.

He studied her with an expression she had not

yet seen. Then he offered her his arm. "Then let us pursue your whim."

Noel barely recognized the Granthams' house when he arrived promptly at eight o'clock to have supper with the family. Garlands of pink-tinged white flowers—to match Miss Grantham's dress—twined around the staircase balcony and continued over door lintels and under sconces, lending a sweet scent to the candlelit air. A glorious bouquet stood behind her pianoforte, which had so haunted the drovers in Oxford. When Miss Grantham sat down, it would frame her perfectly. Five rows of chairs transformed the music room into a musicale.

The plan called for some professional players before and after Miss Grantham, with several breaks for refreshments in the other rooms so that everyone would have a chance to talk and mingle and compliment. If Mrs. Grantham recognized a need for dancing, they would all take a collective breath and clear the chairs.

He barely recognized Mrs. Grantham, either, when she came down the stairs. The sky blue silk made her hair seem blonder and her eyes a smoky blue. And the gown's lines, simple and unadorned except for the intricate pleating around the bodice and arms, created a vision of flowing grace.

Miss Bourre stood with him, and she said what Noel suddenly could not. "Oh, Mrs. Grantham, you look absolutely divine."

She smiled and looked at him. "Let us hope the evening goes easily."

Noel stepped forward and took her hand. "Lord love a practical woman."

And then she blushed, which sent the blood racing through Noel's veins, too, to settle where it should not.

For all that, Miss Grantham's launch went easily. She outshone the other players and managed not to knock anyone down, or offend with speech or manner. The gentlemen, in turn, did their job by her, flocking and listening and praising her. Noel was amazed to find Breshirewood often in the thick of her admirers, which forced some of them to defer to the ducal rank and remain silent while he waxed prolix. And Miss Grantham seemed to like his tune.

Malcolm also joined the ranks of Miss Grantham's admirers; and with a slight look at Miss Bourre, Mrs. Grantham dispatched her to detach him. This suggestion of planning warmed Noel in a way he had to work to identify. He realized it was pride.

He was proud of Mrs. Grantham. She might do things for unfathomable reasons, she might sorely plague him and his need to know, and she might test his patience, but he was proud of her.

He had not been proud of anyone since Anne died. Noel tried to imagine what Anne would have said if she had been here, how she would have looked, and could not. It took him a few moments, watching Mrs. Grantham across the room talking to a group of gentlemen, to remember what Anne looked like.

Guilt buffeted him, left a sick taste in his mouth. Then, suddenly, he remembered instead the taste of the chocolate and sweet cherry from Gunter's that Mrs. Grantham had insisted he have. Mrs. Grantham's whim had taken them there. His own steps had guided them to his house.

He had grown happy in his grief, Noel realized. It had given him a direction. Not a direction with a positive destination, but a direction.

He wanted a new direction.

But first he wanted Major Black to go away. Black did insist on buzzing around Mrs. Grantham. She in turn treated him like a footman, dispatching him on various and sundry errands. He adjusted candles at the pianoforte. He fetched punch. He asked a matron if she was comfortable.

When Noel had a chance to come near Mrs. Grantham, he inquired, sotto voce, "Where is Oxford when you need it?" And she had laughed.

But she was not laughing now that Black clung to her as so many others said their good nights.

"When was your brother introduced to Dorrie?" Fitzhugh asked.

"Hmmm? Oh, tonight, I believe."

"Who introduced them?"

"Black, I think, when Malcolm had her cornered. Why?"

"She looks charmed."

"She looks flattered," Noel said. "Malcolm excels at flattery."

"Your pardon, but Mrs. Grantham was not charmed by his flattery."

"That was Black's doing," Noel said, "distracting her."

"What has Major Black done tonight without Mrs. Grantham's express order?"

That was a point. "Malcolm is no danger to Miss

Bourre, Fitzhugh. You know her mother would never approve it."

Fitzhugh relaxed. "You are probably right."

But probably right or not, Noel decided to keep note of that situation. Fitzhugh considered himself Miss Bourre's brother or its near equivalent. Were her honor called into question, Fitzhugh would take the prerogative to act. Did Noel have to choose between friend and brother, he knew which side he would come down on, whatever he might imagine his mother's spirit to say. Better not to let it come to anything.

A peal of laughter and Miss Grantham sitting back down at the pianoforte redirected Noel's attention.

"Good God," Noel said, "Breshirewood is still here."

"Yes," Fitzhugh replied, "that happens when he does not leave."

Noel pursed his lips. "Do not try to be me, Fitzhugh."

"My oh-so-humble apologies."

"Heh. So, what is he doing here?"

"He does like music," Fitzhugh said.

"He is making himself conspicuous by staying."

"I am certain he can talk himself out of it."

Noel smiled, and went over to speak to Malcolm and Miss Bourre. Malcolm was leaning over to whisper when Noel joined them. He straightened with a guilty smile that flickered into dislike and then false welcome. "Excellent evening, big brother. I was just saying so to Miss Bourre, whose acquaintance I have had the pleasure of making this evening."

"Miss Grantham plays very well. I have not had

the chance to speak to either of you tonight. How
are you?"

"Miss Bourre has been telling me how you and she
have been helping the charming Mrs. Grantham
prepare the chit for this evening. I have never known
you to be altruistic."

"Mrs. Grantham grew up with Lady Reversby,"
Noel said, and was glad he had kept track of Sir
George. He and Malcolm had not crossed paths
that evening.

"Maintaining the family honor?" Malcolm asked.
"Bit of a stretch, don't you think?"

"I shall concern myself with my sense of honor."

"Now that your brother mentions it," Miss Bourre
said, "I must admit I have never thought of you as a
stickler."

In Noel's opinion, Miss Bourre should confine
herself to being the stalwart friend, rather than a wit.

A new direction, he thought. *I want a new direction.*

"Let us say that I have been inspired by my company of late." Noel flashed them both a smile. "And
who says one must be a stickler to assist a friend?"

Mrs. Grantham came up to them, an inquiring
look in her eyes, said, "Miss Bourre, I am in dreadful fear that they will ask Lizzie to play all night do
we not round out our program. I shall ask her to
play 'When Morning is Breaking,' to call the
evening to a close. I need your lovely alto. Would
you gentlemen be so obliging as to excuse us?"

Miss Bourre took Mrs. Grantham's arm readily
enough. They had become closer, Noel realized,
over the last few days. Perhaps Miss Bourre had
asked him that question, not to please or amuse
Malcolm but to protect her friend.

"She is quite fetching," Malcolm said.

"Miss Bourre? She is indeed," Noel said.

"I referred to Mrs. Grantham."

Noel reminded himself that Malcolm liked nothing better than to see him get anxious, but it was a delicate line to tread, since he had come over to detach Malcolm from Miss Bourre. "I hope you said so to her."

"I am certain you know that I did," Malcolm replied. "You have kept careful eyes on her all evening."

"I am here to be of assistance. What assistance can I be can I not be summoned quickly?"

"The Hussar major, he could be summoned more quickly," Malcolm said.

"Well, he is a lackey," Noel said, and he and Malcolm shared a rare sympathetic smile.

Its goodwill faded rapidly. "You want more from her than appreciation," Malcolm said.

"Whatever I want is none of your business."

"I am your heir. Of course it is my business."

Miss Grantham had ended her piece and was bowing amidst applause, most notably from Breshirewood, and Mrs. Grantham was raising her hands to announce the last song of the night.

Noel succumbed to his anger, all of it: at his brother's repeated harping back to money and position, at the situation that existed between him and Mrs. Grantham, and at the confusion it provoked within him. "When anything to do with me is your business, I will let you know. Until then, keep your debts and your gaming and your company well away."

"How kind," Malcolm said.

Noel left him in disgust and returned to Fitzhugh. "It has occurred to me that against all inclination, I should endeavor to remarry as soon as possible for the sole reason of ensuring that Malcolm is no longer my heir."

Fitzhugh's brows rose impressively.

"Someone young and sweet who would think of nothing but my needs."

"One of the things I like least about your brother is the way he brings out the worst in you."

"I beg your pardon."

"Do be quiet. Mrs. Grantham is trying to get us all in formation."

Noel scowled but subsided. Mrs. Grantham announced the last song, and Miss Grantham played a verse before Mrs. Grantham and Miss Bourre sang together. Miss Grantham played with all the élan she used for Beethoven. Noel knew Miss Bourre had a fine alto voice, but Mrs. Grantham's richly textured soprano surprised him. For the duration of the song, he forgot his anger at everything.

Then, the last notes fading, it redoubled for having been forgot. He did not want to marry again. He wanted things to be as they had been: simple, tidy, and understandable. He did not like having entanglements any more than Mrs. Grantham had professed to. Why did she have to make that wretched bargain with him? Why could Fitzhugh not sort out his own Miss Bourre trouble? Why did Malcolm have to come along and make everything seem more complicated?

Simmering, Noel nevertheless put on a pleasant

face and helped the Granthams say good night to everyone else except the Bourres and Fitzhugh.

"That went very well," Mrs. Bourre said. "You should be proud of yourselves."

"The Duke of Breshirewood is divine," Miss Grantham said. "Did you see the way he listened to me?"

Noel and Fitzhugh exchanged glances. It was one thing to have Breshirewood's presence bring others into Miss Grantham's circle, but it was another to have her set her sights on him.

Mrs. Bourre spared them from being the ones to give the bad news. "He is certainly a connoisseur of beauty, be it art or music, especially, but when it comes to people, he tends to be highly conscious of his family honor. You might do better, my dear, not to set your sights along that road."

Miss Grantham drew herself up. "You have all been very kind, and generous with yourselves. Thank you. I am grateful to you, especially since now I know to whom I aspire. I shall marry the Duke of Breshirewood or no other. Good night." And with that, she spun on her heel and retreated from the room.

She did not trip on her pseudodemi-train, nor knock someone's arm, nor bump against a chair or door frame.

With stars in her eyes, Lady Grantham went after her. In overly hearty accents, Sir George offered Noel and Fitzhugh a drink and left without receiving any confirmation. The Bourres excused themselves and left. Fitzhugh showed them out.

While Noel and Mrs. Grantham were alone, however briefly, he said, "You put her up to this."

"I do not understand what you mean," she said, but she was reacting to his angry tones with her own.

"Breshirewood. His reputation. He shows interest in many, preference for a few. Somehow, General, you found the unbreachable fortress, and you pointed her at it."

Her anger froze into an iciness he had never seen, which gave him pause. "I am very sorry to disappoint you, but I had no hand in Lizzie's choice. You made this bargain, knowing what it was, and what she was."

"And I can walk away from it anytime, is that it?"

"You have said it."

"I do not walk away from bargains."

"Neither do I maneuver behind the scenes," she replied.

"Excuse me, but I thought that was exactly what you did."

"I have no desire to argue further with you, my lord, nor to speak with you. Thank you again for your help this evening. You may consider our bargain annulled."

"Oh no, you don't."

"As far as I am concerned, your behavior gives me little to choose between you who would be Hercules and some two-headed monster he has to tame."

"You can say two-headed?"

"Why not?"

"How about two-faced?"

In answer she spun on her heel and went to meet Fitzhugh, who was coming back into the room. She dropped a perfect curtsy, the coldest thing Noel had ever seen.

"If you will excuse me, I must attend to my niece. Please enjoy your drink with Sir George." She swept out.

Fitzhugh's glance asked what Noel had done and conveyed sympathy all at once. Noel wanted neither to answer nor accept. "Please give my apologies to Sir George," he said, and left.

Chapter Sixteen

Learning that Breshirewood, along with the rest of London, would attend Lady Waterbury's ball the next night, Lizzie had dressed for the occasion as carefully as she had the night before. She had also, with surprising, grave maturity, requested that Meg accompany her to visit Mrs. Bourre. There, Lizzie decanted Mrs. Bourre of all she knew about the duke.

As they were leaving, Mrs. Bourre took Meg aside to murmur, "I was reluctant to encourage her to attempt cracking such a tough nut, but if she has set her mind upon this course, I wish her luck."

From Miss Bourre Meg learned that the duke had been interested in her the past Season, but she had fallen in love with Fitzhugh and warned the duke away from making a proposal. That Breshirewood was capable of working his way up into a proposal gave Meg some hope.

Of course, Lizzie could change her mind.

But Meg also dressed carefully, for with the rest of London would come Lord Reversby.

Meg could still taste her fury of the night before, a fury that was no less intense for having been a surprise.

Two-headed monster! Meg patted the curls Hemmie had created in her hair. Was it not better to have two heads than two stomachs, one for eating one's fullest, and one to cramp up at the least little sign of difficulty? At least with Lieutenant Grantham, she had had a full month before he had revealed himself. With Lord Reversby, she had had two weeks.

Why *had* he reacted so badly to Lizzie's preference? She was not known for her constancy. Whatever her rapture of last night, did the duke once not invite her to dance, she would likely declare him the last person in the world she would marry.

Did Lord Reversby not realize this? Apparently not.

But how could someone who could eat chocolates with her that day at Gunter's, after recognizing her simple need to walk, not realize such a thing?

Did he merely feel sorry for himself?

Meg snorted, although silently, for a colorful sea of plumed, beribboned, and scented aristocrats lapped around the ballroom that spread below her as she descended Lady Waterbury's marble staircase. In a moment, she would join it, and her dress, which was the color of creamed butter, would become merely one drop.

How often she had felt the same way as part of a long ribbon of people moving through the Portuguese and Spanish countryside. One's troubles either faded to insignificance in the dizzying anonymity or compounded as one contemplated how many people one struggled with for survival.

Meg resisted feeling depressed, and thrust the notion aside, as she had often done, by taking matters into her own hands. She could do what she could do.

And there was something she had to do, although it had nothing to do with Lord Reversby, but instead his younger brother, to whom Miss Bourre was speaking. No, rather Mr. Dodd was speaking to her, for he had her backed up by the doors to the patio, close to a group of matrons so animated that ironically, they paid no heed.

Meg did not like Mr. Dodd. It was not merely that he was conceited. Conceited people often provided hours of entertainment to Meg, as they described the world with such a definite brush. No, it was the petulance that underlay his conceit. Meg could understand anger and annoyance, but when they stemmed from petulance, she lost all patience. The world owed no one anything.

Was that why she could become so angry with Lord Reversby? She had discovered he had the courage to rescue a boy from a river, the skill to be a potential member of the Four-in-Hand Club, the discernment to understand some of her needs. But did he also think the world owed him something? Is that the only reason he pursued Anne's secret?

She would ponder that matter further. But not now.

Meg finished her descent of the stairs with the Granthams, saw Lizzie established and preparing to accept offers to dance, and crossed the ballroom.

"Why, um, hello, Mrs. Grantham," Miss Bourre said.

"Good evening," Mr. Dodd said. "If you are looking for my brother, he has not come yet. Some new business of his with his blessed reconstruction."

Reconstruction? What reconstruction? "I was not

looking for your brother, sir, thank you," Meg said, "but to say hello to Miss Bourre."

"It is a fine enterprise," Mr. Dodd said. "One which I have been enjoying myself."

Miss Bourre looked self-conscious.

Trying to decide whether she should attempt to separate Miss Bourre from Mr. Dodd and being intrigued by the mention of reconstruction made Meg hesitate before speaking. But she was spared the decision by the sudden appearance of Lord Fitzhugh at Miss Bourre's side.

"Dorrie," he said, "our dance, I believe. Your servant, Mrs. Grantham. Dodd."

"But I do not wish to dance, Fitzhugh," she said.

She did not, though, sidle away from Lord Fitzhugh, Meg noted. Perhaps her defiance ended at her words, or perhaps she had taken stock of the flush growing upon Mr. Dodd's cheeks.

"Later perhaps, then," Fitzhugh said. He bowed and took himself off to a place where he could observe. Meg approved of Lord Fitzhugh's ability to make a good strategic retreat.

But Miss Bourre was embarrassed. "He will insist on standing as older brother to me," she said to Mr. Dodd. "But there is no need to heed him."

No reason other than his reputed sword arm, Meg thought, which reason was also circulating dizzily under Mr. Dodd's too-perfect curls.

Spying Major Black, Meg decided to let them talk it out—or all too politely ignore it—as they would. For reasons of her own, Miss Bourre did not want rescuing. Meg excused herself and went to say hello to Major Black.

After five minutes of pleasantries, she was able to

direct the conversation to a point where she could say, quite casually, "Yes, I believe Lord Reversby mentioned something about that. I understand he has been working on some reconstruction."

The subtle hint that she already knew what reconstruction Lord Reversby was involved in provoked a surprisingly even-handed compliment from Major Black. "From all accounts, he performed quite the miracle. It is quite ironic, too, that he was able to put together the funds necessary for capital improvements on the outcome of a shooting match. All London was talking of it before I shipped out."

"He shoots well, then? That I did not know."

"No one knew it, that was the beauty of the thing. But he can shoot the pips from a card at fifty paces. And with his father's reputation for gaming, everyone assumed there was another Reversby tossing away the family fortune."

Gaming, Meg thought. *How horrible!*

"The only one who bet on him to win was Fitzhugh, and everyone ascribed that to loyalty." Black jutted his bony chin in Miss Bourre's direction. "If you value your friend, you should keep her away from that one. He's a bounder."

"I have tried," Meg said. "Oh, good, there is Mr. Smith-Jenkins."

"Do you know Smith-Jenkins?"

"But barely. I suspect, however, that he will like Miss Bourre's conversing with Mr. Dodd as little as you do."

"It is as well that he has returned to Town," Major Black said, and elaborated at Meg's questioning look, "Some family matter required him in Hampshire."

Meg wondered if Miss Bourre observed Lord Fitzhugh looking at Mr. Smith-Jenkins but tipping his head toward her, for that slight communication was all Mr. Smith-Jenkins required to locate Miss Bourre and approach her.

"So," said Major Black, returning to his theme, "there is quite a bit of bad blood in Lord Reversby's family."

"Lord Reversby has been helpful with my niece, Major."

"Bad blood will out, Mrs. Grantham. He had himself nicely turned around, nicely enough to make him an attractive prospect to your friend, God rest her soul. But from what I heard, they followed quite different pursuits, if you know what I mean."

A deep unease prompted Meg to say, "I am not sure I do."

"You of all people should understand," he said.

Had the poor state of her marriage been known? Meg wondered with embarrassment. Known, that is, past the women? What had Anne done? *Oh, Anne, tell me that you never . . . Why would you? You were married to him.*

Anger at her friend filled her. Had Anne lain next to a husband who whimpered about having to brave the next march, the next skirmish, the next battle? No, Lord Reversby would as soon joke as whimper.

Moody Reversby might be, and not so pleasant when he was frustrated, but that paled in comparison to what he could and did do. If he had heard anything of the rumor Black was telling her, he had good reason to want to know her secret. It did not make her feel any the less frightened for herself, but she had to admit to being ashamed of herself for thinking Reversby would be frivolous in the matter. She was also angry at Black.

But she managed to say, "Do, sir, as a friend, be specific as to what I should understand."

"I beg your pardon, Mrs. Grantham. I should not have equivocated with you over questions of loyalty. Your loyalty could never be questioned," Major Black said with a bow that made his bony frame look awkward.

"What has my loyalty to do with anything?" Meg asked, wishing that Lizzie had another pianoforte, or anything that she could send Major Black after. She despised him and his coy roundaboutations, and herself for despising him. He was not a bad soul, just not very bright.

"Nothing," he replied, flustered. "It was a compliment."

"You pay me no compliment when you imply such things about my friend."

"No, no, of course not. It was meant as a warning, only, because of this friend." Black glanced toward Miss Bourre and Mr. Dodd. "Lady Reversby was, I hear, often in the company of her brother-in-law, Mr. Dodd, at various gaming palaces, playing deeply. More than one gentleman has told me she enjoined them not to mention her appearances to her husband. Now, it is well known how little love is lost between Reversby and Dodd, but what if—"

Meg would not believe it. "You are fishing for intrigue, sir, but it does not swim in those waters."

"How do we ever know what goes on in others' lives?" Black asked, recovering with a bandage of anger.

"I would have known *that*," Meg said. But even as she said so, she doubted it. If Anne had been unfaithful, could she have expected Meg to comfort her?

That was a sore question indeed.

Meg ached for Reversby's ever hearing such horrible rumors. Then she ached for herself. Had she fooled only herself to compare herself to Anne and think herself nobler? No, for she had gone for the adventure. What had she learned? She had learned that trials either made one or broke one, and then there was the next trial. Her complicated feelings for Reversby had become her next trial, and she feared General Grantham could not save her from it.

"Then I daresay you could settle the matter," Black said.

"I am sorry, but I do not take your meaning," she said.

"Nor," said a disturbingly familiar pomegranate voice from behind her, "do I."

Noel should have kept his mouth shut. He knew that. Had he kept his mouth shut, he might have heard something that would give him a clue as to Mrs. Grantham's secret. But instead he had stupidly reacted to the distress in her voice. Her cold tone could not disguise either her fear or her anger. What Major Black had said to provoke such a reaction, Noel could not imagine. The woman who could endure Black's prattling for three months before dispatching him after a pianoforte would surely not be cowed by idle conversation. No, something else had been going on that he had missed.

Mrs. Grantham and Major Black regarded him with expressions of horror. Did they spring from the same source or merely the same circumstances?

Noel polished his monocle, placed it, and smiled his laziest smile. "Close your mouth, sir, do," he said, "and collect your wits. They seem to be scattered all over this fine parquetry. Only look, Lady Pfoff is stepping on them there."

"My lord, um," Black said.

"Such a conversation you were having," Noel said, deliberately not looking at them but at the sea of people dancing and conversing. "You were quite oblivious to my efforts to attract your attention. I do envy you your concentration."

But neither of them picked up the conversational glove. Mrs. Grantham had recovered somewhat. She gave him the same wary glance she had given him when they had walked by the great tree in Leicestershire, discussing reasons to keep secrets. Shortly another lie of omission would hide itself behind the curtain of her words.

Major Black, however, did not pretend to recover. If anything, Noel's words had given him fresh fright. He bowed and took himself off. And Noel did not repress the darkling glee that such a reaction provided.

Mrs. Grantham watched him scurry off, then sighed and said, "Do not bother relating the lengths to which you went to attract my attention."

"It is interesting, is it not, that someone else wants to know your secrets?"

"I will not judge how interesting, sir."

"I suppose that would depend upon the secret."

"I suppose it would," she replied. Then she

straightened. "What secret do you think Major Black fished for?"

"In truth, ma'am, I have no idea how many secrets you carry."

"Please excuse me, my lord."

But before she could curtsy, he said, "I would not do that, were I you."

"Why not?" she asked. "I do not plan to continue here and let you amuse yourself at my expense, particularly when it gives you far too much pleasure."

"Nothing about this situation gives me pleasure."

"Even so, you make my point."

"You are amazing in your ability to carry an argument despite being on both sides of it. It is time for a new field. How shall your niece's chances fair if we are publicly at odds?"

"You seemed less concerned about that last night," she said.

"Let us say I have reconsidered."

She looked away, and her lips moved. Doubtless she was muttering an imprecation.

"Come out onto the patio," he said, "and you may express the full magnitude of your discontent."

"I have no need to express discontent, my lord. I have expressed everything I have needed to express."

"Wanted to express."

"Felt myself obliged to express or desired to express."

He had to admire her endurance and determination, even if he resented its results for him. Then something caught his eye. "Good Lord," he said, and took her arm to turn her around. "Is that Breshirewood leading your niece out for the next set? Damned monocle. I swear I am half-blind with it."

She had stiffened, but now she leaned a little toward him, the better to see through the pulsing crowd, and he caught a whiff of her spicy scent. It sent heady ripples of desire through him, and he stopped caring what secrets she kept or what manipulations she might employ to protect them. He wanted her in a way he had wanted only his wife. He wanted her morning, afternoon, and evening. He wanted her in the fragrant garden, across a billiard table, on his large bed with candlelight limning her honey skin.

"There is nothing wrong with your vision," she said.

Noel reminded himself of where he was, shook off the confounding images, and said, "God save us all from the whims of dark horses."

He thought he heard her mutter, "From all whims," but he could not be sure.

With Breshirewood leading her, Miss Grantham stepped on no one's toes. She looked happy, full of self-confidence, and not the least bit cross. For his part the duke appeared to be conversing at full grandiloquence, a sure sign of delight.

Murmurs were beginning around the dance floor's edges, accompanied by raised eyebrows over furious fans. Even Fitzhugh, from his station near enough Miss Bourre and Malcolm, waggled his brows at Noel's inquiring look.

"They say God looks out for fools," Noel muttered.

"Would that were true," Mrs. Grantham said.

For a moment, the music, the buzz of conversation, and the rhythmic pounding of shoes and boots upon the floor peeled back, leaving only him and Mrs. Grantham. If desire for her body had

tugged at him before with the scent of her perfume, her words, so weary and so wise, made an
equally powerful desire bubble up for her soul. She
did not have the same soul as Anne, not even close.
Where Anne had carried him along with her thirst
to try new experiences, Mrs. Grantham wore away
at him like the spring mist that formed the rushing
torrents he had pulled young Jimmy from. He did
not know what to think or how to feel.

"Don't," she said, resigned dread mixed with
fright. "Oh, please, don't."

It was the resignation that smote him. "I wish I
had met you a long time ago."

"I was less then than I am now."

"Could we take an average? I am less now."

She shook her head but whether denying the
premise or the claim he could not guess. "I am not
yet five-and-twenty. Not until Michaelmas. And already I have seen too much. I have not your optimism, or your faith in the world. If you think you
see things in me, you have been wearing that monocle entirely too long."

"Faith can be shared."

"After it has been transferred," she said. "I am too
many hard planes and edges to press anything into.
There, the dance is ending. I must congratulate my
niece on not tripping."

Had he been arguing with Anne, she would have
left him with some conversational ball he could lob
back at her. Mrs. Grantham, however, had left hers on
the ground, on her side of the net, leaving him feeling vaguely unsporting for wanting to jump across,
pick it up, and shove it at her to get her attention.

Some Hercules, he thought, and followed her.

Chapter Seventeen

For the next three days Mrs. Grantham gave Noel no opportunity to converse with her in private. Leeds declared her unavailable when Noel stopped by in the afternoons. Even a week ago, Noel might have been able to get the man to budge, but Mrs. Grantham had worked her pride and efficiency magic on him.

Noel took to riding out in the mornings in the hopes of seeing her walking, but there was no sign of her. She had anticipated him, he felt sure. In the evenings, she refused offers to dance and remained near her sister-in-law, Lady Grantham, while they watched Breshirewood pay Miss Grantham continuing attention. Or she stood next to Miss Bourre whenever Malcolm tried to pay her attention.

Miss Bourre worried her, Noel could tell, which was not to be wondered at. Malcolm always worried him. Fitzhugh also kept a weather eye on them; and although Fitzhugh and Smith-Jenkins did not converse when Miss Bourre was about, Noel often found them sitting together at White's. Noel did not resent Smith-Jenkins, although he would have liked to ask Fitzhugh if Breshirewood had said anything that could lead him to hope.

* * *

On the third evening, to relieve Fitzhugh and Smith-Jenkins's worried frowns, Noel opined that Malcolm might make a lot of noise, but he never followed through on anything that would require him to be honorable.

They were not relieved. "I should not have gone away," Smith-Jenkins said, and from the way Fitzhugh shook his head, Noel inferred he had said so many times already.

"We neither of us thought she would allow Dodd to so turn her head," Fitzhugh said. "Your pardon, Reversby."

"No offense taken," Noel replied. "I have tried to speak to him, for all the good it does."

"The goat, Reversby," Fitzhugh said.

"Oh," Noel said. "You think he's still trying to take credit for the goat?"

Fitzhugh nodded.

"That's not good, is it?"

"What goat?" asked Smith-Jenkins. "What isn't good?"

"A prank we pulled on two dons at school," Noel said. "Very clever, and—"

"A very long story," Fitzhugh said.

"Right. Goat story later. Malcolm wanted to be part of the prank so badly he told the headmaster he had done it. Headmaster knew he had not, but his coming forward caused us a lot of awkwardness."

"Damned near miss," Fitzhugh said. "And I don't want Dorrie to be another one."

"He does not look strapped," Noel said, "but he has fooled me before, and I have not been paying him proper attention."

"So," Fitzhugh said, "will you ask Sommers if he knows anything interesting about your brother?"

"I have quite frightened Sommers away. It will have to be you, Smith-Jenkins. You can still play both camps. I won't be offended, whatever you find out."

"I begin at once," Smith-Jenkins said, and left.

"He did not ask again about the goat," Noel said, after sipping his brandy.

"Smith-Jenkins has that singular ability to focus on one goal and eschew all others."

"Must be nice," Noel commented.

"You are glum, Reversby. I thought you and the lady were on the mend, now that Breshirewood's preference for Miss Grantham has become so decided."

"Would there be something to mend, I would take out my handy needle and sew it right up. Metaphorically speaking, that is, because I have never figured out how women manage to put those blasted threads into such small places."

"It is one of the mysteries of the distaff side."

"When I first read that letter, I needed to know what it was all about. There was something about Anne that pushed me away before the end. It was subtle, but it was there. I let her, too. That was my mistake."

"You, make mistakes, Reversby?" asked Breshirewood, who had come up behind Noel and Fitzhugh's wing chairs and now leaned sloppily against them. "Not for me, you have not. The young lady is divine, and I am looking forward to knowing her much better." He tried to clap Noel on the shoulder. It turned into more of a swipe. "Owe you a bottle of something. Maybe a case."

And off he toddled.

Noel and Fitzhugh rolled their eyes.

Then Fitzhugh said, "Perhaps she cannot contemplate building a deeper bond by betraying her friend."

Noel tried to remember all Mrs. Grantham had said. Most poignant to him were her words about protecting fools and how little she had left of tender feelings. And yet she looked out for the Granthams, seemed even to care for them. And yet she clung to Anne's secret, protected it as if she were a Nemean lioness and it her cub.

What was more important to him? Did he still want to know about Anne, or did he want to retain Mrs. Grantham's regard? Assuming that he had had her regard to begin with.

"She will insist on keeping the bargain. She is that sort. And once she tells me, she will be as good as gone."

"It is excessively annoying when women decide to claim as much honor as we do," Fitzhugh said.

"You are joking, right?"

"Not really." He sighed. "The trade-off is to marry someone who cares about little more than fripperies. Or live alone."

One of the waiters bowed before them, a salver in one hand. "A letter for you, Lord Fitzhugh."

Fitzhugh took it, thanked the man, and broke open the seal to reveal another letter. "Donaldson," he said, naming his butler, "sent this on." He broke open the inside letter, read, and then smiled broadly. "Esme is heading south on the Great North Road."

Noel congratulated his friend, but underneath his warm speech there lay a bitterness for remembering vividly how he had looked forward to seeing Anne again after they had been apart. Knowing her secret could be akin to seeing her again, but at what price? Then there would never be another reunion with Mrs. Grantham. She would be gone for him.

Gone. As good as dead. Could he stand that? Could he avoid it?

For the life of him, he did not know.

The next morning Meg gave her restless feet permission to wander where they would. She passed through Hyde Park and was soon in the countryside, where her sole company was a flock of sheep and a few ducks upon a reedy pond.

Meg wished she could have felt better about her accomplishments in London. It looked like the Duke of Breshirewood was entranced by Lizzie, quirks and all. He had hovered by the door last night, and after the Granthams were announced, he had spirited Lizzie away for the first dance.

But Meg felt as if she had failed Miss Bourre entirely. The news of Lady Fitzhugh's imminent return had plunged Miss Bourre into wretchedness.

"She must have come eventually," Meg had said to her.

"I had hoped she would not," Miss Bourre had replied. "I know it is ridiculous of me, but there it is."

Meg tried another approach. "Mr. Smith-Jenkins adores you, you know."

"Breshirewood adored me last season," Miss Bourre replied, almost losing her composure. "That mattered naught to me."

Meg had not known how to reply to this, but spotting Mr. Dodd working his way toward them through the crowd, she said, "Above all, dear Miss Bourre, do not set yourself upon any reckless course."

Miss Bourre had promised, but there had remained a wild look about her that Meg had often seen in people about to go into battle. Seeing it had made Meg sick at heart, and yet she had to stand with the others after Miss Bourre left with Mr. Dodd and smile.

Somehow Lord Reversby had known. After dispensing with pleasantries with his customary deft manner, he had drawn her aside and said, "What has happened?"

Walking along the pond, the wind on her face, the ducks wagging their tails at her, Meg shivered again as she had shivered the night before from his pomegranate voice. At once gentle, concerned, and enthralling, it plucked complex chords of desire. Could she but once feel his hands on the bare skin at the top of her dress, have him touch her the way a woman should be touched, she thought she could stand anything.

Meg had to tell Lord Reversby something. Could she tell him Black's rumors? What was one secret as opposed to another?

A second lie, she told herself. She would no longer have even her own version of her honesty.

But how she had been tempted. She was still tempted. But she had said, "Miss Bourre is despondent and with your brother."

"We are working on that," he had replied.

Reversby had asked her to dance, but she had refused all cajolings. Did he actually touch her, Meg thought, she would have let that nasty temptation take firmer hold. She recognized that she frustrated him, but there was little she could do. Did he learn her secret, she would lose both whatever regard he had for her and her last veneer of respectability and belonging.

With these unhappy, swirling thoughts for company, Meg returned to London. The day was growing warm, and she welcomed the cool foyer of the house.

But the expression on the butler's face melted her small happiness. "What is it, Leeds?"

"A footman, ma'am, from Mrs. Bourre," said the compact man, "he came with a note for Miss Bourre, thinking she was here. Then another man brought this for you. It is from Miss Bourre."

Meg broke open the proffered letter and read.

> *When you receive this, Mr. Dodd and I will have left London along the Road for the North. I am leaving a note for you, and you alone, Mrs. Grantham, because I trust that you will keep my whereabouts secret long enough for us to avoid any unpleasantness. Mr. Dodd confirmed my feeling that you are the most discreet of confidantes.*

What have you been telling her? Meg wondered darkly. *What secrets do you know, Mr. Dodd? And how dare you, Miss Bourre, insist I keep your secrets? I do not owe you the same obligation I owed Anne.*

> *You will call me absurd, my dear Mrs. Grantham, and indeed, the possibility of your disapproval gave me pause. But I feel certain you of all people will understand what I am about to do. Mr. Dodd told me he learned from your friend Lady Reversby that you eloped yourself. I want to be married, to have my life settled upon its path, so I can see Lady Fitzhugh again, not as that "poor Miss Bourre," but as the cherished Mrs. Dodd. He does adore me, Mrs. Grantham, in that you may trust.*

You fool, Meg thought, *you little fool.* Some of her anger at Miss Bourre receded, however, to be redirected at Malcolm Dodd. Surely he knew what he was doing. Surely he could not intend to marry her. Surely he was trying some trick on his brother and Lord Fitzhugh. There was no love lost, and envy and resentment aplenty.

> *Think happy thoughts for me, and do not try to stop me.*
> *Your friend, Dorrie Bourre*

Transfixed, Meg reread ". . . and do not try to stop me." Miss Bourre had not needed anyone to keep her secret. She could have allowed herself to go missing, if she had not the decency to inform her good mother. But would there be time?

"Leeds, I need the carriage and someone to carry a note to Lord Reversby. At once, man, jump to it."

The man blinked, said, "Ma'am," but got no more than two steps away before the door knocker sounded loudly.

Meg swore under her breath but nodded to Leeds to get it. Mr. Smith-Jenkins, of all people, entered and bowed, and was about to remove his gloves and hat when Meg said, "Did you walk, sir?"

"Ah, I, um, no," he managed to say. "I drove my phaeton."

"Is it still outside?"

"Yes, ma'am."

"Keep it there. We need it. You're coming with me."

"Ma'am?"

"North. We go north, as soon as I get my reticule and write a note."

Chapter Eighteen

Meg gripped the edge of the phaeton as Mr. Smith-Jenkins climbed back in after receiving a no at yet another inn. A large cloud of irritable dust shortly developed behind them again. Mr. Smith-Jenkins was an admirable driver, but he and Meg did not discuss that subject on their bumpy, hurried ride north.

"I was coming to ask your advice, ma'am, on how to make her hear me," he said again, as he had already in at least ten versions. "I cannot believe she would do anything like this."

"She does not want to," Meg said, as she had replied to each variation. "She wants us to come get her."

"Does she want me to kill him for her?"

With the wind whipping his fair hair against his hat and making him squint his amiable features, Mr. Smith-Jenkins looked about as dangerous as a nut-deprived chipmunk. Meg debated the wisdom of speaking, then said, "No, she wants Lord Fitzhugh to kill someone for her."

He took his eyes from the road. Meg realized he was likely a few years older than she, but in comparison to him, she felt ancient. "My best advice to

you, sir, is to stop trying to be an imitation of Lord
Fitzhugh. You admire him, I know, but you will not
win Miss Bourre's heart by trying to *be* him. She will
always know the difference, and you will always
come second. Be yourself. She'll either love you for
it, or you should find yourself another woman to
love. Now drive, for God's sake."

He drove, and Meg hoped that Lord Reversby followed closely behind. She hoped even more that he
had not taken his friend Lord Fitzhugh. She realized that in her haste to beg his assistance, she had
forgotten to tell him that.

The sun began drawing low, although Meg esti-
mated they had another hour of light. They had
learned that a couple fitting Miss Bourre and Mr.
Dodd's description had asked for directions to the
inn at Biggleswade.

"Either way, we must stop, sir," Meg said. Indeed,
she was surprised they had traveled as far as they had.

Grimly, Mr. Smith-Jenkins agreed. Four miles later
they fetched up to the Crown on Biggleswade's High
Street. The setting sun glazed it with warm light, and
Meg was surprised and relieved to find it new, and
therefore likely to have clean sheets and plenty of
hot food and water. She disliked the feel of the dust
on her face and the emptiness in her stomach. As
Mr. Smith-Jenkins helped her from the phaeton, she
reflected wryly that she had grown soft.

The inside looked every bit as neat and attractive
as the out, with warm beams and white-washed walls,
china, and comfortable furnishings. Several tables
nestled near a comforting fire, and a long bar filled
with polished glasses was already getting a good custom. As Quality the world around received its fair

share of interest, Meg hoped they could obtain a private parlor.

When applied to, the innkeeper, an exceedingly tall, thin man with a sprouting of dark hair, answered Mr. Smith-Jenkins's question about Miss Bourre and Mr. Dodd with a, "Yes, sir, they bid a private parlor."

Meg's hand on Mr. Smith-Jenkins's arm prevented him from surging forward. "Peace," she said, sotto voce, for the innkeeper was still speaking.

"And they have gone for a walk down by the river before supper. I would gladly offer you the other parlor, but it is reserved for a lady and her steward."

"We will be fine in the common, then," Meg said, keeping her pressure on Smith-Jenkins's arm. "After such a long ride, a walk by the river sounds lovely. Don't you agree? What direction is it, please?"

"Is it really Mrs. Grantham, from Portugal?" inquired a husky voice from behind Meg. Meg turned and beheld the beautiful widow she had met almost three years ago coming down the stairs. Now that her hair was not covered, Meg saw that it was a brilliant copper. A stocky, distinguished man of about forty-five stood behind her. Her majordomo, Mr. Williams, Meg remembered, who had remained impassive but close as the Portuguese general had flattered her.

"Yes," Meg replied. "How kind of you to remember me, Mrs. Compton."

"Mrs. Compton?" asked Mr. Smith-Jenkins.

"As was," the woman said and smiled. "How are you, sir?"

"Lady Fitzhugh, Dorrie has—"

"Come to meet you," Meg said, suppressing her amazement to the demands of exigency.

"How lovely," Lady Fitzhugh said with but the barest trace of uncertainty.

"She's with Dodd," Smith-Jenkins said, "Mr. Malcolm Dodd."

There were questions on Lady Fitzhugh's lips, and although Meg envied her their admirable bowed shape, she wished Lady Fitzhugh would display Mrs. Compton's efficiency and enable them to remove their increasingly awkward scene from the public room.

Lady Fitzhugh seemed to understand Meg's silent urging, for she said, "It would give me the greatest pleasure if you would both join us for supper."

"Thank you, my lady," Meg said for both of them.

"Attend us, sir, if you please," Lady Fitzhugh said to the innkeeper. He followed them into a large private parlor as charming as the common, with warm red chairs around a large table, a divan and three more red chairs, and patterned light gold wallpaper.

"It seems friends of ours have asked for the other parlor. It will surely not be necessary. Do show them in here, but do not tell them we are here. I wish to surprise them," Lady Fitzhugh said.

"Very good, my lady," he said, and bowed.

Lady Fitzhugh sat down, tacitly inviting the others to as well. Mr. Smith-Jenkins fidgeted, but sat. "Now, Mrs. Grantham," she said, "would you please tell me what is happening?"

Meg took a deep breath, considered the subtleties of the situation, and began.

In public, Noel hated to look like he had urgent business of any kind. He also hated to be publicly in a brown study. Having learned more than he had wanted to that afternoon about his brother's affairs and Anne's involvement in them, his mood hovered dangerously at the brink of fury. The arrival of his panting footman put him quite over the edge.

"My goodness, man," he said. "This is White's, not Tatt's. You did not need to run like a racehorse to find me."

"Yes, my lord," the man replied. His training bucked him up a bit, but his arrival screamed urgent business and had woken several of the sleeping lords dozing in the afternoon sunlight.

"Do not tease him, Reversby," Fitzhugh said from the chair next to him.

The man was opening his mouth, wanting to interrupt. "I have a letter, my lord." He handed it over.

Noel recognized the writing from Anne's correspondence. Mrs. Grantham. He hesitated a moment, wondering whether his servants thought that any letter from Mrs. Grantham deserved urgent attention. What he read left him in no doubt.

My lord, Mr. S-J and I are headed north on the Great North Road in pursuit of Miss B and Mr. D. I believe she wants us to stop her, but I will not pretend to be sanguine about the progress of the situation. I beg you to render me any assistance you can.

Yrs,
MG

Before this afternoon Noel had held his brother in distaste. This afternoon he categorically loathed him. Now he thought he hated his brother with a passion so thick it could choke him. He took a firm grip of himself and swore thoroughly, although under his breath.

"What is it?" Fitzhugh asked.

Noel handed over the note. Fitzhugh glanced at it, crumpled it, and stood, his expression grim.

"I have my phaeton here," Noel said.

"I might kill him, Reversby."

"No, that pleasure might have to be mine."

"Together is the best I'll do."

"Fine," Noel said. He turned to his man. "Well done."

"What a mess," Lady Fitzhugh said when Meg finished. "I am so sorry."

"It is not your fault, ma'am," Mr. Smith-Jenkins said.

"Fitzhugh has worried long about paining Miss Bourre. The bonds of childhood run deep. I envy them that. I never had a childhood friend." Lady Fitzhugh smiled so that no one would say anything pitying. "Now, Mrs. Grantham, may I ask how you came to befriend Miss Bourre?"

Under Lady Fitzhugh's keen gaze, Meg explained her connection to Lord Reversby, using the most generic, neutral terms she could employ. Meg did not think she had fooled her ladyship. Mr. Williams sat with his fingers steepled, a mannerism Meg recognized from their previous meeting that had preceded some trenchant question.

Then the door opened on the innkeeper, Miss Bourre, and Mr. Dodd. Meg would have been hard put to say which of the new arrivals seemed more astonished. After that, however, their emotions diverged. Mr. Dodd's expression darkened. Then he folded his arms, leaned against the door, and smirked.

Miss Bourre saw Meg first, but as she began a flickering smile, she saw Lady Fitzhugh and Mr. Williams. She tried to choke a sob on an upraised wrist and fled the room. Mr. Smith-Jenkins dashed after her, brushing by Mr. Dodd none too gently.

"Well, isn't this a nice little party?" Mr. Dodd asked.

"One to which you were never invited, lad," Mr. Williams said.

"According to whom? You? Are you not the son of a fishmonger?"

Mr. Williams smiled and quoted, "'Is this the noble nature whom passion could not shake? Whose solid virtue the shot of accident nor dart of chance could neither graze nor pierce?'"

"I thought history was your thing, old man," Mr. Dodd said, although he had lost some of his swagger.

"It is a shallow mind that thinks it must run in the same tracks all the time. You are not convinced? Come, let us go outside and discuss how you may broaden your horizons, shall we?" He clapped his large hand on Mr. Dodd's shoulder and turned him around. "We'll start by figuring out the origin of that quote, hmmm?"

When the door closed behind them, Lady Fitzhugh said, "Mr. Williams used to be a don."

"Oh," Meg said, and, because her legs no longer wished to hold her up, sat down.

Lady Fitzhugh poured them both cups of tea. "Although I deplore the circumstances, I cannot help but admit how lovely it is to have this chance to meet you again, Mrs. Grantham, before we are full in society. Our arrangements in Portugal presented such a neatly wrapped challenge for me, and your company was a pleasure. Nor did I hold that opinion in solo. If no one has told you so, let me be the first. The others within your late husband's regiment and division—is that the right word?—deeply appreciated your efforts."

"You are very kind," Meg said.

"I am lazy, more like, because being kind and accurate amount to the same thing in your case."

The tea was reviving Meg. "You struck me as a woman who appreciated accuracy. Why, then, did you make yourself known as Mrs. Compton?"

"The Dowager Countess of Iddesford carried a lot of baggage, more sometimes than I wished to lug."

"It must be very convenient when one has two names. Legitimate names, I mean. Lord Reversby introduced himself to me as Mr. Dodd."

"Did he? He must have been more Noel than he normally is. He has a most irritating way of deflecting pointed comments. He just says something amusing that makes you feel like you have been caught undressed."

Meg did not want to think about being caught undressed before Lord Reversby. It made her feel hot and shivery together. "I think I know the kind you mean."

Lady Fitzhugh smiled. "Tell me, how long have you been in love with Reversby?"

Meg thought of all the things she could say. That she was not in love with Reversby. That she and Lord Reversby could never have any future together. That the mere thought of him provoked anger, fierce tenderness, and searing desire.

She said, "I am not sure. Possibly when he wondered whether he thought I would ask him to wrestle a bull."

But Lady Fitzhugh did not laugh. She tipped her head, causing the emerald pendant she wore to wink. "Does he know about your failed elopement?"

Meg took a breath. "If Lord Reversby deflects pointed comments and Lord Fitzhugh gives one such a look, then you, my lady, enjoy saying that which will shock and amaze."

"It has been my way, yes."

"How did you guess?"

"I try very hard not to guess about the people with whom I do business," Lady Fitzhugh said. "Mr. Williams asked around after I met with you. It seemed universally agreed upon that you were an excellent woman and such a shame that you had chosen such a man, but that . . ." and here she shrugged, doubtless in imitation of those Mr. Williams had interviewed, "one does make odd mistakes in one's youth."

Meg flushed.

"But it was not until I met your friend Lady Reversby on a ship bound from Calais to Portsmouth that I learned the truth of the matter. She had quite a bad case of mal de mer, but would take no sympathy. 'My friend Meg is enduring worse, I have no doubt,' she told me, and the whole story came out. I was quite amazed to discover my Mrs. Grantham and Lady Reversby's friend Meg were one and the same person. Your not-quite-elopement explained those comments Mr. Williams and I had puzzled over. When we were to disembark, she bade me tell no one what she had told me. I gave her my promise and have kept my tongue about our meeting."

"Yes, thank you," Meg said, choking on the words for her anger at Anne, who had promised never to betray her. "It would have embarrassed her."

"You have been around Reversby too long."

Meg stood. "Never fear, I will not be around him anymore."

"What do you think to do?"

"I had promised him, my lady, that I would tell him a secret, which he knew Anne and I to share, if he performed a few services for me. Now that you know, none of that matters."

"How does that follow?" Lady Fitzhugh said. She had made no effort to rise or to stop Meg from leaving.

"I cannot continue to be Mrs. Grantham when people know it is not my name."

Lady Fitzhugh played with her emerald. "Who is to tell them? I? Certainly not. I have no patience for such pettiness. I know too well how the stench of rumor and gossip wounds, to wish to spray it about and pretend it is perfume. It is why I kept your secret then, and why I have kept your friend's secret as well."

"How much do you think Lord Reversby will care that Anne went to the North with me?"

"I have no idea. That is not the secret I meant."

"What do you mean?" Meg asked.

"Thinking she would impress the notorious Lady Iddesford, Lady Reversby confessed something that would have shaken Noel. She told me she had quite fallen in love with gambling. She giggled over it."

Meg sat back down. From beyond the door, loud singing began, punctuated with dull thuds upon the bar.

"You do not seem surprised," Lady Fitzhugh said.

"She wrote of a general dissatisfaction," Meg said slowly, "and since coming to London I have heard hints about her gambling."

"Noel's father bankrupted his estate gambling, and Mr. Dodd has gone that way, too. God knows how he remains solvent. It is not a pretty thing, gambling like that. It is like those poor women who cannot stop taking laudanum. Noel once joked that his father would have put him up if he thought Noel worth betting on."

Meg winced.

"What made your friend desire to flirt with the edge?"

"I don't know," Meg said.

"No, I suppose you would not, would you? You were constant."

"Not as constant as you would think. My 'marriage' ended almost as soon as it began."

"We cannot all of us find the person who truly complements us, makes us whole," Lady Fitzhugh said. "When you do, however, do not run away. I was something of an expert on running away. That too leaves wretchedness in its wake. If I do not mistake matters, you would be a far superior wife to him."

Meg shook her head.

Lady Fitzhugh said, "That will not do. Know this, when I first met Reversby last year, I condoled with him about his wife. I complimented her, not just for her own sake, but because I had known you and she had your loyalty. Mrs. Grantham, you deserve what you are willing to fight to hold on to. You of all people should know that."

The singing stopped. Meg thought of Lord Reversby pulling young Jimmy from the river, and her own abandon in hugging him to herself when he had emerged. In a low voice she said, "What will he think of me, continuing with an elopement I knew was false?"

"Fitzhugh thought I had lovers across England and Europe, and knows people still whisper about me. I sometimes think only his reputation as a swordsman keeps unpleasantness at bay." She put a finger over her lips and pointed at the door with her other hand.

The door opened abruptly, and Lord Reversby and Lord Fitzhugh spilled into the room.

"Where is he?" Lord Fitzhugh asked. "Esme!"

Lady Fitzhugh stood and held her arms open to her husband, who crushed her to him and picked her clear off the ground. "We were looking for Reversby's brother and Dorrie," he murmured against her copper hair.

"They were here, but Mr. Smith-Jenkins went after Dorrie, and Mr. Williams took Mr. Dodd outside for a talk," Lady Fitzhugh said.

"Yon innkeeper is doubtless enjoying a fine laugh at our expense," Reversby said, leaning against the door frame and looking hooded, "as well as providing a story for the next meeting of innkeepers. Do they wager, I wonder, how many couples one can have come into one's inn looking for each other, and then pair up differently? How are you, Mrs. Grantham? I see you have made Lady Fitzhugh's acquaintance."

"Yes," Meg replied, feeling heat and misery curl throughout her body. "And I am fine, thank you, sir."

"So where did Mr. Williams take my scapegrace brother?"

"Off some place to drill him on Othello," Meg said.

"Not quite the punishment I had in mind," Lord Fitzhugh said. "You say Smith-Jenkins is with Dorrie?"

"Yes, love. She is safely in his hands. And if there's punishment to be given, do let him participate and not keep all the pleasure to yourself."

Fitzhugh responded to the lightness in her tone by saying, "I will content myself to watch. Will that suit?"

"It might just," Lady Fitzhugh said in a husky voice.

"All this excitement," Meg said, "and I never did get a chance to stretch my legs since that long ride. Lord Reversby, would you escort me? Would you excuse us, please, Lady Fitzhugh?"

"My dear, I feel desolate to have kept you," Lady Fitzhugh said.

Lord Reversby's ironic gaze followed her from the parlor into the common room. The singing ceased again when the public room guests saw a lord and lady emerge.

Reversby flipped a guinea toward the publican. "Don't stop on our account, men."

That brought a cheer, and the singing resumed as Meg and Reversby passed outside into the deepening twilight. There on a bench by the far mews sat Miss Bourre and Mr. Smith-Jenkins. She was crying on his shoulder. In the other direction, blocked from that couple's view by the inn but visible to Meg and Rev-

ersby, stood Mr. Dodd, backed up against an out-
building by the burly form of Mr. Williams.

"It is a veritable Forest of Arden out here," Reversby said. "Let us walk this way." He indicated
the cobblestone road leading away from the inn,
toward the River Ivel.

They started walking. "The Forest of Arden?"
Meg asked.

"From *As You Like It.* Your pardon. Once I start
thinking of Shakespeare, I must hit my head at least
three times before it goes away."

"I shall not mind any allusions. Do not do yourself an injury." She promptly tripped over a cobblestone. "Ow. Now there is a jest."

He steadied her by holding her arm. "No one
can walk so far without stumbling a time or two."

The heat rising in her face made her thankful for
the night. "Thank you," she said, and detached herself, "for coming after me. Us, I mean."

"It seems I am extraneous, though."

Meg looked her question.

"Lady Fitzhugh."

"She is an interesting woman and provided quite
the shock to Miss Bourre. Of course I first knew her as
Mrs. Compton, just as I first knew you as Mr. Dodd."

"You never truly knew me as Mr. Dodd," he said,
as they left the cobbles for a graveled cart road that
ran out toward the river. A soft breeze nudged the
grasses growing in high shadowy profusion to either
side, and brought the tang of wood smoke and
water. "You knew I was Reversby. I never fooled you."

"No."

"You agree very easily."

"My pride demands I salvage something from

what I am about to say. You did not fool me, sir, but I fooled you."

"I fail to see how your pride is salvaged by saying you not only did not get fooled, but fooled me." He frowned. "That doesn't scan well, does it? Good thing I have no poetry on my mind. Well, other than the Shakespeare."

"My lord, I am not proud of myself for fooling you."

"Now on that point, you did have me fooled, because you certainly seemed to enjoy it."

"Will you please stop that?" Meg asked, exasperated.

"What?"

"You know perfectly well what. Your 'gift' as you would call it. I would tell you something."

"No, Mrs. Grantham, do not. I have come to think that I should not wish to know your secret. Much better to have parsing and bargains and impossible tasks. Much, much better to only pretend to be Hercules."

Meg had never imagined this reaction. "You startle me, my lord."

"And you scarcely know how to account for it. I am sorry, General, to shift the ground beneath your feet." A wry smile attempted to make his words lighter. "It has come to my attention that I should not spit on loyalty."

But Meg was not fooled. "Our bargain—"

"I cancel our bargain."

Chapter Nineteen

He made motions while they walked as if he were ripping up paper and tossing it away.

"It is not that easy," Meg said.

"It is exactly that easy. Hello, Mrs. Grantham," he said and bowed, "I am Reversby. Pleased to meet you. Tell me, how have you enjoyed the Season thus far?"

The echo of so many of their conversational practices with Lizzie made Meg's heart ache. How tempting it was to take him at his word and let the whole miserable subject drop. But Meg could no longer stay in the middle of the road.

Lady Fitzhugh's assessment of her feelings had hit the mark. Somewhere, somehow, Meg had fallen in love with Reversby, despite her prejudices and fears. She thirsted to sip the promise, the hope of love.

She took a deep breath and said, "As well as I was able, sir, but I am sorry. You must have heard my name incorrectly. It is Miss Neville, not Mrs. Grantham."

A hesitation in his step expressed the whole of his shock. "I must have spoken truly before. Have we entered the Forest of Arden, ma'am, and are playing at

Shakespearian mistaken identities? For I distinctly remember my wife addressing you as Mrs. John Grantham."

"My dear friend, your wife, kept a secret for me, sir." They had reached the bridge, and although the water did not rush with the same force as under that other bridge, it looked deep and inky and nothing to be fooled with. "We eloped together, with officers. She declined to go through with hers upon finding out neither of us had been married properly. We had never crossed the border. The locals played a joke on us."

He set his clenched hands upon the stone wall of the bridge. "I do not need to know this. You do not need to tell me."

"I do."

"You are walking at the very edge of the road now," he said.

"Yes, and there is a very deep ditch, and I do not know if there is rope."

He said nothing, and Meg's heart sank. The rushing of the river seemed to take all her hopes and dreams with it.

But she pressed on. She wanted him to understand what Anne had done for her. She wanted him to have a piece of Anne to treasure. Was that not what had driven him into pursuing her secret? Even if she never saw him again, even if he repudiated her, she wanted to give him this, the image of Anne's loyalty. She had no idea whether she could give him the fact of it. She hoped he never learned about Anne's gambling or his brother's escort. Certainly she would not be the one to tell him.

"Anne never told anyone but me that Lieutenant

Grantham and I were never married properly, not even Lieutenant Grantham," Meg said. "She wanted us to have our chance at happiness."

Reversby unclenched his hands, spread them upon the stone bridge, and leaned into them. "You must have loved him very much."

"No," Meg said softly, standing close beside him, relief beginning to bubble within her. He had not condemned her out of hand. Then as quickly as she felt a burden lift, she realized she had unfairly given him no opportunity to without taking away from Anne's nobility.

"You did not love him?" he asked, looking sharply at her.

"No, I did not, because my feelings did not last a month. But I was committed. I had chosen to go with him to the Peninsula, so I chose to carry on with our farce, even after I caused him to disintegrate. It was my decision, my choice, my fault."

"How? How could any such thing have been your fault?"

Meg told him about Seward, about the horrible deal Lieutenant Grantham had struck, how she had turned it down, and how she could not stop wondering who had been killed instead because of her decision.

He turned away from her. "That was why you turned into General Grantham. You thought you owed them."

"I did owe them. I owed everybody. How could I say I was an honest woman when I was the opposite?"

He shook his head. "No, that I reject. Now, tell me this Seward is alive so I can shoot him."

Meg held her breath. "He was wounded that day

and sent home. I do not know anything more about him."

"One battle? Too kind, too quick."

"No, I do not think Cap—"

"What?"

She had decided today would be the day for honesty. She would be honest, at least about herself. "I have long suspected that Captain Sandeford shot him."

"The dashing Captain Sandeford of the chocolates on the road to Valladolid?"

"The same one. I think he overheard me in Seward's tent. He is an excellent marksman. I think he took the shot that would cause a great amount of pain."

"You never spoke of it with him?"

"No," Meg said, lowering her eyes. "It was better not to. For everyone. As the campaign continued, and the war broadened, I saw him but rarely. Besides, by then I was General Grantham and had all the protection I could have ever asked for. That is the other, equally unflattering reason I did it: I need never fear my husband again."

"How long did this process take? How long did it take you to turn into flint?"

Tears formed in Meg's eyes, tears she had not cried for longer than she could remember. "I never did. I wish I had. Had I, I would not have needed to walk so steadily in the middle of the road."

He was silent long enough for tears to roll down Meg's face, hopefully unseen in the night.

"When would you have told me about Anne's gambling with Malcolm?" he asked.

Meg gasped. "You knew?"

"I learned. This very afternoon, in fact, when I tried to find out more about my brother to head him off Miss Bourre. I can well understand why you wanted to keep this one to yourself, but how convenient for you that you had two secrets to share. What would I have had to do to get the one I came to you to hear? What Herculean task would you have had me perform?"

Anger competed with sorrow, pride, love, and loss. Meg held her head up. "I am sorry, my lord. You were right. We have carried this bargaining entirely too far. I am going back." She turned away from him.

He caught her by the shoulder, not roughly, but so Meg knew that she could not escape either him or the heady feelings he stirred within her. "Would you have told me?"

"Not this. I would never have told you this."

"You parsed and danced and tried everything you could to make me heed that I should be careful of what I wanted to know. You told me not to push. How long have you known?"

"For certain? Only this evening."

"This evening?" Reversby asked. "From Smith-Jenkins? Malcolm?" He would have started back for the Crown, but this time Meg stopped him with a hand on his arm.

"No, my lord, from Lady Fitzhugh. Anne confessed it to her when they met on a packet from Calais."

"But not to you."

"No, never to me. There was only the one secret between us, and we shared it. Oh, I noted that she grew more distant, but I thought that was because there seemed to be part of her that envied me my choice. She wished for excitement and danger, and I told her only ugliness lived near me. I wished her happy to live where there was beauty and love. I never told her about Seward, so maybe she did not believe me."

Meg heard the plea in her voice, and, as it appeared not to move him, said, "She did not tell me what compelled her, and I have no idea why she would crave danger or excitement, not when . . ." She shook her head.

"Not when what?"

"Not when she had you," Meg whispered, and covered her mouth with her hands, felt the wetness on her cheeks. "Oh, I should not have said that. You were her husband."

"Not enough of one, it appears," he said. The words sounded as if they were being pulled from him with red-hot tongs.

"I used to wonder," Meg said slowly, "whether Lieutenant Grantham lost his spine, arranged that horrible bargain, because I somehow let him know my feelings had changed."

"No," he said, gripping her shoulder fiercely, "you will not pity me."

"Pity, my lord, is the very last thing I feel." Brazenly she put her hands against his chest, felt his heart pounding in his solid body, its hectic beat finding its answer within her own. He did not push her away. Her hands continued, twining themselves in the crisp hair at the nape of his neck.

He inhaled sharply.

"We could debate whether we failed our spouses," she said against his neck. He smelled deliciously of lemon and warm man. "Or they us." She darted her tongue behind his jaw and felt his pulse jump. "Or whether the Fates have decreed us to be unhappy." She pulled away slightly, so that she could look at him, his face between her hands. "I do not wish to be unhappy. Will you throw me a rope?"

He took a deep, shuddering breath and stepped away from her. There was her answer. She had done her job of pushing him away too thoroughly. He might not condemn her out of hand. He might not mind being swayed, briefly, by desire. But he would certainly not embrace her. He folded his arms tightly, hands clenched in fists.

Meg wrapped her arms around herself, trying to keep the warmth of him from fading, as it would. She would listen to him, the same way she had listened to Seward, with her head up. Then she would leave, leave London, leave the Granthams, and strike out on her own. Somehow. If General Grantham was the only person in her life who could support her, she would be General Grantham again.

"You know I loved Anne," he said.

Meg nodded. She knew where this subject would tend. All his pursuit of her had been for what she could tell him about Anne. Desire had been a by-product. Meg could never compete with Anne on that footing. After that, there was little to choose between them. She had made as many mistakes as Anne had. Arguably more.

"Learning that she gambled, that she craved it, that was hard. Hard, but not altogether surprising. I had come to figure out that I loved her for her drive to explore new things, new experiences."

"I remember," Meg whispered.

"Yes. Her desiring to elope was very much like

her. But why did she back out? Even before she would have . . . consummated it?"

"I don't know," Meg said. "I can't help you. I can't give her back to you. My secret leads nowhere."

He shook his head, put up a hand, and withdrew it back into a fist. "I begin to think that your secret lies at the beginning of the path. I begin to think she was never mine. I borrowed her for a while, let her blaze her will across my sky, and then she was gone."

"I'm sorry, my lord," Meg said. She had been wrong to think she could stand still any longer. A braid of grief, anger, and embarrassment whipped at her. This time Lord Reversby did not stop her but started walking with her.

"Do you know where you're going?" he asked.

"No."

"Neither do I. I have been looking for a direction for longer than I know."

"I cannot give you one."

"You already have," he said.

"Away from me and everything to do with me, I daresay," Meg said.

"No," he said, and caught at her arm.

She shrugged him off and said, "What is this, my lord?"

He said nothing for several frantic beats of Meg's heart, while the crickets chirruped, the Ivel—not so far behind them—rushed with determined abandon, and the wind brought muffled sounds of merriment from the inn. "The Nemean lion," he said. "Or maybe the golden stag. I can't decide."

"I have little inclination to jest."

"I am not jesting."

"Have we not had enough of bulls, stags, and lions?"

"Strictly speaking," he said, tipping his head, "we have not introduced stags at all."

"And I feel the lesser for the omission," Meg replied, a reluctant smile tugging at her lips.

He touched the corner of her mouth so gently Meg wanted to cry. "You, yourself, have been more of a test than any you have given me. How to make Mrs. Grantham smile? How to make her laugh? How to make her love a man who has nothing that she does not already possess?"

"Do not tease me," Meg said. "Oh please, do not tease me."

"I cannot throw you a rope, my dearest, because you have had it all along. However solid it might have appeared, mine has been the illusion."

Meg drew a shaky breath. "My lord—"

"Hear me out. You have shown me that. Loyalty burns so brightly from you—loyalty and courage to face whatever needs facing. These are the directions I want. I had thought that so long as I was busy and occupied, I had a direction. But it was as ephemeral as Anne herself. It had no staying power. But loyalty and courage—they can build more than mere business, and everything else can follow in their footsteps."

"Do not grant me any nobility for a choice made in the stupidity of youth."

"Whatever your circumstances, you stayed true to yourself. You are an honest woman, *Mrs. Grantham*, or you could never have said that."

"I am not Mrs. Grantham."

"If your surname troubles you, you could consider changing it to Reversby," he said. "I would make sure it is done legally." He kneeled on the gravel at her feet. "Marry me, dearest Meg, and we will walk together, in the center of the road, at its edge, and into unexplored territory. I want to see places I have never seen before, places I have never heard of, places I could never imagine going without you at my side."

Her love for him threatened to choke her. She had suspected that his irony and jests covered a true, deep sensibility, but she had wondered if she would ever see its face.

"Hold me," she implored him. "Hold me so I know you won't ever let me go."

He rose, gathered her in his arms, and she pressed herself against him as she had that other day by that other river, reveling in his strength and solidity.

"My love," he said. "My best love."

And before Meg could put thought to action, she was kissing him and he was kissing her, their lips telling each other more potent sentences than words could ever convey. The passion rose between them as silken ribbons decorating a Maypole, and then wound around and around, weaving them together in an intricate, colored pattern.

"I will never let you go," he said against her face, his hands tracing shivery designs in her hair, which had somehow come down from its confining pins. "Never let me go, either. Let us be together."

"Together," she said, laughing and kissing his roughened cheek. "I like together. I have looked for it long, but I have never had it."

"We will make a whole passel of togetherness, I promise you. Meg, I love you. I do not know when I started loving you, but I cannot imagine not loving you now."

"Is that what passes for a compliment, sir?" she asked, running a finger from his forehead to his jaw.

He laughed. "I am greatly in fear, ma'am, that instead of a lion or stag, I have found myself an entirely different creature. Indeed, one who changes before my very eyes."

Serious again, Meg rested her forehead on his chest. "I always wanted to laugh, to be my own person, free, but of the world. I distrusted you, dearest Noel, because you had everything I wanted, it was so easy for you, and yet you wanted more."

"I did not know what I wanted, nor what I had. It only appeared that way."

She looked up at him, reveled in his hands warm on her shoulders. "We've both kept our own secrets so well. Too well."

"Reversby," Fitzhugh said, "what is this?"

Fitzhugh and Lady Fitzhugh came up briskly to them, Lady Fitzhugh's copper hair gleaming even though the inn stood some distance off.

"Why," Reversby said, drawing Meg's hand through his arm so they stood like a phalanx of two, "the lady was teaching me all about lions, bulls, and diverting rivers."

Lady Fitzhugh put her hand over her mouth. "Have you cleaned out the stables, then, sir?"

"Entirely. With fresh straw applied, thank you, my lady."

"You are being absurd again," Meg said.

"I am not being absurd," Reversby said. "When am I ever absurd?"

Lady Fitzhugh smiled. Fitzhugh merely raised his brows.

"Yes, well," Reversby said, "I suppose it is not absurd to tell you that we would be very pleased if you would attend our wedding. Three weeks' time, love?" he asked Meg. "As soon as the banns are read and a license procured?"

Meg nodded, so happy she had tears in her eyes again. Lady Fitzhugh made a little shooing motion to Reversby and hugged Meg. "Oh, my dear," Lady Fitzhugh said, "this is the best possible end."

Lord Fitzhugh shook Reversby's hand and kissed Meg on the cheek. "You can live with his wretched jokes?"

"If he can live with mine, sir," Meg said. "I have had far less practice."

"I will manage," Reversby said, and again drew Meg to him. She leaned into his warmth, knew that he took comfort from hers. The love in her heart made her oblivious to the fact that the four of them had walked back to the inn. Only the greater light from the lanterns brought her back to reality.

She thought longingly of the rooms above. Reversby must have been thinking along the same lines, for he said in her ear, "Three weeks? Can you endure it?"

"I have endured worse," she whispered back. "But let it not be a day past."

"Not an hour," Reversby said.

And Meg could tell that his blood urged him as hers urged her.

"Mr. Williams has gone inside," Lady Fitzhugh said, "and Mr. Smith-Jenkins and Miss Bourre."

"And Malcolm?" Reversby and Fitzhugh asked together. Grim amusement crossed their faces.

"You two may beat him later," Lady Fitzhugh said. "We have at least one wedding to plan."

"I have a better idea," Reversby said. "It has come to my attention that Mrs. Grantham knows a wonderful marksman who is not me—yes, there are more of us in the world, can you account for it?—who could take care of all our problems at what, a hundred yards, my dear?"

"Reversby!" Lady Fitzhugh said.

Only a half hour ago, Meg would have winced and retreated, all fiery anger, from any mention of what Captain Sandeford had likely done for her. But Reversby's playfulness soothed her in a way she had never imagined. She took three fingers and poked at his chest. "Three hundred yards, if you please, and a nice wounding it would be."

"We must consider it seriously, do you not think?" Reversby asked.

"I would seriously consider going inside," Lady Fitzhugh said. "I want to know if there will be a second wedding to plan."

"Ah, how quickly one's news is supplanted," Reversby said. "Here I had been thinking us quite unique enough to have lasted for a full hour."

The Fitzhughs gave him an identical fondly amused look. "My dear," Fitzhugh said, ushering his wife in.

Meg and Reversby grinned at each other. As they passed inside, Reversby again flipped a guinea to the quieting crowd, then another. "Two rounds, my fellow Englishmen. The lady has consented to marry me, more fool her."

The crowd cheered, doffed hats, and grinned.

As Meg and Reversby paused at the door to the private room, the Fitzhughs behind them, Reversby stopped. "Good God, we will have the Granthams at our wedding, will we not?"

"Well of course," Meg said, and understood exactly what difficulty he anticipated. "Lizzie will play for us."

"That is a strategy suitable to General Grantham. 'Twill serve to keep her away from the cake. Oh, love, can you imagine, Miss Grantham dancing and a cake? Even with Breshirewood there? I do hope she still—"

"Do stop being absurd, Reversby," Fitzhugh said, pushing him into the room, "and kiss your fiancée while we arrange for wine."

"I am never absurd," Reversby said.

But Fitzhugh had closed the door on them.

Reversby shrugged and gathered her in his arms, brushed her hair from her forehead, dusted her with kisses until, when their mouths finally met again, Meg could barely contain the desire to undress him then and there. Panting from their kiss, she drew back and said, teasingly, "Really?"

"Well, except absurdly in love."

"Is it absurd that we should care so much for each other?"

"I was referring to amount, not quality. Are we parsing again? May we tell our grandchildren we met over lions and fine definitions? They will never believe us."

"Reversby—" Meg began in protest.

But he kissed all her protests away.

Author's Note

You may remember that we first met some of the characters in *In Pursuit of a Proper Husband* in *A Delightful Folly*, Zebra Books, March 2005. Since I have heard so many women say all the good ones are married or otherwise uninterested, I hated to keep a man like Noel Reversby unattached. I also regretted leaving Dorrie Bourre in the lurch. I hope you agree that this is a reasonable end for them.

The women's quartermaster's band is my own invention, but Wellington's prohibition on soldiers' wives buying bread is not. The lottery to choose who could accompany husbands also existed. If you want to know more about following the drum, may I suggest: *Following the Drum: Women in Wellington's Wars.* Andre Deutsch: London, 1986.

More Regency Romance
From Zebra